In Paterson

ALSO BY MIRIAM LEVINE

• POETRY •
Friends Dreaming
To Know We Are Living
The Graves of Delawanna

• NONFICTION •
Devotion: A Memoir
A Guide to Writers' Homes in New England

In Paterson

A Novel by
MIRIAM LEVINE

SOUTHERN METHODIST
UNIVERSITY PRESS
Dallas

Copyright © 2002 by Miriam Levine
First edition, 2002
All rights reserved

Requests for permission to reproduce material from this work should be sent to:
  Rights and Permissions
  Southern Methodist University Press
  PO Box 750415
  Dallas, Texas 75275-0415

Grateful acknowledgment is made for permission to quote from the following works:

Lyrics from "Pennies from Heaven" (John Burke and Arthur Johnston) ©1936 (renewed) Chappell & Co. All rights reserved. Used by permission of Warner Bros. Publications U.S. Inc., Miami, FL 33104.

Excerpt from "Sailing to Byzantium," from *The Collected Works of W.B. Yeats, Volume 1: The Poems, Revised,* edited by Richard J. Finneran. Copyright 1928 by the Macmillan Company. Copyright (renewed) 1956 by Georgie Yeats. Reprinted by permission of Scribner, a division of Simon & Schuster, Inc.

Jacket photograph: *Park Avenue* by Morris Engel.
Design by Tom Dawson Graphic Design

LIBRARY OF CONGRESS CATALOGING-IN-PUBLICATION DATA

Levine, Miriam, 1939-
     In Paterson : a novel / by Miriam Levine.—1st ed.
       p. cm.
     ISBN 0-87074-467-4 (acid-free paper)
     1. Family owned business enterprises—Fiction. 2. Remarried people—Fiction. 3. Marital conflict—Fiction. 4. Paterson (N.J.)—Fiction. 5. Stepdaughters—Fiction. 6. Immigrants—Fiction. 7. Fur trade—Fiction. 8. Girls—Fiction. I. Title.

PS3562.E898 I5 2002
813'.54—dc21   2002019374

Printed in the United States of America on acid-free paper
10   9   8   7   6   5   4   3   2   1

For David
dear son, friend

Acknowledgments

THANKS TO
John Lane, dearest love.
For Paterson stories, my mother, Gertrude Levine.
For kindness, encouragement, and savvy—Alan Feldman, Marilyn Harter,
Bernard Horn, Kathryn Lang, Cynthia Linkas, Stephen Love,
Carol Marks, Jo Simon.

I am grateful to the following individuals and institutions for support: National Endowment for the Arts; Massachusetts Artists Foundation; Corporation at Yaddo; Château de Lavigny International Writers' Colony; Hawthornden Castle International Retreat for Writers; Ledig House International Writers' Colony; Villa Montalvo Estate for the Arts; Boston Public Library; Linda Brown, Paterson Public Library; and Deborah Kelley Milburn, Schlesinger Library, Harvard.

PART ONE

en Shein, the furrier, leaned back in the bathtub in his mother's house on Manor Street, in Paterson. Though his wife Tess had been dead for five years, he still grieved. His specific sorrow—for his loss, for Tess's agony—had grown to a sadness that stained and spread, as if all he knew had been soaked in the dyer's vat and hung out blue. At dusk the July heat still had not broken, but he left the hot-water tap on to a trickle. Ben wanted his bath to stay hot enough to numb him. The steaming water lapped his shoulders. He let the heat soak into his slender legs and tight buttocks, and finally he relaxed.

Though Ben was not a swimmer, he had a swimmer's long, supple muscles. Except for his head and hands, Ben had never uncovered himself out of doors. His white skin, smooth as a boy's before adolescence, glimmered in the greenish water that slowly darkened to the color of tea in the dusky light from the window. Drops of water from the tap stirred the surface. The steam rose around his head. His black hair curled. Though he had shaved closely that morning, his cheeks were dark with a five o'clock shadow. A blue shadow.

Ben rested his head against the sloping tub and closed his eyes. He knew what he would see if he looked down. He was hard. He felt a swelling pull from the tip, down through his balls, up, deep in the base of his spine, a silken seam of heat, a flame welted around a cord that branched upward through his spine and bloomed in the hollow at the back of his neck: all one, seeming to burn away sorrow. His penis floated out of its nest of black hair, weightless above his flat stomach. Ben waited, his head, for this moment, emptied of grief. "What's your hurry?" he asked himself.

He sat up and took hold of himself like a lover. He was alone but did not feel alone. He stroked, he labored, his small strong hand oiled by hot water. He put his other hand into his mouth, sucked and bit. Ben was the horse and the rider. He galloped. When he came, he tasted rust, blood, salt as if he were under water. With his eyes closed, he saw waves of white light.

Shaken by pleasure and release, he trembled and shuddered. Though his daughter, Susan, and his mother were in the house, he did not choke his cry. It broke out of him, a sob like a child's. When he felt the sound in his throat, it seemed to come from someone he didn't know, and it made him sad. There was no one there but Ben. Who was he?

He wasn't used to defining himself. When he felt desire, which was seldom since Tess had died, he touched himself. If you asked Ben whether he needed sex, he would have looked bewildered. "Sometimes," he might have answered. "Sometimes, it used to be good." On past evenings like this when the air was thick with the cinnamon smell of sycamore trees, when the sky darkened to gray in the sunset and brightened to pink in the afterglow, he could make love to Tess, speak a few words, and instantly sleep. An immigrant and the daughter of an immigrant, they had burned with work fever, but when they had exhausted themselves, they knew they would sleep. They had given each other sleep. Tess had drawn Ben inside her, all of her open to him. She would be next to him all night; and in the morning, when he opened his eyes, he would see her face. She had taken away his bad dreams.

Ben stood while the water drained away and rubbed himself down with a wet wash cloth. The moist July breeze that blew up from the river sucked the thin, white curtain against the screen.

The Shein house was on a hilly, sycamore-lined street that rose from the Passaic River. Moisture caught in the trees and coated Manor Street's brick houses, whose round entry-hall towers looked vaguely French. Moisture from the river was in the air like a smoky breath—you could see it. Along the tree strips, at the edges of the thick green lawns, under the privet hedges, the random pulses of fireflies made an intricate dissolving web of light under the trees: a trick of the eye—when a firefly went out, it left a trace the brain remembered. The web knit and dissolved, knit again.

A white towel wrapped around his waist, Ben knelt on the bath mat and slowly scrubbed the tub. He felt languid, almost drunk, as if he had been dragged from a deep afternoon nap.

A flicker of old pain roused him. Under the bones of his chest the faint constriction grew to an ache. "It's your fault, Tess," he said to his dead wife. "I'm not blaming you for dying, but I got used to you."

"Me?" Her voice was rough inside his head.

Ben reached for an idea: "With you, I could do . . . everything."

Now Ben strained to hear Tess's voice again. He bent his head, tuned his ear to remember, as he had once waited for the blessing whose possibility had been held out to him at Tess's grave: before the Kaddish, that fierce chant for the dead, came the exhortation, "May the memory of the righteous be a blessing."

"The hell with it," he said to himself. What was the use of remembering? The tightness in his chest loosened but did not let go. On his knees, on the bathroom floor, Ben heard only his own breath. He was as alone as he had been on the edge of that hole in the ground into which Tess's body had dropped. The towel came undone. His penis, the same blood-smoke color as his mouth, curved against his thigh—as if his longing had made him naked again. He looked at his smooth skin: I don't look too bad, he thought. No, not bad. I look pretty good. Maybe I could get married again. "Why not?" Ben whispered.

He clenched his fist to fight off his hidden adversary but instead summoned him. He heard his grandfather Jacob's voice, which had rung in Ben's ears day after day of his childhood, "Happiness comes like a streak of light across a table." He could smell the old man—the woolen pants, the sweet tobacco fragrance that had clung to the old furrier's hands, even on his deathbed when he reached out and touched Ben's head.

Ben answered back: "I'm too old to wait again. A woman could look at me." His eyes tightened in anger, against fate, against Tess. He pressed his hands against his ears—Tess, Jacob, all day, all night. He had dreamed of his grandfather for years, always the same dream: Jacob naked, washed for burial, laid out on the gouged table in the workshop in Lodz, in Poland, where the old man had cut pelts for the family business. Jacob's hair tangled with the fox fur he had sliced and shaped, now pillowing his head, both streaked white as if touched by frost. "At least we don't have to slaughter the beasts ourselves," Jacob had once said. Ben could see inside his grandfather's chest: Jacob's heart beat; blood shone in the chambers like a red night-light, but Jacob was dead. Yet his heart beat as though he were alive. Ben would watch tears stream from his grandfather's closed eyes, pushing out from under the inflamed lids, the lids glowing as if the eyes were burning coals. Tears would slide into the old man's long hair, into the fur, and Ben would wake, the hair at his own temples wet and cold. He was sick of crying. Jacob—he didn't want to listen to him anymore. Ben switched on the light.

Bunching the towel in one hand, Ben used it to wipe the tub. He found a dry corner of the towel and rubbed the steam from the mirror. His gaze slid past his own eyes, which no longer surprised him—the right eye dark brown, almost black; the left eye, a violet-blue flecked with gold and green. When he was younger, his eyes used to remind him of an illustration he had once seen in a schoolbook: the stem of a white flower cut in half vertically, leaving the flower attached. Each half-stem was sunk in a glass vial. One vial held black ink, the other blue. One half of the flower was veined with black, the other with blue, the ink-filled veins as fine as thread. As he combed the curl out of his hair, drops of water ran down his neck along the points of hair left by the comb. He took a fresh towel, blotted his neck and face, and dusted his cheeks with a light coat of talc. If he had planned to go out that night, he would have had to shave again. He put on white cotton pajamas and a dark blue robe, tying the belt smoothly around his waist. In the steamy air, his hair was sleek as a muskrat's. Ben looked priestly in the polished cotton of his pajamas and robe, the dark and the light, dressed for his longed-for sleep as for a rite he could perform to give himself peace. He switched off the bathroom light. The tub gleamed in the dusky dark.

Ben went down the stairs. From the dining room door he could see his daughter, Susan, reading at the table, which was too high for her. At ten, she was still small. She propped up her head with one hand, the other hand curled palm up next to the book, the pale, poreless skin of her inner arm whiter than her grandmother's damask tablecloth.

Years later anyone seeing Susan's picture would say, "She looks like Anne Frank!" The dark chestnut hair parted on the side, a thick lock held by a barrette, the narrow serious face, the deep-set shadowed eyes would seem so familiar. But it was 1940. The world had not yet heard of Anne Frank.

Susan's eyes narrowed. Above the cheekbones, blue smudgy shadows, like dents. She put her head down on her extended arm and looked at the book sideways, her head turned up. She breathed through her mouth.

Ben moved closer, "Susala, Susala." She didn't seem to hear him. He put his hand on her head. "Susan, what are you doing?"

"You can see."

"What?"

"I'm reading." She tilted the book up, her index finger holding her place, and turned the spine toward Ben. "*Heidi.*" Susan opened the book to her place and peeled back the cloudy paper that covered the picture.

Ben stared. A little girl alone in a dark room. Her small hands in her lap. A rag of a dress. Heavy boots, laced tight. Big sad eyes.

"She's an orphan," Susan said in her clear voice. "Like me."

"You? You have me." What did she want, a mother? Ben pointed: "That one's a blonde. Not like you."

Susan ignored him. She put the tip of her thumb next to Heidi's face and stroked the paper.

"It's good quality," Ben said. "That paper."

She nodded her head, her eyes on Heidi.

"Did you eat?" he asked.

Susan nodded again.

"What did you have?"

"Daddy!"

"Are you tired? You look a little tired. Come, I'll sit with you in your room. You'll sleep."

"I'm not tired. Don't want it. Don't need it."

"You don't?" Ben did a quick-step dance around the table, his hands like tipped flags, one on either side of his face, thumbs pointed to his chin: " 'Don't want it. Don't need it. Don't want it. Don't need it.' " Since Tess's death, she had fought sleep—the enemy. "But the Sandman will come," he told his daughter.

"I'm ready. He'll never get me." Susan closed her book and took her father's hand. She spread out his fingers on the table and walked her index and middle fingers up and down across them.

"Susan, you feel warm." Ben pulled his hand away. "Let me feel your forehead."

"I'm burning up." Susan lifted her chin and smiled into Ben's face: Tess's gleeful smile.

Ben couldn't take it. He turned away and went to find his mother.

Brona Shein wasn't a person to hesitate in doorways. Carrying a loaded tray, she advanced on the dining room table. "Both of you, I have to eat. Susan, you are hungry? Yes? It's time." She put down the tray and swept back the gray hair that fell slantwise across her low forehead. Brona had cut her hair in the twenties and still kept the fashion—full in the front, short in the back. Her hairdresser shaved her neck. Her nose was long, bony, and strong; the soft curve of her mouth, surprising.

She had brought them tumblers of milk, a plate with four pieces of thickly cut yellow sponge cake, a bowl of blackish-red bing cherries. They ate with their hands—like children.

Ben looked at his mother and back to the cherries. "Where?"

"From the Italian, on the corner, near the hospital."

"He robs you."

Brona reached for more.

Ben was ready for her to start on him—what about you, how many suits does a man need? But she was quiet. Let her be quiet. She had more than all of them. Not that Ben and Nat minded. The brothers had signed over their shares of the house to her when their father, Eli, had died shortly after the family had moved to Manor Street, just as Eli was about to enjoy the profits from the fur business. He had been a playful man with a sense of humor. His light voice, his jokes—the boys kept listening for him, but he was gone. Eli had left everything to be divided equally among his wife and two sons, who were still in their teens, but Brona had wanted the house for herself. When Ben and Nat had suggested they sell it, Brona refused. "Your father and I worked too hard—I'm not going to lose it," she had told them. "Pa . . . ," Nat had begun, and they had all cried, only that one time. They had no opportunity to grieve: they had to work to save the business, Ben as a furrier, Nat as a driver and handy man. Brona kept the books. Skilled at managing money, the parents had been prudent in buying the smallest house on Manor Street: seven rooms, not twelve. When the Crash came, Brona could pay the mortgage. Ben had listened to Brona and put most of the profits back into the fur business, and now that Tess was dead he and Susan had moved in with her.

Brona's diamond shone against the dark red cherries. She had bought the kind of ring Eli would have given her if he had lived. "What's the use of complaining?" she liked to say. For Brona, there was no use.

She put a handful of the fruit into her granddaughter's outstretched hand, "Darling, do you like them?"

"Of course she likes them," Ben said. "What's not to like? Cherries?"

"What's the matter with you?" Brona asked her son. "Have some."

"Not for me. The cake is enough. How much can a person eat?" Ben didn't know what he wanted.

Brona touched the top of Susan's hand, her unpolished nails rounded, tipped with white. "Darling, take more." Susan opened her hand. Brona dropped cherries into her granddaughter's palm.

"How much did you pay for the cherries?" Ben persisted.

"More money than you could dream of."

"Oh, I have dreams," he said.

"If God can take, I can give." Brona smiled.

She always had a comeback. Maybe he'd find a woman who would listen to him. "He took, all right." Ben's voice rasped in his tight throat.

Brona bowed her head toward Ben only as far as she could and still keep her eyes on him. Her eyes softened, giving him the comfort he craved. Pressing her index finger against her mouth, she nodded toward her granddaughter.

Susan had fallen asleep, ambushed, her head on her folded arms, under her right hand a few uneaten cherries.

Conspirators, they got up from the table. While Brona pulled out Susan's chair, Ben lifted his daughter against his chest. Her head fell back, and he shifted his position until her head came forward against his neck. She was heavy. Brona uncurled Susan's fingers, scooped out wet cherry pits, and wiped her granddaughter's hand with a napkin. Susan grumbled and put her arms around Ben's neck, her thin legs dangling like white roots yanked from the ground. The dead weight of her oxford-shod feet swung against his thighs, and Ben reached down and held her legs behind the knees, drawing her closer to him.

Brona followed him up the carpeted stairs, both of them pausing on the top landing, where Ben crowded against the wall so Brona could get past him. She turned on the light, drew down the blanket. Ben bent down. Pulled forward by Susan's weight, he lost his balance, caught himself and managed to slip his daughter onto the bed without waking her.

Susan's shoulder-length hair had fallen back from her forehead. There was a blurred line of shorter hair at the scalp line, which made her face seem unfinished. In the light of the small lamp the shadows around her eyes were violet.

Brona untied and loosened the laces of Susan's shoes; right, left, easing them off. A shoe in each hand, she held them against her full breasts.

Ben pulled up the blanket over his daughter's feet, over her knees, up to her waist, over the thin yellow dress. Susan lay without moving.

Ben breathed with his mother as if they had been dancing. He waited for their breathing to slow, waited to hear Susan's breaths. Still pressing Susan's shoes against her chest, Brona left the room.

In their old flat on Broadway, Ben would kiss his daughter good night and leave her to Tess, who would read her a story until Susan fell asleep. The bedroom door would be open, and Ben would hear Tess's voice as he washed the supper dishes. Tess's laugh was quick and easy—like his father's. Reaching down, with the backs of his fingers, Ben grazed the side of Susan's face. He bent closer. He couldn't hear his daughter, but he saw her chest rise and fall.

He went to the window and opened it. He wanted Susan to have fresh air, yet he was afraid. A person didn't know what could happen or where the danger could come from, not even a big shot like Lindbergh. *His* baby had been kidnapped and murdered. In the night a man had climbed a ladder into the baby's second-floor room and taken him from his crib. Bruno Hauptmann—some people thought he was Jewish.

Jewish people didn't do such things. Ben looked at his small hand on the window frame: he was no Lindbergh. Holding his hand close to the screen, he stroked the mild night air. The moon had risen and the sky was white over the black sycamores and maples. Making sure the screen was firmly fastened, he left the window open wide: Susan had to breathe.

In Ben's room at the far end of the hall, a pink-shaded lamp cast a mild light on Tess's dressing table, the only furniture he had brought from their old flat on Broadway. Long empty of her things, the glass top now held his thin wallet, keys, a few bills pressed in a money clip, scattered change. The rest of the room looked new, like the future. Instead of "period," Brona had picked modern decor—blond wood, shell pink walls, dark rose drapes.

Ben slipped off his robe, threw it over the footboard, took a clean handkerchief from the drawer and put it on the night table. His hand moved precisely, but he felt unsure. He turned on the small oscillating fan and stood for a moment listening to the fan's whir before he got into bed.

He lay awake, listening, clean, alert, longing for sleep.

Finally he drifted, the night already half gone. Between waking and sleeping, he saw his dead wife, Tess, as she had been before the cancer that had killed her. He could not force her up out of memory or drive her away. She came when she wanted. Her blond hair frizzed around her pink face; her blue eyes were hot, her pale skin tight around her light bones. The Polack, he used to call her. Her feet were firm on the ground, her trunk twisted: she was stopped in a dance. She stood in front of him naked. The hair between her legs, thick and honey colored, always surprised him. It came up to her pupik. Her arms and legs were covered in down, invisible except in certain light, as now. A tender slant of light—like a caress. He couldn't read her face. Ben could hear the ocean, yet he was in the old workshop above the fur shop in Lodz. At the shadowy edges of the room, the finishers, the women who completed a coat by stitching in the lining and facing, sat against the wall. Tess waited.

"Who made the dress?" Ben asked, though Tess was naked.

"Who do you think?"

"Wise guy. Show me," Ben said. "The hem. You're supposed to be the finisher."

"Deeper," Tess said. "Go deeper."

His palms felt wet. He heard himself talking, but could not understand the words. He was crossing over into sleep. He saw himself reaching for Tess, felt his fingers graze her belly. He heard her moan, but it was his own cry. Unaccountably, she smiled. "It doesn't matter," she whispered. Her voice was so light-hearted Ben knew again that she was dead.

Ben heard the ocean once more. He might have been far out at sea on a moonless night, the stars covered by low, thick clouds, so black was his sleep.

Ben jumped awake in the half dark, his pulse racing as if something were running after him. The furniture swelled; the outlines of the windows hardened. He flicked on the small light. In a few minutes he was dressed—gray summer-weight wool suit, white shirt, black shoes, a new blue tie with swirls of black sea horses. Draping a towel over his shoulders to protect the material, he wet and combed his hair. It glistened. He ran from the sleeping house. The night had been worse than a funeral. At a funeral the dead stay dead.

BEN LEFT THE CAR FOR BRONA. SHE WAS THE DRIVER. WITH HER leather gloves and tailor-made suit—covered by a cape in the fall—she looked like a general behind the wheel of the Chrysler. Ben drove well, but would have been happy never to be in a car: he hated the smell of gas.

He walked down Manor Street without knowing he was looking for a sign that might lead him. The mist from the river had burned off, and the sky was blue and pink. A rosy light washed the cooled sidewalk. Ben reached Broadway dug out of the narrow waterside streets, laying waste to much of the oldest part of the city, cut wide through Paterson, stretching east to meet the river again and the bridge to Fairlawn.

He looked ahead and went down the wide sloping street, stopping at the window of the store where Brona bought her choice fruit: a light at the back of the store faintly illuminated the narrow center aisle, the shelves and bins, and the cash register and counter near the door covered with overlapping brown paper bags, which, in the shadows, looked like huge dry leaves. Taped to a wall close to the window was a picture of Saint Francis—brown robe, bare feet, sweet doll face beneath the tonsured hair, a sparrow hovering above his tiny uplifted hand, a cloud of birds around his head. Ben stared into the chapel of the store and felt the shock of strangeness. He felt the same way when he passed the open door of a church and glimpsed the sanctuary always filled with dim brown light.

At the corner across from the library, the deaf-mute paper seller bent over the bound stacks of papers that had been heaved out of a moving truck onto the sidewalk from the gray river of the street. He slid his knife under the tight binding rope and with a sharp upward thrusting movement cut the papers free. Ben took one. The paper seller finally looked up, his silent mouth open. He made a sign with his hand: Give me. Ben pressed change into his palm. The man rocked on his bowed legs and bent again to his papers, as if Ben weren't there. Head down, the paper seller jammed his callused hands, palms up, under the tight cord—there seemed to be no space for his fingers—and dragged the solid blocks of bound papers to the kiosk.

With the paper under his arm, Ben walked two blocks east from Broadway, where the streets narrowed, and came to Sophie and Si

Winik's store at the corner of Fair and Auburn. They had been married so long and had lived so closely with their son that Ben saw the Winiks as one holy family. From habit he looked for the old faded sign, though he knew Sophie's son had taken it down. Ben pulled the door open; the dangling bell clinked.

He went in, as he did every morning on his way to work, went back, back to Europe. Si Winik, like the Sheins and most of the people who lived in the neighborhood clustered around Broadway, came from Poland, from Lodz, a city of weavers, but Sophie Winik was an Alsatian Jew. Now that her husband was sick, her French hand was on everything.

The store looked like a place where you could buy something, but if you were a stranger, you wouldn't know what. The shelves were bare. On the counter, reflected in the downward-tilted wall mirror, was a pair of large scissors, a ball of rough twine, and a white saucer with a small pyramid of salt for Sophie's tomatoes. There were a few wooden tables with scrubbed, worn surfaces, each framed with a pair of chairs painted apple green. The store had once been the Winiks' grocery. Now Sophie Winik made breakfast and afternoon tea for a few regular customers. She "baked sweet" three times a week and served her cakes in the afternoon—deep sheet cakes, bare unfrosted vanilla sponge, apple laced with apple brandy, chocolate so dark it looked black. Bread and rolls came from Sophie's son, Theo, who, just after dawn, would bring them, fresh from the night ovens at his job across town.

Sophie had saved Theo's life. When he was six he had had influenza, which left his legs paralyzed. His hair had fallen out. He couldn't hold his water. "I got a pisher again," Sophie told people. Every day she had hauled Theo from his bed and strapped him to her firm body. His head with its black bristle of returning hair against her stomach, his stocking feet on top of her feet, she had walked him. She had put a record on the Victrola and danced him. Her back straight as a pole, her arms stretched to the side, she had made a cross from which Theo would hang by his small hands. She had propped him up on a table near the store window that faced the street and pushed bits of bread into his mouth, long ago.

Now the store was empty. Ben walked to the kitchen in the back where the Winiks spent most of their time. They lived in the building and slept in one of the two upstairs bedrooms. Si Winik sat just inside the kitchen door. His collarless long-sleeved shirt looked as if it had just been lifted off the ironing board. He had had a stroke and did not talk. Ben touched his shoulder; the old man did not move.

When Ben walked past him, he smelled the carnation scent of fresh soap. She keeps him so clean, thought Ben. The image of Sophie washing the old man came into his mind—Sophie in an apron bent over the bed, old man Winik on his back, Sophie drawing off his pants, turning him, lifting him, washing him, soaping his chest as if he were a baby, her hand on his breast bone. Ben felt again a piercing stab in his chest, then the familiar slow ache. If something happens to me, Ben thought, who would take care of me? He wanted to be held in the wordless fullness of what he imagined to be endless love. He wanted a wife to take care of him like a mother—forever. A sob rose in his throat. He swallowed and opened his mouth for air.

Beyond the open side door was a thicket of tomato vines tied with rough cord to stakes made from old broom handles, pipes, lattice. Sophie Winik came in, carrying an empty pail. She brought with her the raw, minty smell of crushed tomato leaves. She'd been pinching suckers. "Not ripe yet," she said. "Soon."

Sophie looked like a Mongol. Her skin was olive, her face broad and flat, framed by coarse white hair, which hung to her shoulders. Her eyebrows were black, as were her eyelashes. She looked at Ben with slanted tawny brown eyes. With her large head, she motioned to a table. Ben sat down. He knew better than to order: there was no menu, and for breakfast no choices. "It's cooled off," he said, motioning with his head to the weather beyond the window.

Without a word, Sophie went to the back of the store. Her silent self-possession struck some people as cruel; they stopped coming. Sophie didn't need them, they thought. Actually she did, just as she had needed her children. Sophie had gifts: whatever came out of her hands. She had to give these things to someone. She catered to her few regular customers; she didn't need the money. Her husband now seemed her creation—clean, new. If she could have given him speech, she would have. Sophie believed she knew what her husband was thinking. She was sure he could hear her words and thoughts: he made no motion, but the light in his eyes seemed to change in response. All day she answered him. In reverie, she knitted and unraveled their words, knitted them up again, let the stitches drop, picked them up with a different tension. What were the words? She couldn't remember. They were the present. The present disappeared. New words came.

Sophie moved to her own time and the time it took for things to ripen, boil, bake, and brew.

As Ben Shein waited, a young woman came in from the street, setting the dangling bell in motion. Ben took her measure: tall, slim, straight-backed, she wore her clothes well; even that cheap ready-to-wear suit. She faced the back of the store in the posture of an expectant customer, but there was no expectation in her dreaming eyes as she gazed into the space above Ben's head. She seemed newly made, untouched. Her pale brown hair lay flat against her head and curled in toward her shoulders in one soft roll. There were no sharp angles or deep curves; her face was oval, serene, refined. Dark lashes emphasized her light brown eyes; rose-colored lipstick shaded her mouth, which was closed in a small half smile that seemed to contain secrets. She liked to stand in front of the mirror after she had completed her makeup, smiling this quiet little smile.

If her father hadn't died so young, and then her brother, Judith Karger liked to tell herself, she would have become a teacher instead of a salesgirl. At least she was employed at "a fine establishment," her English-born mother, Estelle, would say. Estelle Karger's voice was unwaveringly reasonable, even when she would correct her daughter or refuse her pleas, "No. Understand me. Of course not." Judith, like Estelle and the Karger women before her, had heard that calmly restraining voice since birth. Before she could understand the meaning of "no," Judith had felt that "no" in her solitary room, in the emptiness of the crib into which her mother's hands had dropped her. Unlike Estelle, who also had never felt a mother's love, Judith had become furious, yet numb to her choked misery, lost in her suffering, empty. This morning she wanted something sweet to fill and soothe her, a passion strong enough to cauterize her mother's warning, "Mrs. Winik—too dear, for us. We just haven't got that kind of money." Judith took a step forward, hesitated; she hadn't been in the Winiks' store for years, but today she would spend.

"Sophie, she'll come," Ben said to the young woman.

Judith jumped and stiffened. He had surprised her—this man with dark hair and a white face. "Yes, I'm sure," she said. He stared at her as if he had been watching her for a long time. She looked away, letting her eyes drift out of focus.

"Don't be *too* sure." His voice was soft. "I know you. But what's to know?"

Judith couldn't answer. She looked into Ben's eyes, shifted her gaze from the dark right eye to the violet left eye, where gold specks floated like dust shaken inside a globe, confusing her. She straightened her back, pulled in her stomach. "You might have seen me in Quackenbush's. I'm employed there."

Ben laughed. "I never step into that place. Ben Shein—from the fur salon. Maybe from there I know you, Miss . . ."

Judith took in the cut of his expensive custom-made suit. The lapels lay perfectly, the interlining and padding so beautifully tailored there wasn't a crease. "No, not I. Perhaps my mother—years ago—Estelle Karger. I resemble her. I'm Judith. You have a good memory for faces."

"Miss Karger, in business you have to. But you go to business, and you didn't remember me."

"I never saw you. You took care of my mother." Judith smiled, just enough, the way she smiled at her customers—a welcome and a good-bye.

Her calm face belied her nervous hunger as she walked toward Sophie, who had come out of the back room. With her back to the counter, Judith gathered her strength to ask for what she wanted. She had been trained to wait on others, first at home, now at work. All day, she would lift her face to her customers and ask, "May I help you?" Pleasing people strained her small store of energy. Waiting for Sophie to speak, Judith felt the pressure of Sophie's knowing eyes searching out her secrets. Judith finally spoke: "I want . . ."

"I got chocolate cake. I'll get it. You'll have."

"She knows how to make it," Ben said. "Miss Karger, Winik charges you, but it's worth it."

Judith turned her back on him and faced the counter.

"The real thing," Ben said.

Keeping her back turned, Judith nodded as if she were paying attention. Her hands tightened on her leather bag.

"The best butter. Sweet," Ben said.

"Mmmmm," Judith murmured.

"Fresh," he said.

Judith's shoulders tensed and lifted in a tight hunch, as if Ben Shein had given a command. She nodded again, struggling to shut herself off from his voice. Alone in her own silence she could drift. The pyramid of salt stood on its little saucer, undisturbed. Judith pulled the glove from her right hand, put her bare index finger into her mouth and drew it out wet. A look of girlish hope lit her face and made her tender, as if she were waiting for her father to touch her head, give her the lightest sign of his love, as he had long ago before his weak heart had stopped. Modest, self-effacing Henry Karger—he had never given any trouble until the shocking suddenness of his death. Breaking the neat pyramid of salt, Judith touched the crystals she thought might be sugar. She brought her coated fingertip to her tongue: the salt stung.

"Here." Sophie Winik was back, a brown paper bag in her hand. "Seventy-five cents."

"Pardon?"

"Seventy-five," came Sophie's unapologetic voice.

Judith opened her neat handbag, fished in her little black change purse, and stopped. "I didn't know . . ."

"If you don't want it, I'll put it back."

The odor of dark chocolate, vanilla, sugar, and butter escaped from the bag in Sophie's hand, rising to Judith's nose as if it were a visible substance.

The fragrance came to Ben with the faintest edge, which he breathed in as he watched Judith's back.

She was counting: nickels, dimes, and pennies. Her head spun, black flecks darting at the limits of her vision. She was spending, losing; money could fall through a hole and keep falling as Judith could fall, like the girl who had dropped into the black night from the open car of the white-lit Ferris wheel in Palisades Park.

"Let me." Ben was out of his seat. "I'll pay."

"I got." Sophie weighed the change in her open hand with slight up and down motions, like a child about to throw a tiny ball into the air.

"Give her," Ben said.

"Mr. Shein, I couldn't," Judith said.

"You could. What's a little gift between businesspeople?" he said.

His soft voice reached her. It had been so long since anyone had given her a gift, but it wouldn't be a gift. She'd give something back. "Mr. Shein, I could send you customers. I could suggest." Judith opened her hand, into which Sophie poured the small hoard of coins. "Thank you," Judith said to Ben.

"My pleasure. I bet you can sell, a well-spoken girl like you."

She could. She was the first in sales on her floor, where she sold accessories. She pushed the cake into her bag and snapped it shut. It was no one's business what she had.

"You'll like it," Ben said.

She felt her face burn and hoped the powder she had put on that morning would hide the red.

Ben watched the back of Judith's bent head as she left the store. "You know her?" he asked Sophie when she brought him his food.

"She's a Karger. A Jewish family, but from England." ("Engelandt," Sophie pronounced it.)

"Does she go with anyone?" Ben asked.

"No one." Sophie put down Ben's coffee, steaming with hot milk, and a plate with a floury bialy, a slice of Swiss cheese, and a piece of crumbly sweet butter.

"A nice girl?" he asked.

"What is *nice*?"

Ben had never heard Sophie Winik speculate about the meaning of a word. He pushed. "In all these years, what did I ever ask from you? Tell me."

"Everybody's got a mother," Sophie said. "But."

"But what?"

"I heard about this Judith's mother. My sister is out, pushes my niece in the carriage to get sun on the baby's scarred face—from the forceps it happened—and Mrs. Karger comes by. Takes one look at the baby and says, 'Judith was so easy. Not like having a baby. Slipped out. Not a mark on her.' Mrs. Karger wants a prize. What did she do? Thinks she's the Queen. It's luck."

Sophie knew what she knew. Most infants are pushed and forced out though the narrow channel between spine and pubic bone, their heads squeezed, their sleepy faces often bruised by the tight passage, or—in her sister's time—their foreheads dented by forceps as primitive as ice tongs, or scarred when the forceps slip. Some infants whip their heads in blind instinct, resisting, often cracking a mother's coccyx. Judith Karger had been unmarked. Maybe it was luck. Or maybe my niece was lucky, Sophie thought: the girl was marked and strong.

"But this one from Quackenbush's," Ben said. "A daughter is not a mother."

Sophie stood close to Ben. He smelled her—tomato leaves, coffee, chocolate, sweat. From the kitchen came the sound of the canary singing, a clear spill of notes. "Mazel," Sophie said.

"Luck," Ben said."

"I feed Mazel. He sings."

"I could use some luck."

Walking away, Sophie called back to him, "You got already."

Ben didn't understand. He dipped a torn piece of his bialy into his coffee and turned the paper back to the front page. Though he had touched every page, the paper was spotless, unwrinkled. Maybe he *could* change his luck. He looked up from reading the paper as he ate. The triptych of the bow window framed the street. Under the large maple tree in full leaf, which filled the middle panel of glass, the gold light was laced with green. Anyone who looked in could see Ben, but he, just a few feet back from the window, felt alone, unseen. "I could get married again," he said to himself, and the thought stayed with him as he left the store and continued his solitary walk.

The streets of Paterson had not obliterated the landscape. They lay loosely buckled over red shale and sandstone. Decaying red shale turned the soil of Paterson a raw dark red. The city was bound by a deep curve in the river. Paterson was a peninsula bathed by the river on three sides.

Ben walked down Broadway into the heart of the city. From the sloping street he could see the green woods of Garret Mountain. When he got to Four Corners, he heard the roar of the Paterson Falls, where the rain-gorged river dropped seventy feet into a narrow chasm filled with mist. The buildings at Four Corners—with their deeply carved facades, rosettes, and curving leaf-shapes, their dark recessed windows creating the illusion of open space between the incised half columns— looked like a row of temples leading to the green glades of the mountains and the rushing roar of water.

Farther on, clouds of starlings rose from City Hall, where they nested in the arches, balustrades, and deep cornices. They would come back at dusk, whirling down into a spinning funnel, perching so closely packed City Hall looked as if it were draped in black bunting, as if Paterson were in official and perpetual mourning. Just before night, their raucous cries throbbed like a call to prayer from City Hall to the surrounding streets. A plan to poison them had been opposed by lovers of starlings, who called the strategy "murderous cruelty." It had been replaced by a scheme to frighten the birds away by exploding Roman candles in a gorgeous public display. Again the starling lovers protested and won. The starlings remained sacred—temple birds, protected in their defecating and devouring. Their going out and their return framed the business day.

The Shein salon was on Ellison, the long, fluid curves of its art nouveau facade elegant and spare in the shadow of the massive, ornate, gothic palace of Quackenbush, diagonally across the narrow street, fronting Market. Before they had moved the business to Ellison, the Sheins, new immigrants, had set up shop on Broadway. It was the twenties, before the Crash, when even ordinary people had bought fur coats. "Not just well-to-do women," Ben had said. "Girls. Not even high school graduates. From the factories. They saved every penny. For what? A coat."

The Crash had almost finished all the fur business in Paterson, but Ben, having learned the rigors of fashion design from his father, had proved his skill to Eli Shein's wealthiest customers, who were immune to financial disaster and did not desert him after Eli's death. Ben also had had the good luck to marry Tess: she convinced him to set up a fabric and notions shop next door to the old fur salon on Broadway. Farmers were coming in from the country to buy in Paterson. Even women who had never sewn before were making their own curtains and pillowcases. Tess's shop made money and carried them through the final years of the Depression. When more people had money for fur coats, Ben was ready. Soon he was able to move the salon to Ellison Street.

Ben had learned about the fur itself from his grandfather Jacob. "Do you know what fur-wool is?" his grandfather had once asked him. The little boy couldn't answer. "It's the under hair," Jacob had said. "Feel it." Ben had felt it, stroked it. "The pelage, soft, downy, silky," Jacob had whispered. "The fur closest to the skin of the warm-blooded swimmers—the belly hair of the amphibians."

"I give my customers quality," Ben now liked to say. If a customer could afford only "Hudson seal," so be it. He'd make them a beautiful coat. And he kept the secrets of his trade. A customer shouldn't know that her "Hudson seal" was muskrat. He did his best for wearers of rat as for the wearers of Persian. "Persian" lamb was really from Russia. Lamb was *lamb*. Customers heard that word but they didn't hear. As the skin was cut from the lamb and became "Persian," so the word *lamb* was severed from the actual lamb, from the pitiful youth of the lamb. But Ben did not forget the bloody slaughter. "The best Persian comes from the Karakul. We take the fur from the lamb before the curl loosens," Jacob had told Ben. From the youngest lamb, the silkiest, a week old. A nursling, toothless. The tooth buds still deep in the soft gums. For the best quality pelts, the slaughterer skinned the animal while it was still warm, the skin bloody, the skinned animal bluish red like a fetus. Ripped flesh stuck to the skins. With rare exceptions, the skin of the most darkly furred animal was white. White under dark. White streaked with blood.

The customer didn't know, didn't want to know, didn't have to know. The customer had to pay. Nobody got a break. The furrier had to pay, too: he had to know and lie.

Ben Shein reached his salon on Ellison. Flanking the door of the shop were two bow windows still lit for night, the glass angled like the panels of a three-way mirror. The window on the left was bare except for a dressing table and a plush-covered stool pushed back as if someone had just put down the silver-backed hand mirror, risen from her seat, and passed into the second glass chamber, where she stood caressed by a close-fitting suit of thin violet wool. She looked out to the designer who had made her garment and dressed her: Ben judged his creation:

not right, not yet. He knew what she needed and he would get it. He let himself into the store, chose a long brace of silver fox tails, and, carrying the fur in two hands, climbed through the narrow glass door into the window, where he arranged the thick silver rope so that it fell just below the hem of the skirt.

Turning off the night lights, Ben went out, crossed Ellison, and took as long a view of his work as the narrow street would allow. The fur did not hang right. "Almost, almost," he said to himself, as he climbed back into the window. Hunched in the small space between the wall and the mannequin, with no room to extend his arms, he adjusted the fur, slowly moving his wrists as if he were adjusting the weights in a mechanical clock. Once more, Ben went back to the street to judge the effect. The fur looked wild and fresh against the fine violet wool. Finally he was satisfied.

He looked up Ellison Street, into the shadow of the huge Quackenbush department store. As he rested his eyes on the distance, the memory of Judith Karger came into his mind—her slim arm bent to her waist, the neat handbag holding her change purse tucked next to Sophie Winik's rich cake he had bought for her. Why should a pretty girl have to worry about the price of cake? She had a figure for clothes—that long straight back, a woman's body, and a face like a girl's. For her he could cut out a suit with the right line, because without a line—Ben drew back from the possibility. A pretty girl shouldn't be alone, he thought. But maybe she had someone?

He entered his store again. He walked over his own name set in the tile mosaic.

The salon took up most of the first floor. The vault was at the back and the workroom was upstairs, reached by a spiral metal stairway that rose above the vault. Ben turned on the ceiling fan, opened the back door, and looked quickly around the room, checking the low table between two chairs near the door. The black glass candy bowl was half filled. Ben took a bag from the drawer in the table and heaped the bowl with hard candy, as he did every morning—black-coffee-flavored Hopjes, Tess's choice. He couldn't get away from her, the thrust of her voice. "Tochis, it's the real Hopjes," Tess would mutter under her breath when a customer would ask whether the mink was really mink and not squirrel. She liked to ring changes on the word for ass: a tochis could be fat, skinny, stupid; a person could kiss hers. "The real Hopjes," Ben said to himself as he twisted the bag shut and pushed it deep into the drawer.

July was a slow month. In the summer the Sheins refurbished coats, stored them, and made repairs to the store. Ben's helpers were on vacation, except for his assistant, Moe Black, who would soon arrive. Brona came at nine to open the showroom.

Upstairs at his desk, Ben, who usually took this morning time to sketch new designs and straighten his files, rested his chin on his hands. His skin still smelled like his lemony shaving soap. "Maybe," he said to himself, "I could get married. But then again I don't have to. I can think about it." He played with the idea, imagining himself in a little scene, well dressed, looking younger than his forty years, his step quick, his hand ready for the unseen person who would gaze at him with endless devotion. Held in the possibility, Ben cocked his head against his smooth palm.

He heard the sound of feet, a hum, a whistle, a sigh. Fat, balding, Moe Black came up the stairs. His combed-forward, wetted-down thin hair had dried and lifted from his head like brittle frosting. "Ben," he crooned in a low whisper as if he were meeting him at a wedding or a funeral. It was difficult to know whether he was offering congratulations or condolences. Moe pointed to the coat on his worktable. "Mrs. Gayner, the Behind."

"The same one?" Ben asked.

"The same schmattah."

"She could afford a new one. The woman has money. What it costs her to bring this rag in every year, I could make her a beautiful coat. But no. Look at it. I picked these pelts, I matched them. You saw me. I finessed the shading," Ben said.

"You did." Moe took up the chant. "We cut, we stitched, we soaked the skin-side and nailed the sections over a pattern until they dried. We pieced it. We glazed it until it shined."

"Now look at it. The coat is dead," Ben said.

"Not dead, worn out." Moe held the coat by the collar. He flicked it with the back of his plump fingers. He turned it. The skins were dry. "What does the bat do?" Moe asked. "Put it on the radiator? It's stiff. Like wood. Believe me, this bird ain't got otter."

"Otter," Ben said. He knew what was coming.

"A black like you'll never see. A rhapsody. The silkiest," Moe said.

"I know." Ben's grandfather Jacob had worked on otter; Ben would not.

"A regular pogrom." Moe sighed. "No more. The Russians slaughtered them all. Not one pelt have I seen for years. Nothing."

Ben heard again the elegy of his childhood. "Mrs. Gayner," he said. "I'll sell her a new coat." In order to sell, he had to fit the skin to a woman's body.

"For Gayner, Mrs. Behind, I'll make this one like new," Moe said. "The Behind don't need you, Mr. Designer. Who do you think you are, Chanel? First the black thread then the white thread, the coat is too wet, the coat is too dry, talk to the customer, don't talk to the customer, the store is too hot, the store is too cold."

Ben laughed, "Enough with Mrs. Gayner."

"You know why she don't buy a new coat? She does it to get him, the husband. To shame him," Moe said.

"What kind of marriage is that?" Ben asked.

"One kind. Wait, there's more; you don't know a thing. For years he got someone else. A Polish woman." Moe knew every story. He had once told Ben about a coat a daughter had brought in. Her mother had died in the coat, in a car accident. Thrown through the windshield, over the hood, she had landed face down on the road. The fur was stiff with dry blood, the front of the coat scraped to the skin where she had slid along the rough pavement. She had hit so hard, even the pockets were gritty with dirt. Out of one pocket Moe had pulled a white handker-chief, "folded like a letter. I kept it. Then I lost it. The coat I fixed," he had said, as if he had saved the mother.

Now Moe lifted Mrs. Gayner's coat high in the air. "What's Behind's first name? Dora? How about a middle name—Olga? We'll put in a new lining, with big initials. I'll make it special."

"Next time, send Gayner to me," Ben said. He pressed his fingers against his new tie, the expensive silk, glossy and smooth. The spender answered the saver: "You," Ben said. "You think you can bring back the dead."

AT THE END OF THE DAY, ALONE IN THE WORKROOM WITH MOE AND Brona gone, Ben turned off all the lights except one that threw a single beam of light on the stairs. He would soon meet his brother, Nat, for dinner, but Ben was too tired to think of food. Longing for sleep, he rested in his chair, his hands on his desk, his head on the bony pillow, his eyes closed. If Tess had been there, she would have rubbed the back of his head, coaxed him home. Together they would have gone down the stairs, made sure the window lights were on for the night.

Outside, along Ellison and Market Streets, the owners and managers locked and unlocked their doors, letting their help out one at a time, holding the heavy doors open partway, one arm extended, leaning forward toward the street. To open the door all the way they would have had to step outside like doormen. They were courtly, fatherly, as they performed the good-night ritual, which they believed discouraged stealing.

At Quackenbush's, where Judith Karger worked, the saleswomen had to pass close to the boss as they slipped through the narrow opening. Some laughed their daughterly flirting good nights, while under their dresses, inside their pants, in their bras, next to their skin, they carried things they had stolen—little things: a pair of stockings, a rolled-up belt, underpants, a flimsy pair of earrings. Judith never stole. It was wrong, she thought. And she was afraid of getting caught. She saved for the things she wanted. She liked the feel of silk around her neck. She refused to wear worn lingerie and would buy only white under-things, delighting in them, the signs of her spirit she did not understand.

Among the last to leave, gloved hands clasped in front of her, arms bent so her elbows lay close to her sides—the posture of women of the British royal family—Judith held herself away from the Quackenbush son stationed at the door and, in her quiet well-bred voice, said good night.

There had been a brief, violent storm in the middle of the day. The gutters were still wet, and the sound of the Falls mingled with the noise of the traffic. The day had seemed over inside the store. Now the day began again. Cars drew up to the side entrance of Quackenbush's as if to a theater. Here and there a car door opened; a woman entered. The rest walked, some carrying shopping bags filled with groceries they had bought during lunch hour.

Alone, Judith walked slowly toward home in the bright light of the July evening. Roofers had been working that morning, and the rain had not washed away the smell of burning tar—smoky and sweet. When she was a child, Judith and her friends would gather the hardening tar, glossy as glass. Staring at the weedy, overgrown tree strip, she fell into an old daydream that she would find a treasure tangled in the grass, dropped in the gutter. Money. Something for her. Once, in the playground, she had found coins under the slide. She had gotten down on her hands and knees on the hard, packed ground. It was difficult to get a grip on the coins. She had had to scrape them up with her index fingers. And there wasn't much nail. Her mother had cut her nails close. Maybe she would let them grow—but she couldn't: long nails would catch on the goods she sold.

A loud voice broke into her reverie, "What are you doing with that stick? What kind of child points a stick?" Swaying toward her was an old man, bareheaded, his face flecked with white stubble, his yellow hands shaking. Just in front of her, a boy with a stick. The boy laughed. The old man was ready for him, "You think it's funny? With a stick you could do damage. With a stick you could take a person's eye out. What kind of boy are you? What kind of parents let you go out with a stick? They should watch you. On a street you don't bring sticks. Does a person bring a gun on a street? Does a person bring a rock?" The old man looked at Judith. "You see, young lady, he doesn't answer me. He doesn't know what to say. He could kill someone, and he doesn't know what to say. Listen to me, Sonny." The boy ran across the street. The man stuck his nose in Judith's face. "You, a beautiful young lady, you look like a nice girl, but I know what you are."

Judith's shoulders jerked and froze. "I'm sorry. I have to go. My mother is waiting."

"Who's stopping you?" He glared at her.

Her feet suddenly heavy, she was afraid with a fear so beyond words and reason that she didn't know she was afraid, as a child without language is afraid. She was hot and cold, jolted and still. If she had swung her clenched hand against the old man's head, she could have knocked him off his feet.

"Go ahead. What are you looking at me for?" The old man blocked the sidewalk.

Look at him? She would never look at him. Judith turned away, a scalding heat along her chest bone. Her eyes burned, but no tears came.

Ben Shein and his brother, Nat, walked toward Four Corners, where they ate together once a week at the Ding Ho Palace, two flights up. The relentless rushing glissando of the Paterson Falls grew louder. If the sound of the falls had suddenly stopped, they would have missed its roar, but so accustomed were they to the sound of cascading water they barely heard it.

Nat was the outside man for the Shein businesses. He did the same kind of work he had once done for Paterson bootleggers: he drove a truck; he picked up and delivered. He could not stand to be in the store all day, could not stand to be anywhere. Nat raced ahead.

Ben puffed. "Slow down. What's your hurry? I don't have time to work out like you."

"Why didn't you say something?"

"I did."

"OK, I heard you." Nat Shein reined himself in. His large head shot back. His legs jerked. His glossy, rag-whipped shoes skidded on the pavement.

"Good. We're supposed to be together." Ben laughed. With the smile on his lips, he looked down Broadway and recognized Judith Karger walking ahead of him, in the distance. "I know her," he said to Nat.

"You do?"

"I made a coat for her mother," Ben said.

"What about the daughter?"

"She's got a figure. A nice girl, well spoken. What do you think?" Ben asked.

Nat's eyes found Judith's long back. He sped up, leaving Ben behind, and came abreast of Judith Karger, careful to avoid her eyes. He needn't have bothered: Judith's stare was locked on the distance. Nat passed her, stopped at a store window, his back to the sidewalk. Glancing over his left shoulder, he saw as much as he wanted.

Puffing, Ben caught up as he watched Judith cross Broadway and disappear from sight. "So tell me. You know what a good piece is." Ben believed he was offering the kind of praise Nat wanted.

"You think so?"

"You know . . ."

Nat stopped him, "Later, I'm hungry. Let me eat and then I'll think."

"You're going to think?"

Nat walked faster, swinging his powerful arms. The dressy suit jacket he had put on over his open-collared work shirt strained across his broad back.

"Where did you get that jacket?" Ben called out. "It's too small."

Nat heard the plea in his voice. "From Mendy," he shouted, letting Ben catch up. "Ready-made. He let it out."

"But not enough."

"There was no more. I liked the material," Nat said.

"You're a Shein."

That much Nat could accept.

When the brothers got to the restaurant, they found crazy Joe Mavet squeezed against the wall of the small downstairs hall.

Nat pushed forward to the steep stairs. "I thought you were dead," he muttered to Joe.

"I don't die. I tell." Joe Mavet raised his white index finger and spread his black-sleeved arms.

Ben stopped, already reaching into his pocket.

"Ben Shein, Ben Shein," Joe Mavet sang in his high voice. He wore, despite the July heat, a heavy black overcoat held closed with safety pins. He had pinned a sock around his neck, the large safety pins in front. His long filthy hair stuck out from his apple pie cap, which looked new.

Somebody must have just given to it him, thought Ben. "So how are you?" he asked in a soft voice. Though he had known Joe for years, ever since Joe's sister Yetta had worked in the Sheins' fabric shop, Ben still stared, his heart contracting.

"I've got news for you, Ben," Joe said.

"Mavet, go sing in the cemetery," Nat shouted from the stairs.

"I do." Joe threw out his chest, ready for a medal.

Nat laughed.

"You know Nat," Ben said, his voice low.

"You I know." Joe spread his black-sleeved arms again. "I'm singing now, but you don't listen. And they," he pointed to the ceiling, "they sing to me. In my house, from the icebox, comes voices. From the radio. They know all about me. Also from the radiators. Noises."

Joe had flung the radio out the back window, but he had not been able to move the refrigerator to reach the plug. He had covered the refrigerator with blankets and tied the blankets with clothesline. The sounds of the motor turning on and off came through the blankets. He had covered the radiators to muffle the spit of the steam, to staunch the moist hisses coming up through the pipes sunk deep in the molten center of the earth under Paterson. Wired with menace, the world hummed with murder, the dentist drilled for blood.

"Joe," Ben said in a reasonable voice.

"I know. They tell me. I listen. That dentist Yetta made me go to is not a real Jew. He's a German. The fillings have wires. They are talking. I know what God says. They will kill us. Our children. I don't have. You got. Yours. What's-her-name. Your daughter. You better listen," Joe said.

"Never mind."

"Yours. They'll eat. Everybody. Watch out for her."

"Come on, what do you know?"

"I know. You don't listen." Joe lifted a lock of his filthy hair. "Under my hair is a number. I try to hide it. You have to take a microscope. In the scalp, deep—a number. Maybe you have one too?"

Joe held his hands close to his own eyes and made a fussy motion as if he were tying to pick pins out of the air. His hands were surprisingly clean. When he visited his sister Yetta, she would trick him into washing. She would pile dirty dishes in the sink and coax him to wash them with her as they had done when they were children. They played and washed. She hummed and coaxed. The water turned black; she dried her brother's hands on the kitchen towel. She felt his thin hands through the coarse fabric. Joe left with a package of food. Hers was the only food he would eat. After Joe left, she would wash the dishes again.

"How's your sister?" Ben asked.

"How's your daughter?" Joe answered.

"Fine, fine. Susan is fine."

"A *Susan* you got? I got a Yetta Sister. She's OK too. But she's going to die: Yetta of Blessed Memory. They can go just like that." Joe snapped his fingers. As if they could lift him, he flapped his arms, slowly at first, then wildly, pumping. His eyes were gleeful. He opened his mouth wide, showing his large square teeth. His laugh was a howl. Tears ran down his face.

Ben took the charge of Joe Mavet's galvanic laugh. It thrilled him, the dutiful son, the good son, the tender father. He laughed, too, released from the burden of virtue. He thought he was laughing at Joe's foolishness.

"You're cockeyed," Joe said, pointing a finger at Ben's eyes. "You better hurry up, your brother is hungry. He's not like you. I'm your brother, not him. Go, he'll eat the wall. An animal."

Ben looked over his shoulder at Nat, "He doesn't know what he's saying, he doesn't mean it."

Nat's black eyes turned darker in his pale face. His muscled neck swelled. He shook his head. A lock of his black hair, which he wore combed straight back, broke from its stiff glaze and fell across his eye. He raked it back.

Ben turned away and handed Joe a twenty-dollar bill.

"Ben Shein, Ben Shein," Joe Mavet sang as he walked out to the street.

"Meshuga. How can you give him money? Twenty dollars. He'll throw it away. They should lock him up," Nat said.

"I like to give him. In the hospital, he'd get worse. This way his sister can take care of him. He knows my name; he talks to me. No one should be alone. It's not good. He has good days."

"This you call a good day? You're crazy." Nat's voice rose.

"Don't get excited. It's nothing," Ben said.

"Nothing? What do you need Joe Mavet for? You got me. The fucking stooge. The lugger. You're the genius, the Bar Mitzvah boy, not me."

"What are you talking about? You're my brother."

"Who needs it? Give him money," Nat said.

"I give you."

"For what? Buy yourself another shtarker." Nat spat out the word for strong man, held up loose fists, coyly wiggled his shoulders to mock his own strength as he pursed his lips and made a loud kissing sound.

"You're good for the business," Ben lied. In this family of makers, Nat couldn't make a thing. "People know you. You can make your own time."

"My own? What's my own?"

"You can do what you want," Ben said.

"Leave it." Nat took the steps two at a time, ahead of Ben.

Swaddled in white, the Ding Ho Palace—like a stage room with furniture draped in dust covers when the family has departed for the country—was silent. The tablecloths dropped to the floor. The napkins were as large as towels. Two layers of white curtains filtered the sun that at sunset still burned hot and yellow.

Ben handed his brother a menu. "Whatever you want." He'd make it up to him, he'd take care of him.

When they had slept together as children, Nat—younger, yet sturdy, his muscles already strong—would wake up in Ben's thin arms, his head resting on Ben's chest, in the vee of the pajama top. Against his ear, his brother's smooth skin, the bump of bone, the beating heart. Nat would be comforted. He had turned to Ben in his sleep, never the other way. Yet Nat, years later, had comforted Ben when Tess had died. Ben could remember Nat's leading him away from Tess's coffin into the kitchen. She had been buried from the house, the way they did it then. Nat had cupped the back of his head, drawing him against his chest when Ben had called out, "I don't want my wife in that box, I don't want it." His tears had soaked into Nat's shirt. Nat had not pulled away from his brother's shuddering sobs. It seemed to Ben that Nat had drawn the sobs from him, drawn them into his hard body where they sweetened— once. Once was not enough for Ben. He wanted always. He wanted again.

The waiter, his white apron falling to his ankles, brought the heavy covered dishes that sank into the thick layers of linen without a click or a clatter.

Ben raised the cover of the shrimp in lobster sauce.

Nat repositioned his knife and fork so they lay perpendicular to the table edge. He yoked his restlessness to order. He grinned, inhaled, and for a moment forgot himself.

They both loved the succulent, richly spiced food. They loved the white meat pulled from the shells.

Nat brought the meat to his mouth and ate.

Ben watched his brother's face: "I want to get married."

"You want to get married? So that's why you're looking." Nat pointed his fork at his brother, "That girl in the street."

"You're surprised?"

"You were married."

"So what?"

"So what?"

"Enough already."

"What about Susan?"

"Don't worry."

"I worry."

"Children forget," said Ben, who could not forget. "I'm looking. A man can look. I'm out of circulation. In the store, who do I see? Married women. I don't want to start with them. Where do I go? I'm inside all day, not like you. You get whatever you want."

"I get whatever I want," Nat said. He put his hands palms down on the white cloth. Like Ben's they were small, stroked with fine black hair.

His skin was blue-white—the family pallor. He tilted his head back. His dark brows lifted. The shining cap of his hair slid back. High up close to the hairline, a livid scar, a present from his last lover.

He had been wild to have her on her knees in her father's house, her lace-trimmed underwear disheveled, his cock in her mouth. He had gotten what he wanted and more than he wanted. He had looked down while she knelt, her mouth on him, and he had seen his toes with their thick yellowish nails curled into the floor, like talons, and he had driven his cock deeper into her mouth, hurting her as he came. At the end, he had come away from their lovemaking with his own mouth sore, his back bloody where she had raked him with her sharp, red-painted nails. He had become afraid of his cruelty. "I should put my cock in a sling," he had told himself. "Pack it up with all that." When he broke with her, she had opened up his head with a crystal vase. Drunk when the doctor had stitched up the deep gash, Nat had been ashamed to go back to have the stitches removed. He had leaned close to the bathroom mirror and, with a tweezers, gasping from the pain, he had pulled out the black stitches, reopening the wound.

None of this did he tell his brother.

"Lover boy," Ben said. "What do you think? That one we saw, Judith Karger."

Nat went on eating, his face hard, like a hammer.

"Tell me?" Ben pleaded.

Nat put his fork down. His mouth opened in a crooked smile.

Ben waited.

"Not for you." Nat tried to lend authority to his judgment, repeating the words that had come down from the generations, "Not meant to be."

"Not *meant* to be?" Nisht bashert. Ben laughed. What did Nat know about fate? He was a Shein, but he was no Jacob.

"That one, Judith, wouldn't say shit if she had a mouthful," Nat said.

"That's supposed to be a reason?"

"I know women."

Ben couldn't disagree.

"I have a friend, Lillian Tondow. Works for lawyer Fielding. Divorced from Dave Tondow, the gambler, the one who's in jail."

"Did you?"

"Did I what?" Nat's voice rose.

"Never mind."

"I helped her out."

"You helped her?"

"I talked to her. I listened. After the husband went away. She finally got rid of him."

"A divorced woman?"

"You want a virgin?"

Ben swallowed before he laughed. "I don't know what I want."

"I'll talk to her," Nat said. "Tondow's a good scout, smart. I lent her money. She paid me back. I'll be a matchmaker. Me." He pointed to his broad chest.

"You. It could happen." Ben took courage. Nat would stand with him—a dark blue suit, a white carnation. Both of them in blue.

"Tondow'd be good with Susan. No kids from the gambler, but she's calm. How is the kid?"

"She told me she was an orphan."

"She's half an orphan."

"She wants private art lessons with Miss Moore, the teacher she has in school. Her friend Englander—this Joan—she has private lessons. Now Susan wants. The two of them: together all the time. They love this Miss Moore, a gentile woman. Susan talks and talks about her. Maybe my daughter is looking for a mother." He stared at the table. "What happened to the bill?"

"I got it. I'm fast," Nat said.

"When you want to be."

Nat opened his jacket. He held the bill against his chest. "Let me."

"OK." Ben raised his hands. For once Nat could pay.

Nat had fixed things up. Ben was going to meet Lillian Tondow. He climbed the steep stairs to the flat she shared with her parents on the second story of a two-family house on Twelfth Avenue. The foundation had settled and the house leaned like a bombed ship. The stairs trembled, even under Ben's light step. No one had thought to put a light on; the narrow hall was dark. The thick smell of frying food came from the first-floor flat. Ben stood on the dark narrow landing, close to the door. He felt he might topple backward down the stairs that dropped away behind him. He heard voices when he knocked.

Finally the door opened. Ida Tondow, Lillian's mother, faced him. She didn't speak.

"Is Lillian home?" Ben met Ida's neutral eyes. 'I'll believe it when I see it,' they seemed to be saying.

The proof was on Ben. But he was at a loss.

"Come in, come in. Lillian took out the dog. Sit." She motioned to a chair.

Ben hesitated. The kitchen table was piled high. The stacks of dishes and pots and pans looked as if they would come tumbling down if he moved a chair.

"What are you waiting for? Sit. I'm cleaning my shelves."

Ben obeyed, struggling in the cramped space to turn his chair away from the table so he could see her.

The dark gold walls were crackled like old varnish, the dull red and black linoleum floor scrubbed clean. Early evening light came through the four-over-four pane windows. Ben could see to the horizon—a tender wavering line of treetops.

In his dark blue suit, his pant leg riding up as he crossed his leg to reveal a silky black sock, he looked like a first-class passenger who had accidentally wandered down to the galley where meals for the ship's crew were cooked. He was as sleek as if he had been polished, rubbed with a chamois until he shone.

"I'm working," Ida said. Her flat face was like the lid of a pot, with a nose for a handle; her straight hair, parted on the side, held smooth across the top of her head by a thin barrette, seemed metallic, each strand—gray, white, brown, gold—set into her scalp, like wire. Her body was softer—large round breasts, the cleavage showing, her large head casting a shadow on the fine, slightly stretched skin. The shadow seemed warm.

Would the daughter look like her mother?

"Don't worry, Lillian is coming," Ida said. She kept twitching her head as she spoke, her streaked hair glinting. Between tics, she rapidly inhaled, a hissing, sucking sound through closed teeth. Ida pointed to a restaurant-size soup pot on the stove. "It's empty," she said. "I didn't make anything. I should get rid of all this." The pots on the table were enormous. "I bought from a restaurant. "What do I need all this for? I can hardly lift them. Lillian told me you would be here." Ida pointed to the clean empty shelves. "But why should I wait?" Her next statement had become her philosophy: "I have things to do."

She would not change her plans for anyone. The reason she would not was soon apparent.

The narrow door to the back hall opened. Barney Tondow filled it. He stood in the doorway with his hat on, although he had just come from the bedroom and was dressed in slippers, shirt, and pants. He was not an observant Jew; he wore a hat to cover his baldness. It wasn't clear why he should be so vain: his small eyes were close together above a large nose, bulbous and crooked. His arthritis was bothering him, and he rocked to the table as if he had just dismounted from a horse.

Since his arrival in America from Lodz, Barney Tondow had worked less and less. At first he had blamed the bosses who, he said, expected him to work on a Saturday. "On the Sabbath: I can't do it." Barney was a carpenter. Only once had he been asked to work on Saturday. The shocking request became his defense. He milked it for years, stoking the furnace of his resentment about his failure to find work, hiding his shame, adopting a wise philosophical tone about himself, creating himself as a mensch who could say no, a person of integrity. But in this new, growing world of assimilated Jews with names like "Waldo Fielding"— Lillian's boss—even Barney Tondow realized he needed a new lie. "I'm building a house for a customer," he would say. Lillian paid the bills.

Sighing, Barney Tondow sat down at the corner of the table, "So who are you?"

"I'm Ben Shein." Ben had to turn his chair to face him.

"Shein, Shein?" Barney looked sly.

"The fur store," answered Ben.

Barney smiled at him, showing his small white teeth.

Ben waited.

"Tell me, Mr. Ben Shein, do you shtup those rich women? Your wife's been dead a long time."

"Shah," Ida yelled, banging the table with her fist. "I warned you."

"What a mouth on her." Barney smiled at Ben.

"You should know from mouths. Who asked you? Better you should drop dead," Ida said.

"You before me. I'll spit on your grave. Go, go, peddle your ass with your daughter."

"Me?" Ida laughed. "Mr. Shein, who knows what is inside a man?"

Barney Tondow turned to Ben and lowered his voice. "My friend, I married a whore."

Ben tried to get up, prying himself out of the narrow space with his hands. When he was upright, his right hand flew to his neck, where the carotid arteries brought blood to his brain.

"Don't go," Barney said.

"It's Lillian." Ida waved her head at her husband. "He's afraid of her."

Barney could not keep the spite out of his voice. "A hot day," he said. It sounded like a curse. He was smiling, not like the cat who had eaten the canary, but like the cat who still had the canary in its mouth, the feathers wet with blood and saliva, and was rolling the bird over and over across its rough tongue, and any minute would pop the bird's crushed head out from between its teeth, holding the neck tight, shaking the head.

Lillian Tondow came through the door. Her red pleated skirt looked homemade, but not bad with the round-collared white blouse. A black dog leaped in front of her, ran toward Ben. "Jerry," said Lillian. "Her name is Jerry."

The dog's nose was cool against Ben's hands, her fur silky. "I had a dog once. A long time ago," Ben said as he looked up at Lillian. What a face on her, he thought. White as a behind with those white curves. And that hair pulled back to show it.

She picked up the dog's bowl, went to the sink, poured out the stale water, rinsed and refilled the bowl, placing it on the newspaper in the corner next to the sink.

"She loves that dog," Barney muttered.

Jerry hunched over, her back legs quivering as she gulped, her tags clanking against the metal bowl.

"Sounds like a horse," Ben said pleasantly.

"She's as stupid as a horse," Barney said. "Nothing but a stupid animal."

Ida seized a large fork, held it like a spear, and thrust it toward Barney.

"This one don't cook for me," Barney said. "Big pots, not a drop of food—a stage kitchen I have to look at. Only one child she gave me. Even her own daughter she don't give to eat."

Lillian looked straight at Ben. "Jerry is thirsty."

Ben had managed to turn around in the narrow space. The edge of the table pressed into his buttocks. He motioned toward the door. "We'll go out," he said to Lillian.

"To get out of here," Lillian said, laughing, her mouth open as if she were going to bite into a large apple. She needed to get a sweater and told Ben to come with her.

With the dog squeezed against his legs, he followed her down the hall. She had taken what used to be the living and dining rooms. The sliding doors between them were pushed open partway. Ben could see her bed covered with a chenille bedspread, enormous red roses carved into the nap. He watched as she sat at a dressing table between the two front windows, the dog at her feet. She didn't look at Ben as she let down her hair and combed it up again, fastening it with hairpins, which she took from her mouth. She ran the lipstick over her curving mouth and pressed her lips together as if she were trying to taste them. Never said a word to him. Got up, threw a sweater over her shoulders. She looked right at him.

Ben thought of walking toward her, imagining himself adjusting the sweater on her shoulders. He saw his hands rest for a moment on the tops of her arms, but he didn't move. If only she would say something. Everything he could have done gathered around him as possibility. It wasn't too late yet.

Ben wanted to take her to Caughey's on the Paterson Plank Road to eat fish. "The salmon is so good, the lobster." He could already see the pink meat in her open mouth.

She wanted to drive south and stop at a roadhouse where they could dance if they wanted.

Nat's kind of place, Ben thought. But still he would take her.

In ten minutes they were out of Paterson, driving south into farmland, a strip of fertile land between the ocean and the mountains. When Ben drove, he usually had to think about what he was doing, but tonight he relaxed for a while. There was little traffic. In front of them the sky opened up, dark orange and rose. The clouds stretched into thin black flags and finally, when the sky darkened, disappeared.

Lillian opened the side vent, and the watermelon smell of cut grass flooded the car with its sweetness.

They passed a sign for Vineland, the state hospital. "I know someone there," she told Ben. "My friend Bernice. They put her away when she was still young. She was so skinny her mother used to dress her in little girl clothes, dresses with bows. She wore big glasses and would follow me around and listen to everything I said. There was a thunderstorm, lightning, a sudden cold in the middle of the summer. I was looking out the window. Bernice was standing in the rain without moving. She just stood there like a little tree, dripping water until someone went out to get her. She didn't know enough to come in out of the rain."

"Where was her mother?"

"Who knows? Her mother got tired. Children like that used to die. They would arrange for them to die," Lillian said.

"To kill a child? Who would do that?"

"My father could kill a child. I wouldn't leave my dog with him."

Ben laughed. "You don't mean it."

"You saw what he was like."

"I saw, but . . ."

"He'll do anything."

"He asked if I shtupped my rich women customers. I didn't answer him. Also he also brought up my wife, Tess." Ben's voice caught in his throat.

"How long has it been?"

"Too long."

"So what do you do? It gets lonely," Lillian said.

"Forget it. I went with a customer once, a married woman. I wanted more, or maybe I wasn't ready."

"So you've been alone."

Ben thought of his dreams, the ghost of Tess, her hoarse whisper, and was silent.

"Here." Lillian pointed, but they were already past the low one-story building sunk at the edge of the road. Ben turned back and pulled into the shallow parking lot, nosing the Chrysler into a single row of cars with their front bumpers tight against a wooden fence. Beyond the fence, a field of corn stubble: it was early August, and the corn had been cut.

A red neon sign blinked out Rutt's Hut. Except for the sign and a small light over the door, the building was dark, the windows covered.

"I'm starved," Lillian said as they stood together in the tiny entrance. Her face was so close to Ben's he could feel her breath, but he didn't touch her.

He opened the splintered inner door, and she passed in front of him into the blue-lit smoky room.

Under the low ceiling, couples danced to the music of a three-piece band. The thrum of the bass vibrated. A black woman stepped to the microphone, looked at the crowd, poised, her black dress tight around her heavy body, purple shadows under her eyes. She seemed tired, but as she began to sing, her low contralto, halting at first, smoothed out—seamless.

The bartender was standing on a strip of raised floor behind the bar. His head barely clearing the low ceiling, he looked like an oversized marionette on a small stage, the bottles reflected in the mirror behind them burning amber and red like Christmas lights.

Ben followed Lillian to a table against the wall and sat facing her, his back to the room.

The dancers hunched into each other. They moved their feet in a slow shuffle.

"I like it here." Lillian looked past him to the dancers. "Sometimes I think I could just drive from place to place."

"Maybe you work too hard. Maybe you need a rest," Ben said.

"I do my job."

"Nat told me. For Waldo Fielding."

"He's the front with the degree. He has the suit with the vest, the gold watch in the pocket, the French cuffs with the gold cufflinks. He gets dressed up for court, but he doesn't go to court. He makes his money in paper—wills, deeds, contracts. He calls it The Law. He makes things Legal: Fielding's Law. The Legal Law."

"Things have to be legal," Ben said.

"They do?" She laughed at him.

The waiter came, a heavy man squeezing his belly between the crowded tables. Lillian asked for Scotch straight up, water on the side. Ben wanted beer in a bottle but had to settle for draft. When the drinks came, he sipped. Lillian drank up, in two swallows.

He'd be a mensch. Treat her right. "Another?"

"I'm happy on one drink. I could bum around on one drink. I'm not a drunk."

"I didn't think . . ."

"Forget it." That white face of hers lifted toward him.

"I . . ."

She wouldn't let him finish. She wanted to know who his lawyer was.

"Morty Ploshnick," he told her.

"Morty Ploshnick: he gets the job done. He's no a big I-am, and Ben Shein is not a *big*-time crook. Customers don't sue you. You deliver quality."

"Oh, I'm a real artist. But they get mad when I'm late with a coat."

"For that they don't hire a lawyer. Customers will wait for a coat from Ben Shein."

She had said something good about him. Ben wanted more, but she started on the law again. Her red lips kept moving. "What do most clients actually get from a lawyer? A piece of paper. Bookkeepers—that's all we are. Morty knows this." Her hands moved to the insistent rhythm of her words. "And you can count on him for a sense of—of what? Justice? But of course, we don't have it. Take property law." She stuck out her hand. "What's just about that?"

"What are you talking about? I own. The Sheins own. A house, a business, a car—I worked hard for them. I need Morty to protect me."

"You think you own, but we really don't own anything. We have things on long-term lease. And even then we can lose. And is that really a loss? Maybe that's justice," she said.

"What are you? A commie? What happened to the bookkeeping? The assets? I want what's mine," Ben said.

"Assets?" Her laugh grated on his ear. "I've seen what happens to assets: a lot too small to build on, a dilapidated house with tenants who haven't paid rent in years, a moth-eaten fur coat, a box full of ashes from the furnace, a tooth in a box. That's the estate."

"But some people do well. They have things to pass on. I want my daughter to have what I leave her," Ben said.

"You'd be surprised to see what people leave. A mother leaves her daughter one dollar, the son half a million. She puts the dollar in an envelope for us to hand to the daughter. She wanted a ceremony. I chose not to do it. Waldo has the dollar in the safe—in case the daughter ever asks for it. If you leave a dollar, they can't contest."

"I would never do that. I'll take care of Susan. She's my only one."

"I'm not talking about you." She pointed at him. She waved her hands. "A client takes his dead wife's jewels, divides them, puts them into two velvet bags in a safety deposit box, one for each daughter. After he dies, they stand in the kitchen of their dead parents' house. The younger one holds a gold chain; the older one grabs for it. She grabs so hard she breaks her sister's finger. He should have given it away while he was alive. Jewelry should be worn," Lillian said.

"But the man—he still wanted his wife and what was hers." Ben had kept Tess's clothes. After her death, he had held a hat she had worn to his face and hungrily breathed in the smell of her hair as he rubbed the nap with his thumb. "Where are you?" he had called out like a child.

"I loved my husband," Lillian said. "Maybe I still do."

"Then you still want him?" Ben was careful.

"Never. I've had him. I went to see him once in prison. He looked caved in, gray in the face, but he was cocky, still the big shot."

"I'm sorry."

"Don't be too sorry. Pity can weaken a person. I left my husband just in time. I still have some good memories. I'm not good about changing the past. My father does that—the past and the present. Some people believe him. You saw what he is: a liar. My father slanders dead people. They can't answer him," she said.

"They come back in dreams. They talk to us."

"You dream of Tess?"

At last. The woman had heard him. Ben reached out his hands, palms up. Lillian met him, fit her hands over his, and curled her fingers against his skin. He wanted to turn her hands over and bring the palms to his lips.

They got up to dance. She felt through the material of his suit to his back muscles. He was a lightweight in her arms. Though he danced smoothly, he had to think about what he was doing. She led him, she drew him closer, and he moved with her.

"My brother's the dancer," he said, as they walked back to their table. He longed again to be able to forget himself, to let himself ride on the music. He longed for Nat's easy confidence.

The waiter brought their fish dinners. With her fork, Lillian broke through the crisp brown coat of fried cracker crumbs. Steam rose from the opening in the crust. Her face warmed, flushing, open. She lifted out a thick flake of the moist cod.

"It's good," Ben said. "The potatoes, too." He speared a thick finger of fried potato and brought it to his open mouth.

Lillian ate her potatoes with her fingers, stopping from time to time to wipe them on the paper napkin she had left next to her fork on the table.

She wanted coffee. Ben ordered some for both of them. Holding the spoon level, he poured sugar from the heavy ribbed glass container. As careful as he was, a fine spray of sugar spilled onto the table. Putting down his spoon, Ben brushed the sugar into his other hand, which he held at the table edge and then tilted so the sugar would fall into his saucer. He took a sip, "It's good. Not as good as Sophie Winik's, but good, very good."

"I want to smoke. I'll bum one." Lillian leaned from her chair and asked the man at the next table for a cigarette. He had a big chest and short arms: it would take a genius to cut him a suit. He shook out the pack for her and she took one. He lit it, cupping the flame with his hand. "Thank you," Lillian said, pushing her white, curving face at him. He winked at her: "My pleasure."

"I'm so full." Lillian turned to Ben and undid the button of her skirt. Her breasts moved, full against the thin stuff of her blouse. She stretched and sat taller. "Let's go. I need to walk," she said.

Heat rose from the fields and came in on the breeze. The moon was almost full. They could see across the flat farmland as they stood near the car.

"I forgot to go while I was inside. I'm ready to burst," Lillian laughed, her mouth open. "You don't mind?" Without waiting for him to answer, she left him, climbed over the low post fence, and, screened by the car, squatted down.

Ben could hear it gush out of her. He had never been with a woman who peed on the ground. He had used the men's room. "What are you, a child? You can't hold it?" he asked as Lillian climbed back over the fence.

"I didn't do it in the road. I once read about the Japanese. The Empress would walk in her garden. When she had to go, she would squat down behind a bush, her silk robes around her," Lillian said.

"So it's classy?" Ben laughed. She had a new way of looking at things.

"Aristocratic."

"OK," he said. "You're the Empress." He opened the car door for her. He was ready to turn on the motor when he saw something moving in the field beyond the car. A raccoon. In the moonlight. "Look," he whispered. At first Lillian could not see it. Ben pointed and they saw it together—its humped shape in the stubble. With its sensitive wet-looking leathery fingers, the raccoon found a broken stalk the mower had missed, feeling along its short length. "Oh, he's found something," Lillian whispered, breaking the silence. Oblivious, the raccoon lifted the rough stalk to its small mouth and began to chew.

She and Ben sat still and watched until the humped shape moved through the stubble and was gone.

Ben drove slowly out of the narrow lot onto the moonlit road. Though the air was warm, Lillian pulled her sweater around her the way a child holds onto a blanket. She dozed as Ben drove. Freed from the necessity to speak, Ben relaxed. He looked across at Lillian sleeping next to him, her face half bright, half in shadow against the dark gray seat, refined by moonlight, pure. He drove with care—without shifting out of third gear—not wanting to wake her.

He noticed a dirt road lined with trees, a narrow tractor trail into the cornfields. He thought of turning in and stopping. There will be another road, he thought to himself, as he drove on. I'll stop there. Lillian will wake up. He felt the impulse to take her hands again, to put his lips on her face as she was waking, to draw her tongue into his mouth. He saw another dirt road that dropped deep into the cornfields and rose in the far distance. There wasn't a house in sight.

Ben drove on.

He might have turned into the dirt road and driven deep into the fields, past the stand of maples, past the rows of mammoth sunflowers dropping their seeds.

Ben felt the impulse to turn, but he did not. And he knew the moment was lost. I should have stopped, he thought. Why didn't I? Because she pishes like a peasant, not like the Empress of Japan? Ben heard his grandfather Jacob's voice, "Don't be foolish. You didn't because you didn't. A cloud passed across the moon: say it that way."

Lillian woke. The moon was clear of clouds, and the road was white again. They were almost home. Ben drove to Twelfth Avenue, past two-family houses and apartment houses whose windows were dark.

As Ben parked in front of the Tondows', Lillian put on her sweater. "I was so tired," she said. "It was good to sleep."

Ben got out, opened the door on the passenger side, and reached out his hand. He felt the light touch of her fingers on his arm. "I'll walk you in," he said.

Lillian stopped him, "I'll be fine. You don't have to."

A man's loud voice came from the first-floor flat, "What kind of a person talks in the middle of the night?"

Paterson was a city of interrogators. Ben had heard it and heard it:

Who could do such a thing?

What kind of president?

What kind of God?

What kind of mother?

What kind of father?

What kind of child?

"I'm asking you again: what kind of person talks in the middle of the night?"

"Me, Mr. Solomon. I'm guilty." Lillian's white face flashed in the dark like an enormous wink.

"Don't answer him," Ben whispered. "He's liable to take a gun."

"Never. But you're right."

"I'm right?"

"Ben, be well." She took his hand for a moment and walked away from him into the house. The door on Twelfth Avenue closed. Not even a thank you. "What do you want?" Ben asked himself. She was tired. He looked at the open window of the flat on the first floor and flinched before the interrogator's questions he imagined would come:

What are you standing there for?

What kind of man are you?

Ben looked over his shoulder as he got into the car. No sound came from the window.

The tires made a crunching noise as he pulled into the driveway of his mother's house. Ben turned off the ignition and sat in the sudden silence of the stilled car. When he was ready, he opened the door and slid out of the seat. Just as he stood up, he heard someone calling, "Ben

Shein. Ben Shein." He looked down to the street. Something rustled in the bushes. He heard his name again and walked toward the voice. Crouched on the cold ground, his mud-caked coat pulled around him, was Joe Mavet, his back against the clipped wall of the privet. Ben bent down. "Joe, Joe, what are you doing here?"

"Ben, Ben," Joe mocked. "You want reasons? Everybody wants reasons."

"It's dark out."

"So what else is new? It's going to get darker. Let me tell you. I got news for you. You better be careful. You dumb son of a bitch. Why should you have a daughter? You schmeckel," Joe said.

"You don't mean it."

"OK, I don't." Holding his arms high over his head, Joe rose from the ground as if he were climbing a rope. He stood there, his arms raised, his hands drooping from the wrists. "Don't shoot me."

"Come on. What are you talking about? I'll take you home."

"I'm going home by myself to Yetta, right now," Joe said.

"I'll drive you."

"You're not taking me anywhere. I know you."

Ben reached into his pocket and held out a dollar.

"Keep your money. You can't buy it."

"What?" Ben asked.

"You know what."

Ben didn't know.

Joe ripped the money from Ben's hand. His arms in the air, Joe ran, waving his arms as if he could fly. Ben watched him turn toward Broadway. Joe would be all right. He was going to his sister. He was strong. He runs faster than me, Ben thought.

He went in through the back, into the kitchen. Brona had left the light on for him. The kettle was on the stove ready for breakfast. There was a plate on the table. He lifted the waxed paper to find the piece of apple strudel she had set out for him, took a fork from the drawer and sat down. He could eat better when Brona didn't push him. The strudel was fresh, the thin layers of pastry still flaky. Why should he make trouble for himself with a woman? Ben ate his mother's food and tasted the proof that she had thought of him. Joe Mavet would eat too. His sister Yetta would feed him.

THE PROMISE OF FALL THAT HAD COME AT THE END OF AUGUST—THE changes from morning chill to dry noon heat to golden afternoons—now gave way to swampy heat. The maple leaves drooped a dull, worn-out green. The grass kept its brown burn. It was so hot the squirrels came down from the trees and sprawled in the shade, their small, heaving bellies against the cooler ground near the trunks of the trees. The season slowed, retrogressed.

The previous week's coolness had been a rehearsal: the future in the present.

Even people who were desperate for a fur coat wouldn't come out in heat like this. Ben locked the front door of the shop after the long day. He would go home with his mother, who was waiting for him at the car. She would drive as always, he thought. "Ma, I'm knocked out. It's not the heat; I have the fan. It wasn't too bad. A slow day, it's a slow day that knocks me out," he told her.

She stood there with her pocketbook in her hand. "I want you to drive," she said.

"Me?"

"I don't feel good," Brona said as she walked to the passenger side of the car.

"Ma, where are you going? You'll be fine. Nat's coming for supper."

She didn't answer him, and he had to look at her. Her face was washed out, her forehead damp at the hairline. Across the bridge of her nose, a mottled band of bluish spots. "What's the matter?"

"I don't know. My stomach. Something I ate."

Ben had turned on the alley light, which shone on the car. He got into the driver's seat. His hands seemed naked on the wheel: his mother wore driving gloves even in the hottest weather.

By the time Ben reached Broadway, Brona was gasping. "Ma, what is it, what is it?" he called out. She had to throw up. As soon as he pulled the car to the curb, Brona opened the door, leaned out of the car, and vomited into the gutter. Ben leaned from the wheel and stiffly put his hand on his mother's heaving back. "Get it all up," he said, reaching into his pocket for a handkerchief. He handed it to her, and she wiped her mouth.

"Must have been my lunch. I ate pastrami."

Ben shuddered at the thought of the pink meat edged with black.

"I'm better. Don't worry about me." Brona was quick to reassure him, but at Manor Street, she felt weak again, then nauseous. She barely made it to the downstairs toilet.

While Ben waited for Brona to be fine again, Susan rushed in from the sunporch, her face smeared with paint. The sounds of his mother's retching came through the door.

"What's the matter with Grandma?" Susan's eyes opened big, dark.

"Don't be afraid. It's nothing. Something she ate. There's no reason to worry."

"I'm not. She must feel awful."

It was Ben who felt awful. He had never seen his mother ill. When she had a minor complaint, she would withdraw to her room, emerging—hair combed, face made up—to smile for her son. "It's nothing," she would tell Ben. And he would always believe her. He waited for her to release him from worry. She was taking so long. Ben went to the phone in the kitchen and called the doctor.

When Brona opened the bathroom door, holding tightly to the knob for support, Ben was there.

"I'm so weak," she said. Ben fumbled for his lines, trying to comfort her. "It'll pass," he said without conviction. He expected Brona to sit down in the kitchen and begin talking to Susan. He wanted her to wipe her hand over her damp, pale face and change her expression.

"Susan," Brona said. "I have to lie down." She walked to the foot of the stairs and hesitated. "I feel dizzy. Maybe I have a fever."

Brona reached out her hand. Ben took it and helped her up the stairs. He felt her solid weight against him. He gasped, he coughed for air as if Brona had pushed a pillow down hard over his face. She let go, and the weight of her heavy, damp head rolled against his shoulder.

Sudden burning tears spiked his eyes. He tilted back his head to keep them from falling. Brona—so weak: was she leaving him, as Tess had done? He had nursed his wife during her final illness, bathed her wasted body, carried her to the window so she could see the sky—and now his mother. By the time they reached the top of the stairs, he had collected himself. "You'll be fine. Just go slow," he told her. Her hand was cold on his wrist. He guided her into her room, pulled back the bedspread with one hand. His mother rolled away from him onto the bed, her face darkened with green and violet blotches.

Ben heard his brother Nat's loud voice and went out into the upstairs hall, where Susan stood at the top of the stairs. Nat ran up like a wild man, two steps at a time, his hands outstretched, "Where is everybody?"

"He runs. My brother runs." Ben's mouth tightened in judgment and loosened in pity. Where was Nat racing to? The second floor.

Susan was already in Nat's arms. Nat hugged her, let her go, fast. He looked into her eyes. "Here you are."

Susan put on the English accent she had heard on the radio, a sly half smile on her lips, "Grandmother is ill"—she switched to Jersey brat—"She puked."

Nat's chin flew up. He laughed. "Grandma? She sick?"

"What's so funny? Susan should go downstairs." Ben pointed the way.

"Leave the kid alone," Nat said as he slid past Ben into his mother's room. He had his knee on her four-poster bed, "Ma, did it come on sudden?"

"Yes," she said.

"Food poisoning, Ma. You'll be sick as a dog, then it'll go."

Brona's mouth was clamped shut.

"You won't listen to me." Nat leaned forward. "I'm the lugger."

"What do you want from me? You're my American boy. Go throw a ball." She waved him away with the back of her hand. She tried to get up and couldn't. She groaned, "Help me."

Ben drew back. He had never heard Brona ask for help. Though he had nursed Tess, not since he was a little boy brushing Brona's long hair as it hung over the side of her bed had he taken care of his mother. He barely remembered her long hair as it was before she bobbed it—heavy, crackling under the brush, blue-black in his small hands. He still observed the taboo of adolescence: when he touched her, he really did not touch her. His kisses were pecks, his hands neutral. He was afraid of her body that once had had so much power over him.

"Come on," Nat said. With his legs against the mattress, he held out his forearm so it was horizontal to the floor. Brona gripped it as if it were a bar. Nat hoisted her up. He was smiling. Ben took her arm, but Nat had most of her weight. They dragged her to the upstairs bathroom. Nat let go and now Ben took his mother's weight. Nat ran ahead and lifted up the toilet seat.

"Leave me alone," Brona said. She knelt down on the bare tile and retched violently into the bowl.

"Ma, let me put something under your knees. You'll hurt yourself," Nat said.

"Go away."

"She wants us to go away," Ben said.

"No, she doesn't." Nat closed the door. He leaned against the wall and Ben sat down with his feet on the top step, so that his knees stuck up. From the bathroom came the raw sounds of Brona's retching.

"She's got the dry heaves," Nat said. "She'll get it all up."

A wave of nausea rose to Ben's throat. His mother sounded as if she was throwing up her insides.

Their mother called out, "Where are you?"

"Ma, right here," Nat said. The brothers lifted her from the bathroom floor where she slumped, her head against the rim of the tub.

"Upsy Daisy," Nat said. They hoisted her to her feet.

"Ma, you're heavy. A handful." Again Nat took most of her weight.

"Who asked you?" she answered, sounding like her old self. "Let's go. I have to lie down."

Susan was stretched out on her grandmother's bed with her shoes on. "Go draw a picture," Ben yelled.

"I'm not in the mood," she said.

"That's what I have to listen to. The artist. You and that Englander friend of yours," Ben answered her.

Nat nodded at Susan and she got off the bed. He didn't say anything and she listened to him.

Brona stunk of vomit. She hadn't washed herself. She sat down on the edge of the bed, and Ben knelt down and took off her shoes. She tried to take off her stockings, but she couldn't do it. "I'm dizzy," she said. "I threw up so hard." Her eyelids and the fine skin above them were marked with red pinpoints where the blood had broken through the tiny veins.

"Lie down, Ma," Nat said. "We'll take care of you." Brona did what he said—gave him that look but lay down on the bed.

"Get a basin," Nat said to Susan. "No, a pail from the bathroom, in case she's sick." Susan went.

"Where's your nightgown, Ma?" Nat asked.

"In the middle drawer. No, not that bureau, the other one."

Nat found a pink nightgown with long sleeves.

"No, that's too hot."

Finally he found one that satisfied her.

When Susan came back with the pail, Nat sent her for a basin of warm water, a towel, and a face cloth. He asked her and she did it. Nat tested the water.

"How are we going to do this?" Ben asked. He didn't want to do anything.

"I'll do it. I can wash myself. I'm not that sick."

"Shut up." Nat took the basin and put it on the night table, using it as a shovel to push back the clutter of reading glasses and papers. He dipped the face cloth into the warm water.

"Give me the wash rag," Brona said. "I stink."

Nat ignored her. He pushed back her hair and washed her face and neck with smooth light strokes. Ben watched his brother's experienced hands, his mother's face relaxing as she gave in, and he remembered how Nat had taken care of Brona when their father had died. Ben came closer and Nat handed him the cloth he had moistened again, "Wash her hands." Ben did as he was told. Careful not to let the cloth catch on Brona's rings, he wiped her fingers one at a time.

"Leave me alone. You're wearing me out."

"Take away the basin," Nat told Ben.

Ben moved it to the floor. He didn't want to leave them alone.

Nat rolled Brona on her side and lifted her skirt to just above her knees. Rolling down the thin stuff of her stockings, he managed to get them off without tearing them. He unbuttoned her skirt and eased it down over her hips, her knees, her thin ankles. Without looking, he reached behind himself, handing the skirt to Ben.

"Don't wrinkle it. Put it on a hanger in the closet. I'm so tired. I feel like I was turned inside out." She unbuttoned her blouse. She rolled to her left side as Nat helped her slip her arm out, then she rolled to her other side, and he helped her again. The thin cotton blouse was soiled with vomit that had come through, staining her slip. "I'm a mess." She sat up.

Nat, one knee on the edge of the bed, rolled the slip straps down over Brona's arms, until the slip hung to her waist.

Is he going to take off her brassiere too? Ben wondered. He looked for Susan. She had left. Good.

"You've seen me before," she said, leaning against the pillows, her full, sagging breasts barely covered by the thin bra. She looked lovely, undone, sick as she was. Ben turned away. "Go get me a clean cloth." This time Nat went. He came back with a cloth and a bottle of witch hazel. "This will freshen you up, better than soap." He sprinkled the witch hazel onto the cloth.

"This one knows about witch hazel," she said as she took the cloth.

"I learned it from you. I use it. My beauty secret," Nat said.

Ben smelled the sweet, acid scent and turned back to his mother. She washed her chest, reaching down between her breasts, rolled down her bra, turned it back to front, and unhooked it.

Her nipples were flat like smoothed rose petals.

When she had nursed her sons—heard their hungry cries—her nipples had risen, filled with blood. She had gone to them hard, milk flowing. The fierce suction of their airless mouths had worked a color change, turning her nipples even darker. She had swelled in their mouths; she had fit into them. One by one, she had weaned her sons, a kind of forgetting. All her life she was rooting herself to them and uprooting. It never ended. It would never end. Until she was dead.

Nat gathered up Brona's nightgown and slipped it over her head. As she pulled down her slip, he drew down the nightgown. Brona handed him her slip and her underpants, which she had also removed. They were damp. "I wet myself," she said. Her voice was weak again. "Let me sleep."

Susan came into the room and stood just inside the door.

The brothers—one on either side of Brona's high bed—pulled up the top sheet and the pale yellow cotton summer blanket.

"That's enough," Brona said.

"Are you better, Grandma?" Susan came closer.

Brona raised herself up. "Yes, it's good to be clean. Come here. I'm fine."

"I told you," Ben said to his daughter.

Susan came to the bed. Putting her arms around Brona's neck, Susan felt the bristling hair at the nape of her grandmother's head and gently pulled. "You need a haircut," Susan said.

"Yes, now go eat," Brona said. "Jeannette prepared a salad for you before she left." The Sheins' black housekeeper had gone back to Georgia for two weeks.

"I told her not to go. 'Coloreds only'—it's not good for her, but she wants to see her family," Ben said.

"I called Doktor," Ben told his brother. "He said it's probably nothing, but he'll step in later to see."

"I called the Doctor, Dok Tor didn't come," sang Susan. "Doctor Dok Tor."

"Never make fun of a person's name," Ben said.

"I'm not. *It's* funny. Dr. Doktor."

"Another Tessie," Nat murmured from the kitchen sink. Nat held the blue and white box of Ivory Snow high in his right hand over a shallow white enameled basin rimmed with red. He tipped the box—the moon and stars tipped—and the flakes fell into his cupped hand and overflowed into the basin. He turned his hand over and the soap drifted down. He flicked his fingers to rid them of the rest of the flakes that were already melting on his hands.

"Uncle Nat is washing clothes," Susan said.

"I can tell," Ben said.

Nat turned on the hot water tap, then the cold, swung the basin under the taps, swirling the water into the soap with loose-wristed motions. Dipping his hands again, he tested the water as if he were going to bathe a baby. He lifted the small wilted pile of his mother's underpants, brassiere, and blouse and sank them into the warm water.

"Uncle Nat knows how to wash. He used to help Grandma."

"You did?" Susan asked her uncle.

"Your daddy also, but he was in the house only a little. Fifteen years old—he already went to work with Grandma. We had to, after your grandfather died—pneumonia," Nat said.

"He didn't live to enjoy . . . ," Ben said.

"What are you talking about? Pa enjoyed everything."

"We had to *do* everything. Ma had no one else. Sixteen—I designed and cut my first coat. Good skins—no more practice like with Pa," Ben said.

"How the hell did we manage?" Nat said.

"We were together. You took care of things here."

"Oh, how I washed," Nat sang out, raising his hands from the soap bubbles that gave off a static-like sound as they collapsed. There were soap bubbles on the ends of his fingers. He raised his hands high and flicked the white froth at Ben. The backs of his hands touched over his head as he rose on the tips of his shoes, his back straight, his head steady. "I'm a ballerina," his voice high, like a girl's. He dropped his hands to his hips, threw back his head, and sob-sang, "Buy cheap, buy cheap, and have pity on me, buy my matches." He swiveled his hips, his feet stroking so quickly they never seemed to leave the floor. Ben answered him by grunting out a tango beat, the low sound thrumming off his palate, humming through his nose. With his wet hands Nat swung Ben into the dance.

"You'll wake Grandma," Susan said.

"Never, never, never," the brothers called out. They laid it on thick. They charged at Susan and pulled back just in time. They forced her to the edge of the room. She stood with her back to the window, her face wild and happy.

Dancing as they had years ago in front of the mirror in their mother's room, they turned and tangoed toward Susan again, stopping just short of touching her, and pivoted an inch from her feet to stalk the width of the kitchen and pivot again, glide back to Susan, and drop their arms to let her in. They took hands—the three of them—and whirled with short beating steps, their feet pointing to the center, until the room blurred. For once, Susan did not say, "More!"

"You see, your daddy can dance," Nat said.

"Only with you," Ben said, recovering his breath.

Nat turned back to the sink and bent over his mother's clothes, carefully rubbing them clean.

"Remember, rinse them twice," Ben said.

Nat laughed. "Ma, she would always say that." Nat obeyed and exceeded Brona's standards. Three times he rinsed his mother's clothes in the cold rinse water, squeezing them gently, bending down from the waist, funneling his strength down to the fine, thin fabric.

Ben set the table while Susan went into the sunporch, which she now called her studio. He pulled open the silver-drawer of the kitchen table they had brought with them from the old flat on Broadway. He pulled the drawer out too far, as he often did. The drawer tilted and the weight of the silver was immediate and suddenly heavy in his hand as he quickly braced the drawer with his knee and drew out what they needed from the mismatched collection.

He set three places on the bare deeply grained oak table, a fake-bone-handled fork and a dull knife with a flimsy blade at each place. What would the Sheins need sharp dinner knives for? Whatever meat they ate had been potted to a melting tenderness. The soft flesh would fall apart between their forks and the dull blades of their knives, so dull they could not cut hard butter.

Ben placed the third crackled dinner plate between the borders of fork and knife. The table slanted toward the window and the plates looked as if they would slide off.

Nat was done with the wash. He raised the basin chest high, like a waiter at a wedding. Ben followed him out through the back door and down the short flight of cement steps. Nat stood in the weeds in the side yard, the white basin sunk at his feet in the uncut grass. He bent down from his flexible hips, his legs straight, his hair falling forward. Rising, he drew their mother's blouse from the basin and hung it upside down and dripping from the line. He remembered how to hang the fine cotton bra with one clothespin and the underpants by two. The rough rope squeaked between the wooden pins. Water dripped from the narrow crotch into the grass.

A sudden breeze lifted the clothes and they rose—wet and dripping—as if they would blow away like drenched wind-whipped maple leaves. But the clothespins held the fine cotton to the rope.

"What do you want?" Nat asked Susan, when they were seated at the table.

"A little bit of tuna, a lot of tomatoes."

"Give her," Ben said.

Nat piled up tomatoes on one side of Susan's plate and put one teaspoonful of tuna on the other. The brothers took their forks and, one by one, forked tomatoes onto their plates.

"These tomatoes need salt," Nat said, as if Ben were going to contradict him. He took the heavy shaker from the shelf near the stove and shook out salt onto his tomatoes. "Eating tomatoes without salt is like kissing a man without a mustache," Nat said.

"But you don't have a mustache," Susan said.

"So what? Susy, I can grow one. Can you?"

"Girls don't have mustaches," Susan said.

"That's what you . . ."

"Enough," said Ben. "Enough."

Nat shook the shaker hard. Jeannette had mixed rice with the salt in the shaker to keep the salt from sticking. The rice rattled. "Needs to be filled. There's enough for you," Nat said.

Susan did what her uncle did: she shook and shook until she got the salt. She ate, keeping her eyes on Nat. "I want a dog," she said, her mouth full of tomato.

Ben stuck his fork straight up, "She wants private art lessons, and now—like her friend, this Joan, she wants a dog. Do you think Uncle Nat has a dog in the truck? Right now. A dog?"

"Not now, Silly," Susan said.

"We had a dog. Your daddy and me," Nat said.

"You did?"

"Eat." Ben pointed to Susan's plate.

"Tell her," Nat said. "Rex."

"A long time ago," Ben said, "before Pa died.

"You never told me."

"It's not a secret. Now you know." Ben reached for more food. He didn't want to talk.

Nat stopped, his fork in the thick wedge of tomato. "He chewed the legs of this table. We were supposed to take care of him. We made him wild." He jabbed his finger toward Ben. "Ma and Pa, they should have had him *fixed*."

Ben remembered. Rex's penis would stick out, hard, his swollen balls bunched under his tail. He and Nat had made Rex leap up to the stick they held over their heads. Nat was still small and had to stand on tiptoe.

"Rex needed . . . a bitch," Nat said and bit into the tomato.

"Quiet already," Ben said.

"A bitch is a female dog," Susan said.

"What do I know? Go ahead, go listen to your uncle."

"It wasn't our fault. One day we came home. No dog." Nat threw his head up as if, from his chair, he could butt against the ceiling and knock his mother out of her sick bed. "Ma said she gave Rex to a farmer. So the dog could run. You didn't cry. You believed her. You said Rex was at O'Dowd's, the dairy where we got ice cream. Running like Lassie," Nat said.

"They had peacocks. That's where he was. At O'Dowd's." Ben heard again the flash-wind of the peacock's opening wings and saw the shining fan of eyes. "Ma said."

"She *said*. Did she ever take us to see him?" Nat asked.

"She told me. She told both of us. You were with me. Remember the white barns, the ventilators?" Ben twirled his pointing index finger.

"You woke up screaming. You jumped up in bed. You screamed, 'He's there. The dogcatcher. He's going to kill us.' Ben, you saw him with a noose in the doorway. You knew," Nat said.

"I didn't know," Ben said.

"I wonder how they killed him. Do they chloroform dogs?" Nat chewed his tomato. "Or do they inject them?"

"You know something? I don't really know," Ben answered. "And I don't want to know." He stared at Susan as her head swiveled on her thin neck. Her dark eyes opened wide, wet.

"I hated her. Ma. But Pa did it too," Nat said.

"How could they help with a dog? They worked day and night. Susan, your uncle doesn't understand," Ben said.

"That's what Ma and Pa said. I wanted the dog," Nat said.

"You wanted the dog. You cried," Ben said.

Nat got up and poured himself a drink from the bottle of rye in the pantry.

There was the sound of squealing brakes as Dr. David Doktor's car speeded into the driveway.

"He'll kill himself—a dressed-up bag of peanuts," Nat said. "A doctor, but he can't drive. He's fast though, runs like that guy on the cover of the phone book with wings on his feet."

Susan rushed to the back door. "Doktor," she said, slicing between the syllables with her tongue, sharply coughing the *k*, spitting the *t*. "So glad you could come. My grandmother is upstairs, resting."

Doktor—in his forties—looked like a boy dressed in adult clothing—pale beige one-button jacket, wide loose pants, a green bow tie, lustrous brown shoes whose tips, like polished delicate snouts, barely cleared the cuffs. His slender feet were tiny. The beautiful leather soles of his shoes were smooth and clean, as if he walked on water. The black bag he carried looked too big for him. A life kit, a death kit. It held a syringe, adrenaline, morphine. He waved, tapping his thumb against his own shoulder, like a vaudeville comic. There was barely room between his close-together blue eyes for the narrow bridge of his delicate nose. His thin red lips looked painted, his blond hair, dyed—especially the high bang that slanted across his narrow forehead. He was a brilliant diagnostician with a frightening memory. He seemed to know what people had by quickly feeling them, by sniffing them. But he healed his patients as much by flash and dash as by skill. They loved their lightweight sonny boy so much they had trouble dying. But some of them wanted to die, longed to rest, were worn out with pain. They tired of the bon vivant. "Let us go," they pleaded. Finally he released them, keeping watch at their deathbeds—even the most gruesome—his bright head bent over the blue bodies, his hand on the weakening heart that finally surrendered.

"Don't get up," he said as if the brothers were women at a party. "I know the way." Susan followed him, bouncing her palms off his back so lightly he hardly felt her. They were gone before Ben could stop her.

"Ben, she'll be all right. Ma—she's built like a brick shit house."

"Stop it."

Nat rubbed it in. "There's a bang left in the old lady yet."

"She's your mother," Ben said.

"She's a woman. What happened with Tondow?"

"I liked her, but . . ."

"But what?"

"I don't know."

"You don't know? Why don't you know?"

"I don't know."

"He doesn't know. My brother doesn't know." Nat shouted. "What's wrong with you? She's the best."

"What do you want from me?" Ben felt his face heat up. "Why is it so important with her? Why?"

"Daddy." Susan came through the door, ready to cry, her pale neck so thin inside the loose collar of the smock Brona had made for her, which was now daubed across the chest with wet red paint. "What's the matter?" Susan asked.

"Nothing," Ben said. He pressed his hand hard against his neck as if a mosquito had just bitten him and was sucking blood from the large vein.

"There is, Daddy. I heard you."

Doktor stepped into the kitchen, carrying his black bag. "Mrs. Shein is fine, fine, fine. She needs rest, at least a day. If she can keep it down, a diet of boiled water and rice. I told the Queen what to do. She's sitting up in her royal bed. She should have a coat of arms for her black Chrysler, a silver fox rampant."

He glided toward Susan on his tiny feet. "Susy, come on." Doktor's boyish head darted forward. His blue eyes sparked as he examined her face. "You can walk me out. Give me your hand." Doktor reached out for her. "I want to talk to you."

Susan was too quick for him. She stepped back before he could touch her. "No," she shouted.

"Susan, wait," Ben said.

But she ran from Doktor, ran from the room—her legs thin, white—ran from his healing hand that had saved so many. Doktor pushed open the screen door and was gone.

"And Tondow?" Nat said.

"What about her?" Ben put his hand over his eyes, "She's not the only woman. I could find someone *younger*." As he said the word, he remembered: the image of Judith Karger appeared as if printed on the hand that covered his eyes. She was smiling, grateful, as she had been when he had paid for the cake. What was the harm? He'd look her up. "Not for you," Nat had said when he had given her the once-over. What did Nat know about fate?

DOKTOR HAD BEEN RIGHT: IN A FEW DAYS BRONA WAS WELL ENOUGH to get out of bed. Ben came up behind her as she was rearranging glasses and cups in the pantry. When she turned toward him, he saw that her face looked worn. "Ma, he said. "You don't have to do that. Leave it for Jeannette."

"I can't lay there. Don't worry about me."

"I'm not."

"Then what's that look for?" Brona held an old glass that once had been used for a memorial candle for the dead. Though she could easily afford to buy a new glass, she liked to drink water from this one, her lips on its sturdy rim. The tip of her left thumb fit the small, arched window-shaped depression in the glass. The fingernail was crooked from an old accident. A sash cord had broken, the heavy falling window catching her thumb against the sill, crushing the nail, which had blackened and fallen off. The new nail had grown back crooked, the root carrying the message of damage into the nail. "So? Tell me," Brona said to her son as she placed the glass on the shelf.

The sight of his mother's careful gestures comforted Ben. "Everything's good," Ben said.

"How are you feeling?" Brona asked.

Ben reached for a word about himself, but could not find it. "Susan. She wants private art lessons, talks about this teacher like she's Tess. Maybe we've made a mistake," he said, acknowledging that he and Brona had silently agreed he would not marry again. "Maybe she needs a mother." He stopped himself from saying "someone young." Brona was getting older and so was he.

"Not a grandmother, not an uncle? What makes you think a mother can solve everything?" Brona's back was turned toward her son.

"I don't want a fight."

"You won't get one." She turned to him, her face, which he had kissed when he was a child, now mild, sad, tired in the yellow light from the small kitchen lamp. She had surprised him, and he loved her again. He waited for her to tell him what he wanted to hear: 'Marry. It's OK.' He rubbed his hand against his cheek, felt the stubble, knew his face was dark.

"We don't want to crush her. Such a lively little person. Why shouldn't she have art lessons? You were ready to pay for piano, but she is not musical. She *can* draw, like you. Nat will drive her. Give your brother something to do," Brona said.

"Give him? I give him."

"He can wait for her," Brona added.

"That's what a mother should do. Take care of her."

"What harm? If it doesn't work out, you can stop it. So you make a mistake. So what? You're not cutting out otter. You're not cutting out anything," Brona said.

"There's a schvartze there, too," Ben said.

"A fancy teacher with a maid."

"She comes from money. Nat won't do anything. Not with that one," Ben said.

"That's what you're worrying about?" his mother asked.

Ben couldn't answer. He didn't know what he was worrying about. "She's a teacher. Susan will be all right," he said.

"I'll look into her. I'll make some calls." Brona put one cup inside another. "I'll pay. It'll be my treat. Let me. My pleasure. Before my hands get cold." Brona was too proud to blackmail her son with "I'm an old woman; I won't be around much longer."

Though her tone was light, Ben felt the certainty of her death and bravely dismissed it: "You, your hands must be burning up," he said.

"Look, they're on fire." Brona put down the blue cups, one nestled inside the other, raised her hands, fluttering her fingers. "I'll talk to Susan tomorrow," she said.

They stood for a moment in the night hush of the kitchen. The red curtains, the heavy black and white Chambers stove gleaming with chrome, the deep, double, white sink: solid, immutably domestic—as if nothing could ever change. In the morning, the stove would be lit for Brona's coffee; the blue flames would mount under the kettle; the kettle would steam. Brona would drink her coffee at the kitchen table.

The thought of her death came back to him. Ben watched as she reached up to turn off the light. Brona's hand grew brighter, her palm filling with gold light, which he took as a sign. If he married again, his mother would bless him. He understood: she didn't have to say a word. He would look around. He'd see.

That night, undisturbed by his dreams, Ben Shein slept soundly for the first time in months. Restored by his sleep, he made plans. Nat didn't know everything. "Why should I listen to him?" Ben asked himself. Why couldn't it be Judith Karger—a young woman, but not too young? He would start with her, Judith Karger. *She* appreciated him.

PART TWO

udith Karger leaned over a section of the glass-topped counter that surrounded the high island of cabinets in her department at Quackenbush's, where, since high school, she had sold accessories she seldom could afford to buy. Not until she had been shocked to see a wealthy woman recklessly mop her damp, heavily rouged face with fine, new linen had Judith thought about how a customer might ruin a magnificent handkerchief: if a woman could blot and smear the white square, she could also use it to staunch blood, wipe between her legs with an embroidered rose and afford to throw the stained linen away. On a hot day, she could soak the handkerchief in eau de cologne and press it against her forehead. But some women, Judith told herself, had to do what she did: use her one good handkerchief for show; in her purse, a ragged hanky for dirty use.

Judith ran a clean, white cloth over the glass with slow movements, looking down at the folded silk scarves in the case below. Putting her face close to the glass, she found an angle from which she could see an errant streak or a smeared fingerprint; she wiped it away. Though she kept moving her head, her light brown hair stayed smooth as quiet water. When she stood up straight, the still-clean cloth like a cool, white light in her hand, her eyes widened, and though she looked out, it was difficult to tell what she was looking at.

In ten minutes, the store would open. The lights were still turned off except for the dim ones that always burned at the back center of the first floor, like a ship's light in the most interior cabin. The bright light that came in from the front door lit up the entrance and splashed to a halt against the silvery cosmetics counter, whose mirrored cases bounced light back toward the door. The rest of the first floor was dim. The display windows, dressed with autumn dioramas, were not made for seeing out of.

In the window to the right of the front door, a school-girl mannequin was dressed in plaid skirt, white blouse, and cardigan; her white anklets were snug and spotless above her heavy oxford-shod feet attached to steel-braced dummy legs stuck like pilings into the crude paper leaves.

This was the floor for little things for women. There were no makers here, only sellers. In each department—in Gloves, in Hosiery, in Hats, in Cosmetics, in Perfume, in Jewelry, in Pocketbooks, in Scarves and Hand-kerchiefs—a salesgirl waited at her station to sell what would clothe an extremity; gild a face; scent a body; shine on neck, wrists, ears; give the hands something to hold as a person tried to fit herself to the world.

From counter to counter, pale hands lifted as Mr. B., the floorwalker, held out his straw tray of artificial fall flowers. He suffered from wryneck, a medical condition that had permanently twisted his muscles, making him forever look to the side, so he appeared always ashamed and shy. But it was his near inability to speak that truly revealed his shame. A braver person would have spoken, shouted at a tangent to the listener. He could not. Mr. B. moved on, a gray-headed, gray shadow, one of the sons-in-law of the Quackenbushes.

He had once asked his in-laws, the owners, to put him in the office. They would not. Like everything they did, no matter the cause of the action, it turned out to be good for business: the salespeople usually behaved for Mr. B.; they were his congregation. They didn't lean. They didn't sit—except sometimes at the end of a long day when the store was almost empty. Feet aching, they would pull out a low drawer and use it as a seat, balancing on its sharp, hard edge, knees bent, legs braced against the floor. Although they were not supposed to leave their stations, they would steal brief visits to each other's counters, and no one could muzzle the talkers.

Fritzie Shiffman in Hats turned her head from right to left and back again, making sure she was free from the surveilling eye of the boss. Fritzie was a genius at stealing time and a fluid improviser in a department whose goods were almost pure fantasy. She was never in the fantasy herself. "Judith, look what they bought," Fritzie called out. On the pole of her arm, on the head of her hand, she raised a hat. "How do they expect me to sell this?" The hat was jersey, a cap with a flap across the neck, protection for a knight to wear under armor.

"It's practical. For the cold."

"For the person with a goiter."

Judith turned away from Fritzie's laugh. The manager had once reprimanded Judith for talking. "I saw you from the mezzanine," he had said. "I can see everything from up there." Ever since then, even though she knew he could not stand there all day above her, watching, she had felt the threat of his unseen eyes. She heard Fritzie's loud whisper, "Here he comes. Crooked putz."

Judith spun around, startled, but it was only Mr. B., the floorwalker. "Good morning," Judith said, her voice low, polite.

His head twisted away from her, Mr. B. silently held out the straw tray filled with fake flowers. Judith chose a yellow football mum and, tilting the oval mirror on the counter so she could see herself, pinned the flower to the lapel of her brown military-cut jacket. The angle of the mirror narrowed her chin, swelled her forehead. The flower pulled down the lapel, so she unpinned it, pushing the sharp point deeper, down through the double thickness of the lapel, down through the thin material of her suit. She smiled. "Thank you, it's lovely."

Mr. B. concentrated on his movements. He lifted his eyes to the next counter. He could not lift his head. When he saw his route, he looked down again and walked to his destination.

Judith could hear her own "good morning" and "thank you" inside her head, her voice low and even, as she dreamed her connection with Mr. B. She knew how to speak to people, unlike Fritzie, who made fun of crippled people—Fritzie with her loud vulgar mouth.

She checked her stock. One by one, she slid open the doors of the glass-topped counter that faced the front of the store and ran her fingers over the better scarves, making sure they overlapped without concealing each other. The yellow and orange were in for fall. "Brighten with accessories," Judith would tell her customers. "A touch of color, not too much."

She went back over her work, scarf by scarf, rearranged, so that the pile began with the pale yellows and ended with the darkest oranges. Her hands, with their clear-polished nails filed smooth so they would not catch on silk, moved again over the scarves. She chose a heavy saffron silk, drew it from its soft folds, closed the door of the case, and pulled the silk through the loop of the display stand so the fringed edges would not touch the glass. She stood back, contemplating. Saffron was the day's signature. I'll sell it, she thought.

As she bent down to the side-counter's challis, wool, and cashmere, she stumbled over a box of gloves she had forgotten to put away. "Look where you're going," she said to herself and, with a quick, fierce thrust of her foot, kicked the box under the counter. Again she moved her hands, this time over the heavier winter scarves, and brought them down, flicking, checking, aligning edges.

With her back to the glass counter, she slid open one of the wooden island's small cabinets, revealing hidden goods Judith's well-to-do customers bought for mothers and grandmothers who would not give up their peasant tastes: heavy cotton head scarves, black printed with solid reds and blues. Some prosperous children of immigrants were ashamed to ask for the hidden goods that exposed their origins, and some customers were embarrassed to ask the Jewish salesgirl for the large white linen handkerchiefs to send to nuns. Tied with a black ribbon, the plain handkerchiefs, which had been sent up from the Men's Department, lay, like the babushkas, in the dark of one of the closed arks. Judith had learned how to sell to these customers. When she was first hired, the Quackenbush son had praised her speech, free of a foreign accent: "We have to sell to everyone," he had said. Judith had found a way; her voice neutral, kind, she would try to interest her customers in something for themselves before discreetly asking about their relatives. Referring to a nun, she would say, "And the one who is away?"

Across the floor, the salespeople looked forward, toward the door that most of them could not see. If there were believers among them, they might have prayed; if there were a clear window, a few might have gazed out like schoolchildren holding on to summer's blue sky, but they had to stand and wait, silent, their hands at their sides or clasped in front of them. They were bored. The boredom was endemic: there was only so much stock to straighten and glass to polish. Even when there *were* customers, not every department was busy at the same time. Back-to-school buying was only a small rush. A crowd of customers, gullible enough to line up at the locked door to be among the first for a sale, quickly thinned out as they raced into the hush of Quackenbush's.

They ran to save money on goods that had originally been marked up so high they still would bring a profit when sold at a markdown. The customers didn't save. They bought the still-overpriced leftovers—odd colors, odd cuts, unfortunates. The strangest, most shopworn items that had not been sold were eventually sent to the basement counters. There really was no ultimate graveyard for soft goods—unless there *was* a fire that burned them to carbon dust. They kept circulating—sent on to other stores, schlock houses, "fire" sales, "flood" sales, and finally to the rag man who sold them for reprocessing. The dresses with drooping peplums, the acid green sweater, the ripped tulle, the buttonless blouse, the stained sleeve—all were shredded to their fibers and reborn in another form.

Over the high islands of closed arks, weak pale blue light washed in, almost as transparent as water. The incandescent lights went on.

The light inside Quackenbush's turned dull yellow.

Judith waited, hungry. If she had stopped at Sophie Winik's again, she would at least have been able to look forward to a rich treat with her lunch of two hard-boiled eggs and an apple small enough to fit into her handbag. But that morning, though she had considered stopping, tempted by the thought of the dark sweet cake, she had mentally counted her small hoard of change and locked herself to the routine that helped her feel safe. Needing to check herself, she had searched for her reflection in a shop window and found it—slim skirt, square shoulders, white-gloved hands. She had bravely straightened her back against Sophie's outrageous prices and walked to work with a quick step. Judith hadn't allowed herself to remember that Ben Shein had paid, let alone imagine he might pay again.

Judith had avoided men since before her elder brother Saul had died when she was sixteen, and soon after—much too soon—her father. Saul had been twenty-three, engaged to be married. "The slightest fever," her mother had said as she took the thermometer from his mouth: no need to bathe his head with alcohol. In the morning he was dead of meningitis. Judith had loved him, when she had believed that he loved her. She had begun cleaning his room when she was small, scrubbing on her hands and knees with childish devotion. With her small hands, she had maneuvered the broom under his bed and fished out apple cores, dusty black socks, loose sheets of newspaper. Saul had rewarded her with smiles, petted her head, and taken her to Bradley Beach, where he had taught her to swim: "Let go, the water will carry you." He would reach into his pocket, telling her to close her eyes and put out her hand. With her eyes closed, she swayed, then balanced, her slim legs shifting in the dark—anchored, yet floating; faithful, she had waited until one by one the coins dropped into her cupped palm.

When a fruit store had opened near their house, Saul had sent the eleven-year-old Judith for strawberries. She had taken the basket from the fruit man, his skin tan against the white of his shirt. "These are the sweetest—from Jersey, from right here," he had said as he slipped the berries into a brown paper bag, his teeth a white lure in his tawny face. The gold hair on his forearms gleamed. "Bring back the basket. I can use it." She felt his dry fingers against her palms as he handed her the bag.

When she returned the basket, its thin, pale wood was blotted with red.

She would come back again throughout that long summer: June, July, August, her brother's money in her pocket. One night, though the shades of the shop were already drawn, she had knocked on the fruit man's door. "Go home," he had told her. "I'm closing, go." But he had let her in. Brown paper bags lay over the fruit. She had felt his breath on her face and backed away before he gripped her arms, pushed her against the door, his mouth on her face—the smell of overripe strawberries.

"You want?" he asked.

Judith twisted her head away, unable to speak.

"What's the matter with you? Are you sleeping?" he asked her.

One kiss might have done, or none. But he ripped her blouse and undershirt free from her skirt band and pulled up the soft cotton. He rubbed the flat of his palm against her nipples, which hardened to his touch. She felt his hand between her legs and was afraid.

Look," he said. "You've never seen." Letting go of her, he backed away, unbuttoning his fly. Carefully he lifted his penis out through the opening in his trousers. He held it as if its hardness were not his. At the tip was a swelling and something that looked like an eye. When he eased back the foreskin, a clear drop of liquid pearled at the delicate pink opening. He laughed at himself like a child; he seemed helpless, and Judith walked toward him, curious, free in her desire to know.

Judith heard the door opening, and her brother's voice. "What the hell are you doing?" he yelled. Judith felt his hand on her head as Saul grabbed her by the hair and pulled her away. Her scalp burned. "Cover yourself up," he yelled at her. "You stinking guinea, I'll kill you," he said to the fruit man.

"No, you won't." The fruit man had a knife in his hand, his disheveled hair damp, his lips red. Finally his eyes focused, and he took a step forward: "Get out of here, both of you." He pointed the knife at Judith. "Go home."

"Slut," Saul shouted at her.

The word echoed in Judith's head, as he dragged her from the store.

So great, so human was Saul's need, he had wanted her to be one thing only, adoring—of him. Still holding her by the hair, he hit her, his clenched hand against the side of her head.

"I'm not, I'm not," she wept, yet, in the years ahead, she could not purge herself of shame when daily Saul humiliated her with his aggrieved silence.

After Saul's death, she had clung to her father. When she was eighteen, Henry Karger had died suddenly, without warning, as he was about to start his car on a freezing winter morning. Judith had run out to the car, the frigid air burning her lungs. She had been lost without her father. For months he appeared in her recurring dream: Judith herself in a hot room lit with blinding heavenly light, waiting, as if she had died, but she had to be alive. She was so thirsty, with a living thirst. Then she would find herself swimming, stroking out, happy, until she saw her father, swollen, his white feet tangled in the rocks and weeds at the bottom, a thin ribbon of blood swirling from his blue mouth. She woke, terrified, unable to get out of bed. When her mother tried to coax her to her feet, Judith screamed at her, but gradually, after Estelle had taken her away to Brown's Hotel in the Catskills for a rest, for once not stinting on food, spiking their tea with brandy, Judith had begun sleeping again.

Eventually she had made plans: she would continue to work at Quackenbush's; she would help her mother—they had so little. Perhaps some day she would meet a man who loved her, but that day seemed so far in the future the prospect of change hardly existed.

Now at her counter, Judith got ready for her first sale of the day, arranging the carbon paper between the thin sheets of her receipt book, careful not to dirty her hands on the purple-black ink. She straightened the page and looked up to see Ben Shein walking toward her, his shiny black shoes on the polished floor; dark hair sleek, close to his head; his hand raised in greeting; face pale, expectant above his meticulously tailored suit. As he came nearer, Judith spun around the island of closed compartments so that she was facing in the opposite direction, the receipt book in her hand. She remembered how he had paid for her cake at Sophie Winik's, his eager hand outstretched, pushing its way into her business, but she knew what to do: she would treat him as a customer was supposed to be treated. "May I help you, Mr. Shein?" she said, looking over his head as she came around the counter, her neat receipt book in her hand.

Ben Shein scrutinized his immaculate white cuff and tried to reassure himself: she's shy, a young woman, but why shouldn't a young one look at me? "Miss Karger," he pointed at the book, lifting his eyes. "You're ready for a sale. I may not be so easy." Ben appreciated the pink flush that colored her smooth, girlish cheeks. He sensed his own power to the extent that he could use it to unsettle her. "You can sell?"

His words slid out—soft, insinuating. The tone caressed; the double meaning stung, tipped her off balance. Judith tried to recover: "I do my best." She formed her words so that their distinctness played against Ben Shein's slight Polish accent, but she could meet his confusing eyes only for a moment.

"I want something for my mother. She's been sick." Ben would see how well she could sell, this young one who looked so fresh.

She could face him now, taking in one eye at a time, first the dark and then the light. "It's not every son who comes to choose a present for his mother. May I suggest a scarf?" She pointed to the display stand that held the saffron silk. "This is very nice for fall."

Ben Shein fingered the silk, deliberately taking his time. She didn't open a sale like a Shein—a Shein could sound natural—but she could learn.

Judith moved the stand away from Ben's reach, the back of his hand black with hair. "To brighten a brown suit. A brown coat?" Judith eased the scarf from the metal loop, wrapped it around her neck, her hands on the ends.

"Obvious." Ben Shein pointed at her chest.

Judith crossed her hands in front of her breasts. She yanked. What was she doing? She could ruin the silk. She let go with one hand and pulled the scarf away, sliding the silk along her throat.

"*You* should try a white flower. White would suit you."

She held the scarf out toward Ben.

"No, no scarves. Scarves she has." He could teach her not to oversell.

"We have some beautiful handkerchiefs. Initials are elegant."

"Show me *S*, please."

She turned her back to Ben, bent over, and took a tray of handkerchiefs from a drawer.

He watched how her strong back bent to serve him, the smooth roll of her light brown hair hiding her neck.

Judith put the expensive linen in front of him. Always show the best first, she had been instructed. She folded back the layers of the deck—*A* to *T*—lifted the stack on the back of her hand and drew out an *S*. "Hand stitched."

"Madeira?"

"Italy."

Ben ran his finger over the welting. "Something with color. No initials."

Judith had to take him through the seasons, handkerchief by handkerchief, dozens and dozens—fall, winter, spring, and summer. Her head began to throb, just over her right eye, shooting pain straight down into the right side of her face and into a top molar that held a large filling. "Mr. Shein, I can't . . . ," Judith began, and stopped when she heard

Fritzie Shiffman loudly insulting a customer, "That's a ridiculous hat for you." Judith forced her face into a calm expression. "Let's try again. Perhaps we missed one."

Ben had already chosen, but he hadn't told her. He watched her smooth hand slip under each handkerchief, curl, as she lifted the material, pulling it away from the stack with her knuckles, straightening her hand so that the linen lay flat. It was up to Ben Shein to close the sale. "This one," he said, pointing to a pink rose, satin-stitched on white openwork linen, the most expensive handkerchief in her stock. Ben Shein put money in her hand. "Ten dollars. You sold me, and it wasn't easy."

"Ten dollars." Satisfied, Judith looked directly at Ben.

"So you can smile like a person?" he teased.

"We're all people," she answered in her serious way. Her head still throbbed as she rolled the bill inside the duplicate and carbon and tucked the paper inside a small, hollow metal tube. The tight roll of paper loosened, filling the narrow space. Twisting its soft-padded ends, Judith closed the container and slipped it into one of the pneumatic tubes at her station. There was a sucking sound as a vacuum pulled the paper and metal up into the pipes that pierced the ceiling. There were no cash registers at the counters. The bosses had taken them away to stop the help from stealing.

A vacuum system sucked air at a steady regulated pressure through the dry, smooth plumbing. In a cage at the top of the store, where the bosses could watch her and make her feel watched, a cashier read the green paper, counted paper change with a rubber tipped finger, counted metal change from an enormous rack into a tiny shoot like a V-shaped water spout, and slid the coins into the returning container.

The tube shot back, down through the pipe, down to Judith. "Six ninety-five, seven," she put a nickel in his open palm, then counted out three singles, "eight, nine, ten."

"A bargain."

Judith fitted a sheet of tissue paper into a shallow box, expertly making a cross of folds. The white linen splashed with pink, fit the box exactly. Judith folded over the little doors of tissue and eased on the tight cover. "Roses are always a good choice."

"Who could hate a rose? She loves pink. It'll make her feel better. What's your favorite color?"

Judith was confused. She felt her confusion as a wave of irritation. Why was he pestering her? "Blue," she said without conviction. At school, she had anticipated the questions and memorized all the answers without investigating her own intelligence. "I like pink, too," she said to Ben. Judith could have gone on naming all the colors: her counter held them all. What difference did it make? She felt a piercing emptiness in her stomach. Her irritation grew to anger. "Do you want it gift wrapped?" She was already turning to the spools of ribbon.

"Just ribbon. No paper. Red. Do you have it?"

Judith drew a length of red ribbon from the spool and cut it free with a small pair of scissors. Her back to Ben, she tied the box with an intricate corner tie, framing the name "Quackenbush's" stamped into the pebbly cardboard.

She handed him the package in its stiff paper bag, "Just the right gift. Your mother will enjoy it."

"She'll use it. She's not like those women who would leave it in the box until they were dead."

"I hope she will be fine. Shop at Quackenbush's again. Handkerchiefs cannot be returned."

"She doesn't have TB," Ben said.

"Of course not."

"I know, I know. She'll keep it. You're a smart girl—I'm not easy to sell."

Judith allowed him his pride, an indulgence that cost her little: soon he would leave.

"You could do better than Quackenbush's; clothes look good on you, you know how to talk," he told her.

Judith straightened her back. "Thank you."

"But you could wear better." Ben Shein knew what he was talking about.

Judith read his eyes as they swept over her, assessing, erasing.

"You should step into the shop for a coat. You're tall. You can carry it."

"Fur?"

"Why not? Every woman is not Mrs. Roosevelt. Besides, who knows what Madame President has in her closet? They serve hot dogs to guests in the White House? Only in the movies," he said.

"Mrs. Roosevelt is really a plain person. When would I wear a fur coat?"

"In the winter. I'll make you a blue coat. Blue you like."

"Blue fur?"

"From blue buffaloes, like the Indians had."

"What?"

"Miss Karger. I'll give you a break."

"Oh, you don't have to."

"I know I don't have to. Maybe I want to." Ben Shein hesitated, caught himself: he had broken a Shein rule—there were no breaks. "Maybe. I'll see. Depends what it costs me. You should have a coat, a pretty girl like you. Think about it."

"I will," Judith said.

Ben sighed. "Maybe I could call you. We could take in a movie." He held the box against the interlined fabric of his tailor-made suit.

"I don't know. I'm the only one at home. My mother . . ."

"Your father?"

"I lost him. And my brother."

"I lost someone, too. And your mother, is she a well person?"

"She has more strength than I do," she said.

Ben Shein's dark eye was sweet and warm.

"You see, you don't have to be there every night. Besides an old person can fall down with you right there watching them; they can eat the wrong thing," Ben said, smiling at her, as her brother once had.

"Yes," Judith admitted.

"What did I tell you?" Ben nodded and brought his hand to his head as if he were about to tip his hat, but he wore no hat. The box was light in his hand.

"Thank you, Mr. Shein." Judith picked up her receipt book and with her index finger pushed the top sheet so that it glided back and forth over the purplish-black carbon paper.

"Call me Ben. Ben."

"I will."

Ben Shein turned and walked toward the entrance, his faultlessly tailored jacket barely moving, the fabric so finely woven that it seemed to have no warp or weave.

STARLINGS ROOSTED IN THEIR NESTS IN THE DEEP NICHES OF THE CITY Hall facade. The streets were quiet except for the rushing sound of falling water. If there had been any sunlight, there would have been a rainbow. The day had been warm. The night was cool. But this late in September, the pavement did not keep the heat of the day, and the streets and sidewalks gave off a damp chill.

Inside Quackenbush's, in the Dress Department on the second floor, the armed security guard and his girlfriend were "shopping." Walt Sokolik's brown uniform was correct, but his hair was damp under his police hat. Theresa Neradka followed him through the dimly lit store in platform heels, her hair raised in a coronet of braids above her fierce, flat face. She had not bleached the black hairs at the corners of her down-curved mouth. Above her lip she had drawn a dark beauty mark, unsettling her face. Walt Sokolik had been stealing—carefully—for years. Now he was raising the stakes—against himself—and had to drink to get up his courage. He was flying. "Come on," he called out.

"I'm right here." She had her dress unbuttoned.

"No, no trying on."

Theresa tried to choose, then she grabbed. Excited and afraid, they rushed from rack to rack, until Walt's arms were full.

He dumped the clothes on a chair and ran back to the racks, smoothing dresses back into place. Drunk as he was, he checked to see if they had dropped anything, getting down on his hands and knees, feeling along the floor. He had to be careful: the manager would inspect in the morning before the salespeople came in.

The inventory is a joke, Walt thought. And he was right. But he didn't realize it was the salespeople who really protected him. When they saw something missing, when they found an odd belt under the dress racks, they didn't say anything, not even to each other. They suspected Walt, but they weren't sure. It could be one of them. They went along.

Walt piled the clothes onto Theresa's outstretched arms. They were still racing—past mannequins in niches, on platforms, clothed in dresses, still, blind, their plaster faces softened by the dim light.

Leading Theresa to the elevator at their floor, Walt opened the outer door, pushed the folding grate to the side, and turned on the light. He took her down, the huge ring of keys swinging on his belt, and let her out into the dark alley. He had turned off the alley light. "Leave the car lights off," he told her as he walked her to the car. "Go slow. Very slow." He was too excited to kiss her.

IN THE BACK SPARE BEDROOM THAT HAD ONCE BELONGED TO HER brother, Saul, Judith and her mother, Estelle, stood at either end of the curtain stretcher, a huge wooden frame, like a picture frame on thin legs. The wood was studded with needle-sharp spikes.

"Ben Shein was in the store today," Judith said as she faced the starched net.

"I would think he could afford to buy in New York."

"He bought from me."

"Oh, did he? Judith, the curtains." Estelle reached out.

Her daughter took hold, and, as both women pulled and lifted the topmost of the stiffly starched curtains from the stretcher spikes, there was a sequence of sharp sounds like the rapid fire of a gun.

"Not an easy customer. He said he might call." Judith moved to the other side of the stretcher; her mother's body was cloudy behind the net.

"Not now, dear." Estelle Karger stretched out her long arms and took hold of the top curtain panel.

Judith didn't move. In the open space under the stretcher, her mother's narrow feet were distinct in their polished, laced-up leather shoes.

"Dear, we have to finish," Estelle said. "No one will do it for us."

Judith came around to her mother's side, gripped the bottom corner of the top curtain, jerked, and let go, so that the curtain wrinkled. Before Estelle could speak, Judith blurted out an apology: "I didn't mean to." She hadn't.

"Of course not. We know how to work together."

"I know, Mother."

The two women took hold together. Panel by panel, they ripped the curtains from the stretcher and carried them into the dining room, which still smelled of the vinegar they had used to wash the windows—Judith the top sashes, Estelle the bottom. They were getting their rooms ready for fall.

Judith threaded a rod through two curtain panels, holding the rod between her knees. Standing on a chair, she fastened the rod to one of the dining room window frames, while Estelle watched. With quick pinching movements, Judith adjusted the curtains.

"Too much on the right."

Judith got down from the chair, looked up, judged her work, and stepped up onto the chair again, holding on to the chair back as she climbed. She eased and adjusted the fabric until the gathers were even.

"Good. Just right. The hem is fine as well. We measured right."

Estelle held the next curtain in front of herself. The light had changed, outlining her tall body sharply against the honeycombed net. Her arms were open, as if they could gather Judith and hold her. Her graceful long neck and beautifully molded head, which Judith could not ever remember touching, rose over the curtain edge.

Judith faced her. Smaller than her mother, she had to stretch her arms to meet Estelle's hands. They stood for a moment, the cloudy curtain between them, Judith looking up into her mother's calm, distant face before she took the curtain from her. "I could eat, Mother."

"We'll soon have our tea," Estelle said.

When they had finished hanging the curtains, Estelle struggled to unscrew the tight wing nuts that held together the curtain stretcher. "I don't have the strength in my fingers," she said.

"I do." Judith twisted the metal wings and, one by one, pushed the screws back through their holes. The threaded metal grated on the wood, which was marked in inches like a yardstick and bristled with shining silver spikes. As Judith slid the flat sticks into their storage box, she pricked her finger. She sucked in her breath with a loud a sissing sound as she held up her hands. "I hate these things."

"*Hate* is such a strong word," Estelle said. "Is the skin broken?"

Judith looked at her index finger. There was a small red mark where the tip of the spike had pierced the skin. "It didn't go deep. No blood," she said.

"Put some iodine on it, dear."

"It's nothing."

"You don't want an infection. Better to be careful."

Judith leaned the box that held the curtain stretchers against the bed where her brother had died.

Her mother's lips barely moved. "Don't," she said.

Judith let the box lean.

"I've spoken to you. I don't want you to do that," Estelle insisted.

Judith let the box fall to the floor.

Her mother pulled the combs out of her thick, white hair and raked the combs back so that the teeth dug deep. "Saul was your first love. No one will ever love you the way he did," Estelle said. Her face was smooth and distant, her black eyebrows like the large black check marks one of Judith's teachers had left on her papers. "You're tired," Estelle Karger said.

"I'm not. We have to do the woolens." Under her brother's bed was a cedar-lined box where the women stored their foldable winter things. In the closet were zippered garment bags that held their coats and suits.

"We'll have our tea now." The black check marks of Estelle's eyebrows drew close together. She glided through the door into the kitchen, "It's time we took a rest." The polished kettle seemed to float at the end of her long arm, as she sailed it toward the sink. After she had filled it halfway, she lit the burner, turned it up high, and put the kettle down quietly—the softest clink of metal on metal. When the water had heated to a furious boil, steam billowing from the forked spout, Estelle scalded the teapot, dumping out the water into the sink, sending up a cloud of steam that warmed her cheeks to pale pink. She took down the tea tin, tilted back the lid, and measured out the tea. She had bought it on special order, the way her English mother had, India tea. She did what her mother had done. Resting the spout of the kettle against the teapot's rim, she poured, and replaced the china cover. While the tea brewed, Estelle put out the white china—rimmed with gold, painted with roses—arranged five cookies on a plate, which she put on the table in front of Judith. "First, your finger. We don't want you to get an infection."

"It's nothing, Mother."

"Don't tell me it's nothing. I want you to take care of it. You're so careless."

"I'm not careless," Judith said.

"You are. You are careless. You like to worry me. Such a small thing I ask of you. Soon you won't have me to bother you. I'm an old woman. Blood poisoning is a serious thing."

"It was so clean."

"You never can tell."

"Why are you making me nervous?" Judith asked her mother.

"I'm not making you anything, Judith—not anything."

Judith went into the bathroom and shut the door. Her mother's voice followed her: "Did you find the iodine?"

Judith grinned through tight lips, put her fingers into her mouth, and bit down hard. She felt relief—for a moment. She went to the medicine cabinet and took out the brown bottle of iodine.

"Did you?" her mother's voice came again, close to the door, "Blood poisoning. It's a serious thing."

"Yes. Yes." Judith heard words inside her head, "You whore, you rotten whore." She shook the bottle in her fist and twisted it open. Attached to the lid was a glass rod dripping with iodine. Holding her hand over the sink, she rubbed the glass rod over the tiny puncture. It stung. She dipped again and pressed the rod to her skin. She mopped the length of her finger until it was stained wet yellow-brown and the webbed furrow between her index finger and middle finger was dark with ragged drips. She held up her index finger, waiting for the iodine to dry. Her skin was now the color of raw calves' liver. She kept painting, coat after coat. Her finger darkened to muddy brown. The bottle was nearly empty. The glass rod did not reach the bottom. Judith shook out the last of the iodine onto the back of her hand. Drops splattered against the sink. Satisfied, she went into the kitchen.

Her mother poured out the dark tea.

"Just half for me." Judith hooked her iodine-painted finger through the handle of the pitcher and poured milk into her cup until the tea turned white. She bit into the cookie, tasting the vanilla cream at the center, and waited for her mother to notice what she had done to her finger.

"It's so good to have a helper like you. You're such a good daughter. I know you'll always do the right thing." Her face smoothed by a soft smile, Estelle sank heaping spoonfuls of sugar into her tea, chatting about their cleaning as she stirred and sipped.

Judith stared at her hideous finger.

Her mother drank her tea down to the fine dregs that had escaped the strainer.

Judith quickly cleared the table and piled the dishes in one side of the double sink. In the other side she filled a pail with steaming water and poured in ammonia. She used very little, but the acrid, poisonous smell—like burning—filled the kitchen.

Two thick rags under her arm, Judith took the pail and carried it into the living room. With one of the rags, she made a pad to kneel on. The other rag she sank into the ammonia and water. Kneeling, she seized the rag, pulled it out to its length, folded it in half and, with a vicious jerk, twisted it. She batted the rag against the floor the way she used to beat her dolls. She relaxed for an instant and twisted the rag again until no water ran from the tight knob. Moving the rag in wide circles, she scrubbed the blue-flowered linoleum, which, no matter how hot the water, stayed cool. As she worked, the water grew tepid. Judith's scalp was damp with sweat. Crawling on her hands and knees over the floor, she dug the rag into corners, scouring, gripping the rag so tightly that her fingers cramped.

In a few days the rug would come out of storage. With a sharp knife she would cut through the rough jute that bound it. She would slit the brown paper, releasing the smell of mothballs. She and her mother, both of them on their hands and knees, would roll out the rug across the immaculate floor.

Kneeling at her dead brother's bed, Judith lifted the thin green spread and folded it onto the bed so she had an opening. She reached under the bed for the box of woolens but felt only air. She put her head down and looked. The box was there, toward the head of the bed. Dust puffs caught at the edge of the linoleum, loosened when Judith pulled out the box. She opened it, lifted out the sweaters, and piled them onto the bed. Still kneeling, she put her head down on the bed and turned her eyes to the window.

A moth fluttered against the wall near her hand and was still. Judith plucked it from the wall, her index finger brown with iodine. She squeezed hard and opened her hand. A wing moved. She had to stop it. She closed her hand. Opened her hand. The gray thing didn't move. She dropped the moth into the dust, where she kneeled. She would have to sweep the dust away. She would have to wash the floor.

BEN HAD RUSHED TO GIVE BRONA HER PRESENT. HE WASN'T USED TO buying for her—both of them liked to buy quality for themselves and criticize each other for spending too much. But this time he had splurged for *her* and stood like a child, longing for her approving love, watching her face as she opened the box. She didn't disappoint him. "It's a beauty," she said, opening the folds as she gathered the handkerchief at its center and brought it just under her nose. She ran the fine fabric over her sensitive top lip. "Fine." Brona sighed.

"You're still tired," Ben said.

"Not me. I'm better. You know, the doctor was right. Nat said . . ."

"You like it, you're sure?"

"I told you." She gazed at him, quiet.

"I got it at Quackenbush's—a pretty good salesgirl."

Brona stared at her hands folded around the handkerchief. "Such a beautiful deep pink." She raised her head, her full mouth rosy without lipstick. Ben breathed in—quick, as if her smile were the air that kept him alive.

Early one morning Ben waited for Judith on Ellison Street. She came toward him in the chilly air, her handbag on her gloved wrist, her face fresh as new bread. "It's me," he said to her.

"I know." She wanted to laugh.

"We'll take in a show? What do you say?"

Judith avoided his eyes, glancing to the side to check her appearance in the store window. The morning light still hadn't reached the window, and Judith could see them both reflected in the black glass—Ben without a topcoat, his white shirt matching her white scarf. "White," she said, pulling the scarf from her collar's hold. "You suggested it."

"White is good on you. We'll go right here." He pointed to the end of the block away from Broadway. "It's just around the corner, like everything in Paterson. We'll go from work. What do you say? What's to lose?"

He barely turned his sleek head, but enough for Judith to catch his dark brown eye. "Yes, I'd be delighted."

"You see: it wasn't so hard."

It wasn't. Ben Shein had made it easy. She would tell her mother she had to help dress the Quackenbush windows.

"I'll meet you right here," he said.

Judith looked back at a window that was now being washed with first light, whitening, brightening, erasing their reflection.

Judith and Ben sat in the crowded, half dark Montaulk, once a vaudeville theater—still gilded, rococo, painted French blue, carpeted in red velour. Judith looked straight ahead, drew in her arms and legs, holding her hands in her lap. They were too close to the screen, but there was no place to move to—they had come too late. The aisle lights went out; black numbers leapt out against the white face of the clock; the exit lights glowed a deeper red in the brief moment of darkness before the screen filled with images.

Their heads tilted back, they watched while the news rolled across the screen—the *March of Time*—one story after another. Band music, the sound of horns, tanks, planes, ships, bombs, smoke, Poland, England, Germany. A man's voice barked through the theater—rapid, nasal, tense. The news from Europe seemed far away.

But not for Ben, who recognized the curve of a Polish road, the cobbled marketplace of Pabienice, the spire of Lodz, the grainy smoke pouring from the factory stacks. He remembered the Saturday Sabbath hush, the fury of Sunday bells, the clean smell of frost in the workshop above the Sheins' fur store in Lodz, when, as a small boy, he had been sent up to light the stove—all that the Sheins had left behind, along with most of his imperfect Polish. What could he do with these memories? Here he was in America, in a theater, a young woman at his side. Who knew where life could bring a person? Ben adjusted the coat that had slipped from Judith's shoulders. "I could hold it," he said in a low voice.

"Don't worry," Judith answered.

"Who's worrying? It's warm."

Judith leaned forward, lifting herself a few inches off the seat as he pulled her coat away.

Ben folded the coat so that the lavender-scented lining lay across his lap.

His sleeve grazed her wrist. "Here," he whispered. "Kisses. Take some," he insisted as he had at the stand in the lobby, urging her to pick what she wanted.

The sharp corner of the candy box pricked Judith's palm as she fumbled in the dark. She took a small handful of the kisses, put them in her lap, and unwrapped one of the chocolates from the tight foil. She ate in the dark, losing track of how many she was eating.

Fear came on.

Too close to the screen, deep in the strange silvery light, Judith felt seasick: daylight was moonlight and night was a darker day.

Claire's face floats on the watery screen.

Tommy loves her.

She is laughing.

She looks out into the night sky, her eyes starred with light.

Beads of silver rain collect on a black window.

She is crying.

Tommy is going to kill her.

She swoons, her blond head down, her black velvet evening dress dragging her to the floor.

Tommy climbs the curving stairs, shadows on the wall like blades, in his hand a tall, narrow glass of milk glowing like a nightlight on a silver tray. His hair is sculpted, like wet black clay. He bends to kiss Claire, his teeth white as Chiclets.

Claire's eyes spin. Terror—there's poison in the milk! She's sure—but she can't move, weighted down in her gauzy, bridal-white nightdress, caught in the huge, white, smothering bed with its headboard thickly padded in quilted white satin, the white satin spreading like slithering water, covering her to the waist.

Tommy is talking, his black eyes like fresh-poured tar, his black eyes shining like murder.

Judith groaned, hunched, pulled her head down between her tensed shoulders, and closed her eyes, sealing them with her hands.

Ben watched, in and out of the illusion, alert and distanced. "It's only a movie," he whispered to Judith as he reached for her arm, touching her elbow, bony, jutting inside her suit jacket.

She jumped, her heart pumping so fast she had to pant to catch her breath. She opened her eyes, closed them again to shut out the dazzling silver light.

Ben lightly cupped the back of Judith's head, her smooth hair cool under his fingers as he drew her closer.

Under his light touch, she leaned sideways, so that her head rested on his shoulder; she sank down, twisted her head, her closed eyes pressed against his upper arm, the fine material of his jacket sleeve silky against her lids.

Her head and the little bones in the back of her neck were as light and delicate as his daughter Susan's.

"What's he doing?" she asked, afraid to open her eyes.

"Nothing. Driving."

Judith watched.

And it seemed as if the couple would go on riding in their gleaming convertible, the top down, the wind in their faces, Claire's hair wrapped in a turban against the wind. But Tommy speeds faster and faster, the little car barely holding the road on the sharp curves at the edge of the high cliff.

Terror in Claire's spinning eyes, the stars gone.

The speedometer needle quivers and jumps clockwise, past higher and higher numbers, the black sea churning far below, crashing on the rocks. Faster and faster—the needle jumps again, the car door bursts open.

"No," Judith moaned, sitting upright, covering her eyes with her middle and index fingers, sealing her ears with her thumbs, but she couldn't block out the shrieking and shouting, the mounting crash of music.

"Look," Ben said, "it's over." As he leaned toward her, her coat slithered off his lap, and he bent to retrieve it, his head against the metal back of the seat in front of him. His muffled voice grew clearer as he straightened up. "They trick you. Nothing happened. They drove back. She was afraid for nothing."

Judith opened her eyes to a blank white screen.

"What are you worrying about?" he asked her.

"I get nervous."

"You're cute, like my Susan," he said, as if he had not been frightened himself.

AT BEN SHEIN'S SALON, JUDITH STEPPED ONTO THE SHALLOW, CARPETED platform in front of the three-way mirror. She never would have been there if Ben hadn't persuaded her. He measured her, while her mother watched. Mrs. Shein kept her eyes on her son and took down the numbers in a slim, bound ledger.

Neck to shoulder, shoulder to wrist: he knew his business, and he had felt the angle of those shoulders, the circumference of those wrists. He looped the tape around Judith's upper arm and stopped, "For a slim arm like this I don't have to measure."

"You should," Brona said. She raised her pencil, dotting in air.

"Of course, Mrs. S.," Ben answered. He tightened the loop and measured. Careful not to touch her breast, he moved the tape to Judith's underarm, "Inside to wrist."

Judith felt saliva collecting in her mouth. Finally she swallowed, hearing the creak of her own throat. Ben's fingers were so light she could barely feel him, but she wanted to run. She had to stand still while the two women watched her. Through the draped curtain at the back of the store, she saw the closed, ceiling-high door of the vault. It gleamed dully, its massive round handle like the wheel on a submarine hatch.

"Please lift your hair," Ben said to her.

"What?"

"So I can measure."

With both hands, Judith lifted her hair. She had washed her neck with alcohol and it was white and clean.

"Thank you," he said.

She stretched out her arms.

"Like this," the furrier said and let his arms drop. "Just stand naturally."

She did, and he measured from the back of her neck to just below the back of the knees. She was a good student; she knew how to listen: he would make her a beautiful coat.

Brona wrote down the measurements, her large diamond dull white in the evening lights of the store.

Judith felt the pressure of the tape in the sensitive creases at the backs of her knees where the veins bunched, where the mosquitoes bit.

Brona continued writing.

"Lift your arm. Please, the right one." Ben said.

Judith lifted her arm.

Again Ben stretched the tape—underarm to calf.

"Now if you will look straight ahead."

Judith checked her posture in the mirror. She saw the back of Ben's sleek head, felt his fingers in the hollow of her neck, above her collar bones, saw the back of his hand, felt and saw the tape snaking over her breast. She tried not to breathe. She looked down at him.

"Look straight ahead." He wanted to wink at her but stopped himself.

Judith did as he asked. In the mirror, she saw him, a dark shape kneeling on one knee, beneath her.

Ben's mother put out her hand, and Judith, clutching her by the wrist, stepped down.

Estelle Karger rose on her long legs, her flat envelope handbag pressed under her arm. "I don't know why a fur coat," she murmured.

They had already chosen black Persian and the design Ben had sketched. Judith wanted the coat, but she wasn't sure she should have it. "You don't think?" she asked her mother.

"If you want it, dear."

"I don't know," Judith said.

"You could wear the coat Mr. Shein made for me. There's nothing wrong with it."

"Mother . . . ," Judith tried to speak.

Ben interrupted. "Mrs. Karger, we could fix it up. There's plenty of wear in that old coat. An old style is interesting. An old style has value."

Her mother sighed, "Maybe she *should* have her own."

"Something new. Something warm," he added.

"For winter. Will it be ready?" Estelle asked.

"Of course, of course."

"November?"

"Before the snow," he said. Without touching her, his arm outstretched, Ben guided Mrs. Karger to the desk, while Judith followed them.

Brona drew out a large sheet of pale violet paper from the curved-front drawer.

Ben dictated. "One fur coat. Persian lamb. Black."

Brona wrote the words in the bottom half of the page. At the top she printed "Judith Karger" in large letters. "Your address, Miss Karger?"

"164 Tenth Avenue."

"Phone?"

"Sherwood 3642." She tried to read the upside-down letters of her name.

"Judith," her mother began, "do you think Persian will be all right? Are you sure? Is this what you want? The cost . . ."

Ben answered, "Quality. For a refined girl like your daughter—elegant."

"But isn't Hudson seal more practical? Not so expensive?"

Judith had already heard it. They had gone back and forth all afternoon: Persian, Hudson seal, Hudson seal, Persian. "Mother . . ."

"Mrs. Karger": Ben would get this fly with honey. "Not so expensive? Yes, you are right. More *practical*? No."

"But she's only seen *my* Persian," Estelle said.

"I may have something to show you. Do we?" Ben asked his mother.

"Let me think." Brona paused, looked past Judith. "There is one. It's a special design. Not for a customer. Something creative. A furrier has to work out an idea." She turned to her son, her pencil in her hand. "Mr. S., show them Shein Five. The latest. You know what a Ben Shein coat is." Her voice dropped, respectful, confidential. She deferred to her son.

Judith moved closer to the desk. She smelled Mrs. Shein's perfume, something light and something heavier. It was long past teatime and she was hungry.

Ben Shein swung open the heavy door of the vault. Cold air came into the room, making her shiver. Deep in the darkness of the vault a light went on. In the spotlight, Ben held up a black sheath of a coat on a hanger and glided into the room, lifting the coat higher, like a banner. "One slim stroke, no lapels," he began.

Brona Shein jumped out of her chair. Her right hand shot out, the dark green pencil pointed at her son. "That's not the one, that's not the one I meant."

"Feel, Judith, the real *Persian*. I'll make one for you, but fuller," Ben said.

"Miss Karger!" Brona Shein had her hand on the coat.

Judith stroked the cold, black sleeve.

"Silky, tightly curled—the young fur," Ben said.

Judith opened the coat to the large, raised white initials. In cursive: T. L.S. She ran her fingertips across the chilled stitches.

Ben pulled the coat away from her hands, then came back to hold it close in front of her so she could see—in the mirror—her face above the black sheen.

"May I try it on?" Judith asked.

Ben eased the coat away from Judith. "It belongs to someone else. A special customer. An original. In storage. Persian. Did you feel it?"

Judith nodded. "I like it."

"I know you, Judith. How can you be so sure? You like it now, but later is another story. Don't look so sad. It's only a coat," Estelle said.

"I'm not sad."

The door of the salon opened. A man came in, a newspaper under his arm. He wore wire-frame glasses like Judith's father's.

"An old customer, Miss Karger. You'll excuse me." Brona Shein got up from the desk in one smooth movement and went to him, her hands clasped in front of her as if she were going to rub them together. Judith couldn't hear her, but whatever she was saying must have pleased the customer: he smiled and nodded. It took skill to make a waiting customer happy. In a moment Brona Shein was back. "Miss Karger, the Sheins will work with you. We want to work with you so you will have the right coat. The coat for you. Mr. S., show the Hudson seal. The better one," Brona said.

Ben brought out the Hudson seal and held it open so that Judith could slide her arms into the sleeves as she faced herself in the mirror. The cut was wrong, the fur was mud. Her face was mud.

Her mother appeared in the mirror, behind her, her face to the left, above Judith's head. The check-marked brows rose as Estelle's smooth voice purred, "Judith, it's handsome on you."

"That seal is a *dog*." The customer spoke from the front of the store, his bass voice gathering power, as if he were on a stage. "That's not the coat for you. What kind of coat is that to show such a beautiful young lady? Tell them what you want," he said to Judith.

"The Persian." Judith slipped off the Hudson seal, which she didn't know was muskrat.

Mrs. Shein sat down, and Ben pushed in her chair. As he stood in attendance with his hands on the back of the chair, his mother wrote numbers on the violet paper. "We ask for a twenty percent deposit," she said.

"Judith, we'll be paying for years," Estelle said.

"It will last for years," Ben answered.

"Like yours, Mother."

"You may not live as long," Estelle said.

"A deposit isn't necessary." Ben bent down to Mrs. Shein's ear as if to whisper, but he didn't whisper, "We know the Kargers."

"Of course, we do. As a special courtesy, the Sheins ask fifteen percent," Mrs. Shein said and stood up, the paper in her hand.

Ben reached around his mother. "I'll take care of it. No deposit. Judith isn't going anywhere. We know where to find her."

"Yes, we know. Mr. S. knows." Brona stood there, her coarse hair like a dog's. "We need your signature, Miss Karger." She pushed the paper across the desk and, with one whirling hand, spun the paper so Judith could read the numbers.

Judith took the pen, hesitated, and then, in her round, girlish hand, signed her name. Her mother and Mrs. Shein had nothing to say.

ON A FRIDAY NIGHT, A MONTH AFTER JUDITH KARGER'S FITTING, BEN Shein threw his topcoat over his shoulders and, holding it closed with one hand, hurried across Ellison toward Quackenbush's to surprise Judith. The street was almost deserted, dark except for a yellow light that burned in the distance, magnified by a splintered halo blurring in the moist air. One at a time a few saleswomen came through the door; the good nights dwindled, and Ben turned away, sure he had missed her.

"So long, see you tomorrow, if I live that long," a woman yelled. She had lungs for the opera. Ben turned back to see the loudmouth wave to the slim figure whose measurements he knew. Judith was already hurrying down Ellison, and he had to run. Gaining on her as he struggled to keep his coat from falling, he gasped her name, but she didn't hear him. "Judith," he called again as he reached her.

At the sound, Judith turned around and saw Ben Shein, out of breath, his forehead and nose pale above the dark-shadowed upper lip, cheeks, and chin, his coat hanging from one shoulder. "What's the matter?" she asked; then, to hide her irritation, "Is everything all right?"

"You didn't see me?" he asked.

"I didn't."

"Maybe you need glasses," he said, pulling his topcoat over his shoulders.

"Ben, it's late." She had worked until nine, one difficult customer after another.

"You don't look tired." Her face was smooth, fresh, as if it were morning. "You look good. Your coat . . . the Persian," he began.

"It's ready?"

"Not yet. Don't look so disappointed. Soon you'll have it. Ben Shein never breaks a promise." He felt his topcoat slip, pulled it back over his shoulders, and held it closed with one hand against his chest. With his other hand he reached for her arm. She stepped away from him. The sidewalk had emptied. All along Broadway the window lights dimmed. "I wanted to see you. To tell you. Let me take you somewhere. For ice cream, for coffee." He touched his cheek and felt the stubble of his night beard.

"It's been a long day. You could have called me," Judith said.

"I have to make an appointment? We've both had a long day. I didn't even have time to shave. Come, you can call your mother from the salon. You know the number?"

"Of course . . ."

"Come, you'll see the salon when it's quiet. I'll show you. Be my guest. You don't have to be a stranger," Ben said.

"No."

"No?" Ben said.

"No, I'm not a stranger." She faltered, "If you say so."

"I say so." He swept his hand toward Ben Shein Furs as if he held a wand.

"Then I'd love to."

"I'll show you, then we'll go for a little ice cream. It won't hurt us."

"Not ice cream. I couldn't," she said.

"Couldn't? You *like* ice cream!"

"I do."

"We're talking about an hour. After, you can go. I won't send the police for you."

He made her laugh. He buttoned the top button of his coat, and took her arm, his step light and quick as he led her along. "Look, we're dancing! Fred and Ginger!"

Ben's coat swung like a cape, the dark blue cashmere draping in waves. Judith, stumbling at first, fell into step, giddy, rushing with him past the half-lit Shein windows, where the mannequin stood, now wrapped in a full-length silver fox that seemed touched by frost.

Ben took her hand and led her through a narrow passage that opened into a damp, unpaved alley smelling of earth and cinders. Judith shivered in the moist cold, afraid. Above the back door, a light filled a small cage suspended from a metal bracket shaped like question mark. She heard the clink of keys, then the grate of metal as Ben opened the door, his back to her.

"Wait, you'll see." He left her standing on the threshold as he went first through the back door, turning on the ceiling lights, which filled the cold room with hard, bright light—too bright. He flicked off some of the switches. Better.

Still shivering, Judith stepped over the threshold. "Ben," she called, "it's getting late."

"I'm here." He took her hand. "You're cold."

"It's worse inside," she said. Her legs trembled in their silk stockings.

"Take this. We turn down the heat at night." Ben held out his open coat.

"No, really," she said.

"Go on." He fitted the coat over her shoulders, and she let him lead her in. The salon—dove gray and violet, empty of fur—looked like a sitting room. The drape was drawn over the entrance to the vault holding riches.

"Miss Karger." Ben played proprietor.

"Mr. S."

"Call your mother from the desk. Sit down. Make yourself comfortable. Have a candy. The real Hopjes."

Judith reached into the heaped bowl.

"Take," Ben said, when he saw her hesitate.

Warmer now, Judith grasped the plump lozenge, peeled the thin wrapper, and brought the candy to her mouth, lifting it from the paper with her lips, the taste sweet and bitter.

"Just tell her you'll be a little late." He pulled the coat forward, button-side and buttonhole side, as she sat down, wrapped in his cashmere. "Tell her you're with me." He rubbed the cold receiver in his warm hands and gave it to Judith. "You know the number?" Ben teased again. "Show me. I don't believe it."

Judith spoke the number to the operator and waited. "Mother, I'll be late. Mother?"

Ben slipped the receiver out of her hand. "Mrs. Karger, it's Ben Shein. Don't worry. I'll bring her home." He winked at Judith, his dark eye closed, "I'm a good man."

As if Estelle stood over her, Judith could see her mother's face, the smooth forehead wrinkling, the black eyebrows lifting.

"I'll take good care of her. You want that, don't you?" Ben bobbed his head up and down. "Of course, we agree." He put down the receiver. "What a pill."

"She has no one," Judith said.

"She has you."

There was a sharp rapping noise at the door. Ben spun around. For a moment he thought he was seeing his own face, but it was Joe Mavet. He had something in his hand and was tapping it against the glass. "Ben Shein, Ben Shein," Joe sang. Ben went closer. He could see the coin between Joe's thumb and index finger. The sound was sharp, like a hammer on a nail.

Ben opened the door. "Maybe you want to buy something, Joe? How are you?" Ben reached into his pocket and pulled out a ten-dollar bill. "Here, take it," he said.

Joe did something he had never done before: he pushed away Ben's hand. "I don't need it. I got a quarter. I sing in the cemetery, with the crows. Money drops from their wings. You should sing to them. They'll give you. The hell with this fur business. I saw the light. I thought maybe you were here. Hello. Ben, how are you?"

"You know me, Joe." Ben put his money back in his pocket.

Joe stepped to the side and looked around Ben. He covered his ears. "I'm good. I'm quiet. I'll be a good boy." Joe put his finger across his lips. "Oh, oh, she's big. She's so big." He pointed the same finger at Judith. "What a big girl. Look at those arms on her. She's a strong one."

Judith crossed her arms over her chest. "I have to go," she said.

"He won't hurt you. Don't worry, I know him. He's fine," Ben said.

"I am fine. I'm a father," Joe said.

Ben laughed.

"How is your smart, beautiful daughter?" Joe asked.

"Good. Susan is good."

"They're all good. You better watch her," Joe said and held up the quarter. "I'm going to give *you* something. Take it. Take it."

Joe reached across the threshold, and Ben took the quarter, rubbing his fingers across the hot metal. Joe hopped from foot to foot. "Nobody listens to me. You take good care of that Susan. Now? I've got to go. You don't forget me—but you will. Nobody listens."

From the doorway Ben watched Joe cross Ellison. His army coat dragged on the pavement. Joe stopped, the coat seeming to stand by itself on its thick, heavy hem. Joe turned around and shouted, "Remember!" Then he laughed out loud and drew his finger sideways across his throat. His head rolled to the side, his mouth open like a dead rabbit's. Joe moved on, the coat dragging behind him.

"I should give him a good coat. He's exactly my size," Ben said.

"Poor Joe. I used to see him in back of Quackenbush's, picking through the garbage," Judith said.

"Never mind. 'Poor Joe.' Come on, he's not so poor. He gets around. He's still walking. You saw how quiet he talked. His head is twisted, but he's happy. He laughed. You heard him," Ben said.

"He *was* happy."

"That's what I tell people. That's what I told my brother. Nat thinks they should put Joe away. You, you know what I mean. Joe's just very nervous. He worries. *You* understand."

"I do, Ben." His name came easily to her lips.

"That's who I am!"

"Ben," she said, smiling at him.

Joe Mavet was wrong. She wasn't big. She was a slim girl. "We'll spend a few minutes together, and I'll drive you home," Ben said.

"I won't say no."

With a light touch, Ben took Judith's arm and together they left the Shein salon.

"Anything you want, order anything you want." In the Madison Sweet Shoppe, Ben held the open menu in front of Judith, two fingers in the vee of the crease. The blue-shaded lamp threw an icy light onto the marble-topped table where his treats would be served. He wouldn't let her have plain apple pie and tea, "Have it à la mode, vanilla. Try a little coffee." When he gave the waitress their order—a black and white ice cream soda for him, apple pie for her, and two coffees—he asked that Judith's pie be warmed. "Just a little," he said. "You don't want mush. The ice cream shouldn't melt."

Judith tasted. "It's delicious. I never had it this way. Just that little bit of heat."

"A little brings out the taste of the cinnamon and apple. A little makes everything more. Here, use a spoon."

She ate quickly, spoonful after spoonful. Ben Shein was a generous man.

"You see, you're not so tired. You have some color in your face. You like it." He loved her look of surprise. "You'll like the coat. It's making up. Beautiful. Have some coffee."

"I'm not used to it."

He told her to try it black with sugar and watched as she stirred three spoonfuls of sugar into the cup. Above the rosy circle of light on the table, her face was bright. She sipped then took a big swallow. She liked it.

"You could help me. It's busy. Moe Black knows the business, but he's no good downstairs. If you ever want to leave Quackenbush's," Ben said, shocking himself. His voice caught in his throat and he coughed, covering his mouth. He felt Judith's eyes on his hands and moved them back so that only the tips of his fingers curled over the table edge. "I have a daughter. Susan—she needs . . ."

"If you wanted to add a line of accessories, I could advise you. Handkerchiefs, scarves, the little things. It's important to complete a look. But I don't know anything about the fur business. Nothing at all."

"Never mind, you could learn. You're smart. Like my Susan."

"The little things are important." Judith knew how to choose them, she was sure. "But not too many. Elegance, not fussiness. A bag, a scarf must blend and yet accentuate."

How do you blend with a fur? Ben wondered. Accessories he didn't need; they could get stuck with those little things. He didn't want inventory. He'd teach her the fur. He could already see her in the shop, talking to customers, her voice low, polite. She had manners. She'd keep Susan nice. "You make a good appearance."

"Appearance isn't everything."

"But in our business it's important."

"In our business, it takes skill." Judith brought the spoon to her lips, finishing the last of her ice cream.

BEN BOUGHT JUDITH FLOWERS FOR HIS FIRST VISIT TO THE KARGERS'. He picked out spider mums, which he loved, not heavy football mums. He chose each stem himself, from the buckets in the back room of Krieger's. He and Tess used to buy them in the fall. They would fill the plain, tall glass vase with a huge bouquet—one color—and carry it to the desk near the door so that it was the first thing a customer saw. Ben had stopped buying flowers after Tess's death.

He handed the wrapped bouquet to Mrs. Karger just inside the windowless foyer, where he stood in the dark hall. She seemed not to know what to do with them. "Flowers. For you and Judith."

"Yes." That was her answer. "Judith will be out in a minute. Maybe you could help me with these. We're not used to such large bouquets." She held the flowers straight out in front of her. "Mr. Shein, Judith is . . . quiet."

"So are the flowers. Please, Mrs. Karger, it's Ben. Call me Ben."

"Well, I suppose I can do that." Taller than her daughter, she glided ahead of him into the kitchen and put the bundle of flowers on the kitchen table. With a paring knife, she began to cut at the dark green layers of tissue paper.

"Please, let me." Ben unwrapped the tissue, releasing the cold scent of flowers. The blossoms opened from their tight white centers, thick as stuck pincushions, to yellow petals that uncurled in lavish fringes. They were so fresh, the green, notched leaves crisp, unbroken.

Estelle Karger began to look through the cabinets for a vase. "I don't think I have anything large enough," she said. "They're lovely, but . . ." Reaching high, she brought down from the top shelf a small vase with a pinched, fluted opening. "We can cut them to fit," Estelle said and picked up the knife.

"Not for these," Ben said.

"It *would* be a pity. You might find a container under the sink," Estelle said.

Ben drew up his trouser legs and got down on his hands and knees. He rummaged under the sink and pulled out a large jar with rounded sides. He cocked his head to the side and looked up.

Estelle Karger stood over him. "It had pickles in it. My husband brought it home. It took us a year to eat them, but we did. Can you smell the pickles?"

"It won't hurt the flowers," Ben said and filled the jar at the tap. Now he took the sharp knife and cut the bottoms of the stems at a slant. He picked off the lowermost leaves and, one by one, dropped the flowers into the jar. They made their own design, the strong, thick stems against the wide-mouthed rim of the jar, the blossoms tilting out over the sides, a wheel of flowers. He was satisfied.

"They are pretty, but I don't know where to put them," Estelle said.

"Right here," Ben said, sweeping the paper, leaves, and stem bits into the trash bucket. He put the jar of flowers in the center of the kitchen table. The pale disks of the flowers floated over the dark green stems. Judith will like them, not this miserable mother, Ben thought. Judith would like what he and Tess liked.

Mrs. Karger lit the burner under the kettle, her back to Ben when Judith came in.

Judith looked like a schoolgirl in her pale blue tweed skirt and dark blue cardigan over a matching sweater. A string of tiny pearls, like little white baby teeth, encircled her neck. Her smooth hair fell straight from a side part and curled under at the shoulders in a pageboy. Ben stared down at her bent head, at the clean part in her light brown hair. When she lifted her head, he saw that she wore her half smile, and he thought she was smiling at *him*. "Ben, you shouldn't have."

"I wanted to."

"A small bouquet would have pleased her. Mr. Shein, we live quietly, we live small." As she tilted her head toward her daughter, Estelle Karger's eyes turned as cloudy and soft as they had been when her son Saul had died.

"My mother has her own way of doing things."

"Sometimes you have to let go," Ben said.

"Sometimes, if you can," Estelle murmured.

"The hell with it," he said.

"Ben, there's no need," Judith began.

"Dear, shall we let Mr. Shein speak?"

"We shall, of course, Mother."

Ben recovered, "I bought these from Krieger's. I used to buy a lot from them. For the salon. I should do that again." He thought of buying flowers with Judith.

"Now it's time for tea." Estelle Karger opened her hand as if she were giving him something.

Amidst the stacks of pink and white china crowded on the small table in front of the couch, Ben finally found the cookies: five little pale brown ovals on a large plate. Ben asked for lemon. There was none. Milk he didn't like. He blew on his black tea. He bit into the hard cookie. He dipped the cookie into the tea, soaking it until the end broke off and sank to the bottom of the cup, dissolved. He swallowed the soft end that was left.

"Do have another, Mr. Shein," Estelle said.

"Next time I'll bring you some from Boyarsky's."

"I haven't had their butter cookies for years. Too dear for us, Mr. Shein," Estelle said.

"We have our own treats, Mother." Their rituals—the India tea, embellished only by heaped spoonfuls of sugar and a few packaged cookies—had kept them apart from each other in a discipline that bound them. As Ben and her mother talked, Judith reached for another cookie.

For these cookies, she needs sharp teeth, Ben thought.

As Judith reached for yet another, she saw her mother's eyebrows rise, and her mouth pucker. Though Estelle didn't speak, Judith answered her: "I've had enough."

"Of course, dear." Estelle Karger tapped the back of Judith's hand with her long fingers.

"I don't want to get fat."

"You'll never be fat like some women with bellies out to here. Nobody likes a fat girl," Ben said, demonstrating the size of an enormous belly by extending his arm in front of his own stomach.

Judith jerked back and knocked the cup and saucer out of her mother's hand. The tea spilled across the carpet.

"No harm, Mrs. Karger. Such white tea, so little." Ben pulled at the tips of the handkerchief in his outside breast pocket and pulled out a large linen square, the edges hand-rolled. Crumpling the fine fabric, he got down on his knees and blotted up the tea. "Look, it doesn't sink in. There's oil in the wool. It sheds liquid like a sheep. You'll see: it won't stain. I promise you."

For a month, on Sunday afternoons, from precisely four to five-thirty, Ben came to the Kargers' for tea, rather than taking Judith out.

"My mother hates to be alone on Sundays," Judith would say, avoiding the truth: this ritual hour-and-a-half left her most of the precious day to spend as she pleased. She was used to having her Sundays undisturbed, a welcome rest after Saturday's rigorous housecleaning. Morning and afternoon, while her mother left her alone, she would wash and groom herself, paying special attention to her hands. While her hair dried, she would manicure her nails, pushing back the cuticles with a slant-edged wooden stick until the white half-moons showed, filing the nails close and straight across, rubbing them with her grandmother's narrow chamois buffer until they gleamed, dainty and clean, before she painted on clear polish. Finally she could rest in her good robe, stretched on her bed until teatime.

Though Ben would have preferred to take Judith to a matinee, he agreed to come to the Kargers' on these late Sunday afternoons. For years Ben Shein had managed customers. Not patient by nature, under Brona's direction—relieved by Tess's humor—he had learned the discipline imposed by the trade: how and when to keep his mouth shut, how to wait. Now he would wait for Judith and enjoy the pleasure of generosity, which, in business, he had to check. If customers wanted to believe they were getting a bargain, Ben Shein would help them believe it. But if he gave them a real break, the Sheins would lose. With the Kargers, he didn't have to think. He could give and give. He knew how to bring food—pastry from Boyarsky's, fruit from Oppenheimer's, chocolate for Judith from Barricini's. He enjoyed himself, assuming that the Kargers would take and always love taking.

Yet what could Judith give back? Every week, though she had asked him not to, he would bring a new box of chocolates—truffles, soft centers, nuts—too much. It was difficult for her to eat just one piece when the smell of chocolate filled the room. He wanted her to open every box. When she protested, he would say, "Put it out, you don't have to eat it all."

On leaving, Ben would kiss the women's hands, as he had learned to do in Lodz—first Estelle's, until she came to expect it, reaching out just before the end of their hour-and-a-half together. When it was Judith's turn, she would rise, glad for Ben's graceful attention—and relieved that he would soon leave.

One Sunday afternoon, he wanted more, and kissed her on the mouth at the door, her lips tasting of tea and white frosting.

Judith heard the rattle of dishes in the kitchen and stiffened, unable to move or speak.

"You're shy," Ben whispered.

Judith smelled chocolate as he reached under her sweater, covered her breast with his light hand, and quickly moved his hand away.

He had to get her away from there—then she'd relax. Slowly, she'd get used to him. Sometimes on the nights they both worked late he would meet her after work for coffee; instead of coming for Sunday tea, he would send flowers. Occasionally on a Saturday night they would go to a movie or to dinner in one of the local restaurants.

Soon Judith longed for the feel of his skilled fingers. A virgin's pleasures were enough, complete in themselves: sweet, slow-mounting desire, her hands on Ben's warm neck, the shivering, pulsing heat between her legs as he released her. Once she had cried out when his beard raked her cheek; ever since he had been careful when he kissed her, pressing only his lips to her lips.

When he would sit across the table, she would tell him how well dressed he was, praising his shirts as "immaculate and ironed to perfection." Judith liked the way they looked together: they were a pair, Ben on his side of the table, she on hers.

He bought her little presents, a pin for her lapel, a silver pen from Tiffany's. "To write your receipts," he said.

When the Persian lamb coat he was making for Judith was ready, Ben told her he would pick her up on Sunday—they would have lunch in New York—and this time she agreed. He came into the Kargers' apartment with the coat over his arm.

"I want to see you in it," he said as he held out the open coat to Judith. Her initials were a welted flourish on the satin lining, white against black. With her back to Ben, she slipped her arms into the sleeves. Ben lifted the coat onto her shoulders, and she pulled it close. "It fits so beautifully. I can hardly feel it."

"You could be a model."

Smiling, with her right hand hip-high, Judith swung the right side of the coat open. "I love it."

"A coat from Ben Shein," Estelle Karger said. "I guess it's worth it."

"I'm not charging you. It's a present." It was Ben's proposal of marriage. He was making it through Mrs. Karger, who would understand the terms.

"Ben, I have the money. It's only right." Judith held on to the coat.

"What's right? Let's go out. Comb your hair and get ready." He took her hand with a flourish, bowed and kissed her perfect skin, white against the black fur.

As soon as Judith went to fix her hair, Mrs. Karger started on him. "My daughter is not strong. She's used to a quiet life with me. My Judith was going to be a teacher. Mr. Shein, you'll go slow."

"I do."

"She has to get to know you. She's used to being alone with me. She's a very sensitive girl, a nervous girl. She's always happy to come home."

"You'll see her. She'll be all right. It's not good to be alone."

"She's not alone."

"I'll take care of things. The salon does good. You'll do good." The woman would be crazy to refuse him.

That day Ben took Judith for Sunday lunch at Rockefeller Center, where they sat across from each other at a small round table in the cafe overlooking the skating rink. Judith kept her coat over her shoulders, the black fur over the pale blue sweater.

"I'm buying you a cordial—Cherry Heering," Ben said when they had finished the meal he had ordered for them. "You'll like it. Sip it slowly. First a little coffee, with sugar, the way you like it. Then a little drink."

Judith listened to him.

Ben took her hand in both of his hands. "I want to marry you."

Judith looked out the window to the skaters gliding by, the intricate maze of curving lines incised in white ice. She had once begged her mother for lessons, for white skates with silver blades, but there hadn't been enough money. Out in the freezing air, at the center of the rink, in the midst of the skating pairs, was a lone woman, the short swing-skirt of her white skating costume lined with pink satin, her hair completely hidden by a close-fitting jersey helmet that accentuated the angled planes of her face, the white curved forehead. Judith stared, entranced, as the skater spun on her strong legs, her head back, her back arched, her skirt rising, flashing pink. She spun alone, so fast her body blurred, pulling Judith into the vortex as the skater disappeared into the whirl. As she came out of the spin, her white-gloved hands emerged first, then the rest of her—clear but not clear: the whirling blur remained for an instant, even as she came to a dead stop, her silver blades scraping cloudy wings from the ice. Instantly, the skater extended her arm, her finger pointing, inviting, as she led herself toward the next movement. Primed for the push-off, Judith waited, her eyes fixed on the solitary skater.

"Judith," Ben cupped her perfect hand.

She startled at the sudden pressure, resisting the impulse to pull away from his moist, hot touch, Ben's knuckles white among the black hair.

"We wouldn't be alone," he held her.

"No." Judith drew out the O in a soft exclamation as she pulled her hand out from under Ben's grasp.

Her answer confused him, but he did not ask her what she meant; instead, he made his point again: "It's not good to be alone."

Straightening her long spine so that her neck lengthened, as if she herself were skating, Judith looked beyond the window to the scraped ice, where the white-clad skater executed her dizzying turns.

"What's so important out there? I'm trying to talk to you."

"Nothing, Ben. Nothing."

"Didn't you hear me? It's not good to be alone."

Her answer was a little smile.

"I've been alone." He blinked and his shoulders rolled forward. "I know what I'm talking about," Ben said.

Ben's dark eye frightened her: wide-open, naked, pleading. Her ribs tightening from long habit, Judith stopped breathing, holding herself in the tense embrace that for so long had kept her upright.

"Listen to me," Ben said.

"I . . ."

Ben's head sagged forward on his bent neck, exposing the crown where hair whirled out of his scalp: soft, white, defenseless. Judith sucked in a breath through clenched teeth that stopped her exhalation. "Ben!" The sound shot from her mouth.

"You're tired," he said as he lifted his head.

"It is late." She lowered her voice, grateful he had given her an excuse.

"I'm telling you. I know what I mean. We could help each other. You wouldn't have to worry."

With this he reached her.

"I wouldn't."

"We could work together. We could be a couple," Ben said. He faced her, upright in his chair, his suit jacket smooth, the cashmere fitting squarely on his shoulders.

Judith saw the couple they would be, the couple they were: dressed to perfection. She would be with him, arrange his things, lay out his shirts. They would sit across the table from each other. They would do everything right. She pressed her fingers lightly against Ben's fingers, losing herself in a dream.

"That's it?" he asked.

"Yes."

"You will?"

Now she lifted her hand for his kiss, allowing the quick touch of his lips.

A week later Ben bought her a ring, a blue-white diamond mounted between blue sapphires, not as big as Brona Shein's, tasteful for a young bride.

He helped her with her lists for the wedding, for her clothes, for their new house, for every detail of their life together. She would have what she wanted and never have to worry. "We'll put your mother on the books," Ben said, as if he had the power to erase all trouble.

They both could not stop themselves from giving advice, a way of responding that, while promising to be helpful, drew them apart. In her serious way, Judith would tell him about her work—her successes, her customers, the new line of merchandise. Though she would be leaving Quackenbush's once they married, Ben would lecture her in exhaustive detail about what she should do and how she should do it. Open the sale this way, close it that way. She would nod her head in seeming agreement, as she shut out his advice. Yet she would deliver her own. His mother should not have taken the housekeeper to New York so the two women could shop together; it wasn't right to be so friendly with servants. Moe Black should buy a new suit. Ben should add a line of dresses to his stock. Ben shouldn't work so hard.

Susan should behave. "She uses disgusting language," Judith said.

"My Susan?"

"I asked her to hang up her coat and she swore at me."

"She doesn't know what she's saying."

"Your daughter runs wild with that Joan Englander."

On this point Ben agreed. Susan couldn't leave that Joan alone. The two of them wanted to do what they wanted, wear the same clothes, eat the same food. Mostly Ben would humor Judith when she gave him advice. "Oh, you think so?" he would say. He could afford to let her talk. What did it cost him? "You mean well," he would tell her. She could talk, and he would do what he wanted. After all, he knew more. He had so much to teach her, and she was young with so much time to learn.

One night after work, Ben drove with Judith into Eastside Park. It was chilly, and he kept the car running, the heater on full blast, until the car was so warm he had to open the little side vent and turn off the engine. Piles of leaves had been raked to the side of the road. They gave off a musty smell of decay.

Ben reached inside Judith's coat and put his hand on her bare neck. He pulled her toward him and turned her face to his.

Judith wanted his touch, his skilled hand on her breasts, the melting heat between her legs, the dream releasing her.

Ben had shaved at work, but already he could feel his prickly beard. He would be careful of Judith's tender skin. "Come closer; I won't hurt you. I promise. Let me. I won't kiss you—my beard." He stroked her hand.

"What?" She laughed, opening her mouth.

He stared at her perfect teeth and touched her bare neck again. "Just like a baby," he said, stroking along the hairline. "Baby skin. Baby hair."

Judith shivered.

Ben reached under her sweater. "I know what you like."

He gently tugged at her nipples, over and over, rhythmically. He watched her face change.

Judith closed her eyes, her face against Ben's cashmere coat as heat pulsed between her thighs, sending her in and out of herself. She spun alone.

Though he had promised himself patience, Ben could not wait. He took hold of Judith's hand and brought it to his penis buttoned inside his trousers.

Judith came out of her spinning dream, Ben's hand on her wrist, her hand pressed to his hard penis. Her head went blank; mute, she pulled away, shivering in dark space.

"You're a baby."

"I . . ."

"What are you?" Ben raised his voice.

Judith's scalp tightened; she put her hand on the cold window, her throat closed to stop a sob.

"What's the matter?"

She couldn't answer.

"You're a sweet little girl. Don't worry. You'll be my little wife. I'll take care of you."

"You're not angry?"

"Me? Don't be silly. But we shouldn't wait until we get married to do everything," he said. "You should get used to it. I don't want to hurt you."

In the weeks before their marriage he would take her back to East-side Park, to sit with him in the dark. He thought he was doing the right thing—teaching her, little by little.

He asked her to sit still while he touched her. "You'll be my wife," he said. He could barely make out her face in the dark as he listened to her breathing quicken.

Judith spun in her dream, her eyes closed.

"More," he said. "Please open your legs more."

"No more." She had gotten where she wanted to go—shivering virgin release, forever young, bud unbroken.

"Please. Listen to me," Ben said.

And she did, sitting straight and still, her legs open. Ben stroked her and she relaxed a little.

He tried to put his finger inside her, but she was too tight. He put his finger into his own mouth and then he tried again. This time he got in. A little.

She sat still while he stroked her breast. She closed her eyes, longing to forget him. Ben was adept, he was patient—soon she spun into herself, her legs shook and shook again. In this way, with his hand, he entered her. There was very little blood, very little pain.

"I promised you," Ben whispered.

IN THE HOUSE ON MANOR STREET, IN FEBRUARY, LESS THAN A YEAR since he had thought of marrying again, Ben stood under the wedding canopy his mother had made from a length of old lace. He didn't like the lace. It was too old, he told her, but Brona wanted that lace. She bothered him until he gave in to her. She wanted light to shine through, and it did. White winter light on Judith's dark blue suit, on the white roses in her hands. Not a mark on those hands. He tried to find Judith's face through the short veil. It was like smoke under there, like the gray silk her mother wore.

The clarinetist put aside his instrument and sang to the accompaniment of the violin, *Ah! Sweet mystery of life, at last I've found thee*. Barely conscious of the music, Ben waited for Nat to look at him, but Nat didn't move. Standing close to their mother, his face turned toward the window, watching the gray sky, Nat looked young again, his eyes on nothing—like morning. Or night. And Ben watched, as he used to in bed, Nat's first look of the day, or his last.

The music came to an end, *For 'tis love alone that rules forever.*

Ben faced the rabbi, Monte Gelfand. "Monte" for Moses, Moishe. Who could be a Moses? Tess used to bring in Moishe Pumpernickel from New York. She loved it. The rabbi started. His Hebrew like a conversation: loud, soft—makes no difference. Most of the guests wouldn't understand it.

Ben said the words in English:

Be thou my wife according to the law of Moses and of Israel.

I will faithfully promise that I will be a true husband unto thee.

I will work for thee.

I will protect and support thee and will provide all that is necessary for thy due sustenance, as it becomes a Jewish husband to do.

"What's sus-ten-ance?" The loud whisper came from Susan's friend, Joan Englander, the bigmouth, her hand on Susan's arm. Louder, Susan's whisper: "Suss, tiss."

He wouldn't let her bother him. Ben went on:

I also take upon myself all such further obligations for thy maintenance as are prescribed by our religious statute.

Now the rabbi spoke for the bride:

And the said bride has plighted her troth unto him in affection and sincer-

ity, and has thus taken upon herself the fulfillment of all the duties incumbent upon a Jewish wife.

The rabbi placed a small brown paper bag next to Ben's foot. Inside the bag was a wine glass, not a shot glass. He might not have the strength to break a shot glass. Ben raised his foot and brought it down.

There was a loud cracking sound, like a gun going off. Joan jumped out of her seat. "Wow," she yelled. Moe Black pulled himself up from the chair that barely held him. He gripped his own lapels and pushed out his chest as if he were a cantor and this house were the grand synagogue in Lodz. He chanted, "Mazel tov!"—deep, long, slow.

Another schlemiel who thinks he's Al Jolson. "Moe, OK, thank you." Ben pulled Judith by the arm as he pushed past her mother, making his way toward Susan. She turned away from him, her chin on her hands on the back of the chair. She got up and stretched out her arms to Jeannette. Today the housekeeper was a guest—Ben had made sure. Jeannette put her knee on the chair, leaned, and wrapped her arms around Susan. "Such a handsome couple," Mrs. Karger said. Susan turned her head sideways, her cheek against Jeannette's breast, and whispered, "Bitch."

"Susan," the new bride began, "you've been so good."

"You don't mean it," Mrs. Karger said to Susan.

"Yes I do. I'm an orphan. That's what orphans do. She's my stepmother." Susan pointed at Judith and laughed as she wagged her hand.

Judith clutched her bouquet, crushing the roses against her stomach. "Ignore her," Ben whispered. Susan liked to torture him. He wouldn't let her. He wouldn't eat his heart out. "Susan, you're an actress. You should go on the stage."

Mrs. Karger looked down at Susan, "You will love your new house, and new school, new friends."

Susan's eyes were full of tears. "I'm going to live here with my grandmother."

Judith tried to answer those wide, wet eyes: "You'll visit. You'll have two homes."

"No, I won't."

"Susan, you should be happy for me." Ben touched her head, and she jerked away from him. "You wanted red, and I made red dresses for you and Joan. It looks good: red, white, and blue—patriotic."

"You can take our picture," Joan shouted, her voice high and wild.

"Someone should teach her manners," said Judith, looking to Ben for confirmation.

"She's only a child. They're both children," said Ben. Judith's veil was pushed back, and he noticed a crease between her eyes he had not seen before.

"Susan," Judith said. "This is a wedding."

"So what?" Susan smirked at Joan.

"You will see what," Judith's voice shook.

Ben looked down the length of the double rooms to the window-less wall where Brona years ago had hung a print of *The Blue Boy*. Pink and fresh, he was dressed like a prince in blue satin, his dog at his feet, fine lace at his neck—an innocent. So young, Ben thought: the way I used to be. His throat closed and his chest tightened.

He pulled away when Judith reached for his arm, so that her hand slipped across tense muscle. He looked beyond her to Jeannette, who had both girls by the hand: the three of them were smiling together. There was his mother in the doorway, Nat close to her, both of them waving the guests toward the food. Ben finally took Judith's hand, but he did not look at her. "Come," he called out to the guests, "there's everything."

Two waiters, one on each side of the wide dining room door, held up silver trays with filled champagne glasses. The guests took their wine as they passed through the door toward the food, moving aside as Ben led Judith to Brona's table, "My mother, knows how to throw a party," he said.

"We planned together," Judith said.

"The little things—she was glad you helped her."

Brona Shein's feast dazzled, stunned, enticed: plumped, piled, pickled, stuffed, sliced, spiced, chopped delicacies—all on the pink cloth Judith had chosen. It was a Shein party. Judith couldn't catch her breath. "Too much."

"Nobody's asking you to eat it all. You'll take a little." Ben kissed Judith's cool cheek.

The light touch of his lips reassured her, and she held on to his hand. On the console table were the white roses she had asked for, a large bouquet to match the one in her hands. In Brona's crystal cut glass vase incised with arabesques, they had opened only slightly from their swirled buds to reveal the faintest pink, whole, complete.

Ben stood with her, their backs to the sideboard on which a borrowed epergne held red grapes and persimmons in its little dishes fluted like seashells. On either side of the gold and red extravaganza was a bouquet of crimson roses. Ben had pulled each strong stem from the tall metal buckets at Krieger's.

Nat's big voice boomed, "Ma, this isn't rotgut." He had a glass of wine in each hand. As quickly as he emptied them, the waiter gave him two more. He took a swallow from each glass and passed them to Susan and Joan. "Kiss," Susan called out. Nat bent down, his red lips on Susan's cheek, near the corner of her mouth.

Ben put his hand to his neck and swallowed. His throat felt raw. He leaned toward Nat, yearning to touch him, the longing like a taut rope that pulled him forward, but he held onto Judith's hand. Married to her, he suddenly felt lonely.

"Toast," someone yelled. Nat lifted his glass and held his arm in the air, moving his lips before he spoke the way he did when he read. At last he said, "I want to get this right. To the bride and groom," he paused again, searching for words. "Good luck." He hadn't mentioned their names.

"Good luck, good luck, good luck, good luck." The song went around and around the room. Susan gulped down the wine. Nat emptied another glass and swayed toward Ben and Judith. "From Ma, for the bride." He held out a plate heaped with smoked sturgeon and chopped liver.

"It's really too much for me."

"You might like it," Nat said.

The liver was as brown and dense as wet earth.

"The best pleasures are conquered repugnancies," Nat said.

"What?" Judith asked.

"Nat, leave her alone," Ben said.

"A lady should always have what she wants." Nat handed the plate to Ben and left him.

"My brother."

"Your brother is drunk." Judith's eyes burned.

"There's nothing wrong with my brother."

Now the clarinetist played while the violinist crooned, his voice a husky asthmatic wheeze he just barely controlled to achieve a faultless timing, *Every time it rains, it / Rains pennies from heaven.* Nat pulled Susan into his arms. "Don't look down. Just follow," he said, swinging her out. He twirled her. Susan threw her head back. He spun her again, dipped her, lifted her, and swung her into Joan's open arms.

Joan shook her head, and her hair fell into the straight lines of her Buster Brown bob, no break in the exact thick bang that divided her forehead. The girls held each other, their heads together, Susan's hands on Joan's shoulders, Susan's face as flushed as if she had a fever. She pressed her lips against Joan's cheek, their gathered red skirts that had taken so much material blending into a full red velvet bell, from which the girls' narrow trunks rose as if one.

Nat whipped a handkerchief out of his pocket and whirled it above the girls' heads. Joan tried to lead, but Susan started and stopped, looking at her feet. "Like this," Joan swayed. One finger under Susan's chin, she raised her friend's head until Susan laughed, swayed, her eyes on Joan, who pulled her closer and started off. They didn't stop, they were gliding together, Joan's arm around Susan's waist. Nat waved at Ben: "Come on," he shouted.

Ben shook his head at his brother and held onto his wife's hand.

Judith gazed at the whirling dancers. Humming a waltz, she drew away from Ben and turned in place, conscious of the picture she made, long-legged, fair, her small white and pink bouquet in one hand. As if she beheld herself in a full-length mirror, she turned again in waltz time. "Why don't we?" Judith lifted Ben's hand so that his arm swung open.

"Not now."

"But . . ."

"Later."

"I . . ."

"I told you. What did I say?"

Judith put her free hand over her ear. Gold flecks jumped in Ben's blue eye.

"What a face on you—I committed a crime?" Ben's head spun, a wave of nausea rose from his stomach. Maybe it was the wine that was making him sick. No, it could not be, not from one glass. Maybe he was coming down with something. "Judith, wait," he said.

IN THE TRAIN THAT TOOK THEM TO FLORIDA, BEN LAY ON THE OPENED bed, burning with fever. Their compartment was dark—the light hurt his eyes. No light penetrated the shades, and the stations they sped through were dimmed. The train dropped south.

Careful to keep the lavatory door closed so the light would not disturb Ben, Judith soaked a washcloth in the sink and wrung it out. Closing the heavy door behind her, she felt her way to the opened bunk, which took up most of the compartment. "Ben, this will help."

He groaned as she placed the wet cloth on his forehead. "No more with that rough cloth." He pushed her hand away. His right eye throbbed; the pressure in his ears narrowed to spiking pain.

"Do you have a headache?" Her brother's illness had begun with a terrible headache.

"Not bad."

"That's good."

"What's good?"

"It's probably a little flu." Judith fumbled in the dark and found her small fitted toilet case. With her thumbs, she pushed the buttons; the twin catches sprang open with a clicking sound. She lifted a bottle of lavender water out of its restraining strap, and from her pocket took a new linen monogrammed handkerchief—the kind she used to sell to wealthy customers and would never have to sell again. She twisted open the bottle and held the folded linen to the lip, tilting the bottle back and forth, back and forth. In sweet revenge, she wet the expensive new linen. "This will be better." Judith dabbed Ben's temples, then held the handkerchief under his nose.

He coughed. "Please, no."

His hot hand was heavy on her wrist. She'd let him sleep. Shutting herself in the lavatory, she held on to the small sink fitted into the tiny metal compartment, gleaming, modern, disciplined, the mirror bolted to the wall. Everything was in its place, unmoving, yet the train speeded south. Judith shivered and felt her forehead—no, she had no fever. It was excitement: she had never been this far from home before. Opening the door, she heard Ben's rough breathing.

The train lurched, and Ben groaned, "What is it?"

Judith stepped into the compartment, quickly shutting the door to a crack, so that only a streak of light escaped. "Nothing," she said.

The train shook again and the door banged. The noise shot into his head. "Stop it," Ben said. It hurt him to breathe.

To avoid making noise, she twisted the door handle, retracting the catch, releasing it when she had closed the door, shutting the light behind her. Judith's cool hand was on his burning head.

"Rest is the best thing. And water." She knew the little things that would help him.

He turned his head away. What else could he do but rest? "Leave me alone. I'll be all right."

She took him at his word and went out into the narrow corridor where the air was better. The flat of her hand on the wall, she walked, leaning forward, pushing against the motion of the train, her long legs strong.

Ben couldn't find his own handkerchief and felt too dizzy and weak to get up. She had left him alone in the dark. Phlegm burbled in his chest. He was so hot. He opened his pajama top and put his hand on his chest, the hair thick, growing in swirls. Stretched on his back, his mouth open, he finally slept.

In feverish sleep he dreamed of Tess. The infant Susan sucked her breast, a thin line of milk where her lips met Tess's skin. Susan's open hand, like a star, made tender dents in her mother's breast, as it was before the surgeon cut her, before the cancer ate her. No one saw him. Soft, so soft—Brona took Tess's hand and said to her, "You, I loved. When I looked at you, my nipples stung—you were so lovely—but I would never hurt you. As God is my witness, I would kiss you. Like this." Brona put her closed red lips against Tess's cheek. "See, not a mark." Ben reached out and touched cold glass.

The train sped south through Jersey. Along the tracks, the pine trees were shagged with snow.

Ben's fever rose. He woke soaked in sweat and slept again, shivering in his sleep when his fever dropped. Susan came back, this time with Joan, the girls kneeling at Susan's bed, drunk, naked, their red dresses at their feet—dark red shadows. They crossed their ankles for balance, the top of the outside foot on the ankle of the inside foot. They faced each other in profile, like a pattern cut out of folded paper, then spread open. Susan stretched out her right arm, palm up, the pale blue veins branching darker at her small wrists. Her face was streaked with tears, "Mommy, Mommy," she cried.

"You'll be OK," Joan whispered, her lips against Susan's ear. Joan stroked the fine skin of Susan's inner arm down over the wrist into the palm: "I promise you." Joan's hair was so black the constellations of tiny freckles dusting her high cheekbones looked frosty.

"You don't know. Nobody knows," Susan said.

Joan lifted the loosened coils of Susan's braids, stroked the bare, faintly creased skin under the blurred hairline at the back of her neck, and ran her fingers over Susan's back. "Everything will be all right," Joan said, using her own mother's comforting words.

Susan quivered. "Don't tickle," she said.

"All right, all right." Joan rested her hand between Susan's shoulder blades.

Susan sighed, and Joan patted her back the way you pat a baby. Susan nuzzled against Joan's neck and finally was quiet. Joan reached over and pulled the shining blue spread over them. Folded inside, they held each other.

Ben felt a dark shape above him like the shadow of a huge bird, its wings outspread as he stretched out his own arms to the side. He felt the shape bear down on him. The leering face of Joe Mavet spun toward him, his mouth open for a song, then Judith's face, the crease between her eyes, the bridal veil flying behind her. Ben wanted to scream, but in the dream no sound came when he opened his mouth. With his lips stretched open, Ben struggled to wake. He gasped; his lungs worked for air and he opened his eyes.

Judith sat on the edge of the hard bed. "You have a high fever." She pressed her hand against his neck.

He pulled away from her touch. Who knew what she was? "What's that smell?" he moaned, coughing.

"The cake."

Ben recognized the sweet, white vanilla smell of the frosted wedding cake. She had been eating in the dark from the basket of wedding food Brona had packed for them. "What are you eating in here for?" His shouting strained his throat.

Judith couldn't answer; she sat frozen, bracing her legs against the floor to keep herself from falling, the crumbling cake on a napkin in her hand.

"The smell is making me sick."

"I'm sorry." She squeezed the cake inside the napkin.

"My chest . . ."

"You'll get well in Florida." She had found the right tone, the Quackenbush tone. In Florida Ben would kiss her hand, they would swim together. It was the flu that was making him cranky. She took her new lightweight traveling coat and found her way to the club car, where she sat alone, mentally composing the letter she would write to her mother in the morning. As she found the words, she saw herself in the place she was, dressed for the trip, the first real one of her life, until, lulled by the motion of the car, she slept, her head falling forward.

ALONG OCEAN DRIVE THE PALM TREES—GREEN, YELLOW, MOIST, AND dry—curled landward. The little hotels, sea villas, their flat planes here and there bent into delightful curves, faced the ocean with their answering language of modest beige stucco and metal: porthole-shaped windows, dolphins, tender waves—the trim of pastel lyrics in violet, yellow, pink, and blue.

Nightly, at the Park Central Hotel, moving her head to the music, Judith watched from the curving, narrow balcony of the mezzanine as the guests danced on the terrazzo, each couple a part of the current that circled the floor. The couples came close to colliding, but did not. Sometimes Judith would go down, skirting the crowd, as she made her way to the door that would take her out to Ocean Drive. Clasped in each other's arms, the couples swirled past her, so close she could feel the current of air generated by their dance. Sometimes they grazed her—the passing couples.

All day Ben lay in bed in their room, the ceiling fan whirring above him. A constant moist breeze blew in from the ocean, stirring the thin, white curtains.

Judith called the doctor, who agreed with her: it *was* flu. Even though Ben felt worse, he was getting better. The phlegm in his chest had loosened. Judith washed Ben's face and hands. She had seltzer sent up to calm his stomach. She nursed him efficiently.

She wanted to have a cot sent up for herself, but Ben refused. "Stay with me," he kept telling her. He couldn't bear for her to leave him alone, but when she touched him, he did not feel comforted. Yet he would not let her go. Weak as he was, he held on to her. He wanted her there while he slept, while he was awake.

"The doctor said you're fine," she told him, restless, longing to move. She would leave him only for an hour at a time to walk down Ocean Drive, to swim, losing and finding herself in the waves. Though there was little she could do for Ben, she would rush back to their room, walking as fast as her wedge-heeled espadrilles would allow, her bathing suit still wet, a jersey snood covering her wet hair, her body chilled.

By the end of the week Ben felt better but still tired. He would sleep deeply most of the day. When he woke one late afternoon, his fever was gone, and he was alone, angry and tense with desire. She had left him while he was sleeping. Did she expect him to sleep through their honeymoon? Did she plan to bring him back to Paterson a sick man needing a nurse, not a wife? The ceiling fan whirred; the shades were half drawn. He heard her come into the room and closed his eyes, pretending to be asleep.

Her legs warm, her chest and back chilled to goose bumps, the taste of salt in her mouth, Judith looked down at Ben. His appearance shocked her—so Jewish, so foreign, his thick beard so dark against the bleached white skin of his nose and forehead. His closed eyelids were like the white convex shells she had seen on the beach.

Ben sensed her standing at the side of the bed, but he kept his eyes closed. He didn't know what to say to her. When he heard her walk into the bathroom, he watched her, the straps of her bathing suit dark against her white skin. The bent curve of her powerful back spoke to Ben, but he didn't yet know the language.

Tense with the effort to be quiet, Judith bent down to untie the ribbons of her sandals, longing for her hot bath.

Ben pushed himself up, put on his pajamas, and followed Judith into the bathroom. He stood behind her, slipping his hand up to the damp hair just above her neck. The rest of her hair was dry.

Surprised, she gasped and swung to the side, her arm raised, her fist clenched.

"Don't be afraid," Ben said. His lips were red inside his beard.

He pushed her toward the bed ahead of him. He didn't want her to see him.

"Wait."

"I've been waiting. All by myself." Her back was cold under his hands. Ben pushed her down on her stomach and began to stroke her buttocks. He kissed the back of her neck, he bit, his hand between her legs as he searched for an opening. He felt her tense as he entered her with his fingers. But she was wet from her swim, moist with sea water, and he did not hurt her.

Ben warmed her and she turned into herself as she had rolled in the waves. She turned on her back for air.

"That's right," Ben whispered in her ear, as he opened her legs. His tongue darted against her sex.

He lifted his head and saw her closed eyes. Ben heard his own moan. When he began again, his head down, Judith looked at him between her spread legs; she closed her eyes against the dark furry head, let herself spin into herself as her thighs trembled. When he pulled himself up, she put her hands around his neck and hid her face against his chest so that when he entered her he could not see her face.

He knew he was deft and slow. He could go for a long time. He listened for her. Judith's breathing was even. He moved inside her. He put his hands under her and pulled her to him. Now Ben rolled on his side, still inside her. He kissed her. "Do it to me," he whispered, his lips against her ear, as he drove into her.

The rhythm of his strokes broke Judith's pleasure. Just as he came, she jerked away from him and his sperm wet her thighs and stomach.

Now he saw her face, pale except for a red blotch on the side of her cheek where his beard had raked her. Her lips were closed and her eyes staring, angry. He saw what he might have known all along: she was not for him. "Go wash yourself," he said.

Judith looked at her upraised hands as if she could find dirt. "I need to bathe. I was cold from swimming." Alone in the bathroom, she adjusted the faucets, regulated the temperature of the water, letting the tub fill before she poured in lavender bath salts. Expecting heat, she put one foot into the deep water and had completely lowered herself into the tub before she realized the water was tepid. She had let it run too long. From habit, she soaped the washcloth and rubbed it over her skin. She turned the faucet; the water was cooler still, but she had to rinse away the soap that clung to her skin. She soaked the cloth and stood, the cloth across her breasts, letting the tepid water run down her body. Shivering, she reached for the towel, holding it around her shoulders as she stepped out of the tub. Warmer now, she took a dry towel and rubbed it across her stomach and along her thighs until the skin was pink. She lifted her hair from the nape of her neck and pulled it back. Wrapped in her white robe, she found Ben still in bed. "Do you need anything?" she asked when she saw his drawn face.

"Nothing," he said. Her face was smooth, untouched: white tinged with pink.

"You should drink more water. I can order some food, something light."

He didn't answer her.

The next morning, when she was barely awake, he tried again, his hand on her neck, his hand between her legs. He went soft.

"Those things aren't important," Judith said to him, as she touched his forehead with her lips.

His first time in the ocean, she led him into the warm foam, encouraging him. She knew how to swim and would teach him. He lay on his back over her arms. She took her hands away and he floated. A wave hit him and he thrashed in terror to find the bottom, the saltwater stinging his eyes. She took hold of him, held him tight in her firm arms. "I've had enough," he said. "I have to get out."

Just before sunset, when the wind died down, Ben watched Judith from the beach. She stood at the edge of the ocean, the curling waves lapping her feet. Ben dug his hand into the sand. The waves came in and she walked out to meet them. She stretched out her hands, diving into the swell. She swam out until he couldn't see her. The low sun was gold on the water, and the distant horizon violet. She was gone. The horizon shifted and he saw her again. A weight bore down on him as if he were caught in the pressing machine.

Judith swam back, her powerful stroke pulling her through the chop. She turned onto her back, caught in the slap as she glimpsed the thin clouds above her, the pale sky. She slashed at the waves; her sturdy arms lifted and fell. She turned onto her stomach, her feet pumping as she swam parallel with the long pink horizon, the white shore. Tired, breathless, heated, she turned and floated on her back for a moment before she rolled again, face down, stroking and kicking toward the beach.

She came out dripping, releasing her hair from the tight bathing cap, and lay down on her stomach next to Ben, her face turned away from him. He spoke into her back: "You're a strong girl."

"I'm really not, Ben." She turned to face him and lifted her arm, making a shallow dome of the back of her hand for him to kiss. "Ben?"

"What? You are. A good swimmer."

"My brother taught me." Judith lowered her hand.

"You told me."

"I learned when I was young." Judith shrank from Ben's frown, a ferocious hunger knotting its fist in her stomach.

Ben saw only her smooth face. She was still young and healthy. She'd live a long time. Maybe she'd change, maybe she'd learn to care for him the way he wanted her to care. The thought did not relieve the weight that pressed down on him.

He stayed on the beach after Judith went back to the room, watching the waves come in. He heard the dying hush of the foam and saw the clouds, wind-whipped now that it was getting darker, mount above the ocean. Then the clouds went away. Sky and water became one dark violet and the horizon disappeared: he didn't know where he was—the waves and the sky darker and darker, no end. Near the shore were a father and daughter. The father carried the child on his back, and she clung to him as he swam out. "Daddy, Daddy," she sang, her little mouth open in the last light. Ben looked back to the pretty little hotels along the drive: no Rockefeller Center here. Who needed skyscrapers with that big ocean?

Toward the end of their stay Ben and Judith had their picture taken. In the black-and-white photograph, they are wearing bathing suits. They look young. They stand with their arms around each other, smiling. Pictures lie, Ben thought.

Judith sent the picture to her mother with a note: "Lovely here." It *was*—her solitary pleasures, her virgin devotions to the waves, the long pink and violet twilights.

Ben wrote a card to Susan: "Stay well, Love from your Daddy." He licked the stamp and pressed it into the corner. She would be all right. His mother was watching her as she had watched him and Nat. Tess was gone, but his Susan was alive. He took the pen again and carefully made a fence of Xs along the bottom of the card.

EARLY THAT SPRING THE NEW HOUSE IN FAIRLAWN WAS READY. THE bunkerlike houses on Fourth Street were built so close to the ground that at twilight, even though the houses faced west, the light of the setting sun did not reach the windows. The sky on this evening in April was yellow and rose colored, the small windows blue and black under the low roof.

The neat concrete sidewalk dropped so gradually toward the river that the drop was nearly invisible. The newly planted maples lining the street formed a paling with such wide gaps it seemed as if there were no line. From a distance, the new grass on the tree strip looked like mist.

It was twilight.

Ben raked the topsoil in front of the house. He reached down to pick up the loose stones rattling against the teeth of the rake and the few tangled dry roots that had come from somewhere else, somewhere outside Fairlawn. He saved some of the larger stones to edge a flowerbed; the rest he piled with the torn roots. He moved on with his rake, turning back to throw more stones onto the pile. Judith collected the stones and dumped them into a box. "You missed some," Ben said. "There's a right way and a wrong way. You have to get every stone."

Judith obeyed, though she knew it was impossible to please him. She had suggested they hire a gardener, but Ben had refused. He wanted to do it himself, yet he did little by himself. "You'll help me," he had said. She went back and picked up more stones, raking the dirt with her hands to get every pebble.

Ben walked the few steps to the street and looked back at his work, judging how to grade the loose soil. While Judith watched him, he raked the small, brown plot again. He found more stones. Again Judith picked them up. He raked again.

Judith watched him smooth the surface, driving himself until it was nearly faultless. Finally he stopped, rake upright in his hand, face damp. He looked at her waiting.

"It looks fine." She tried to give him the approval she knew he wanted.

"It's not. Go, get me grass seed, near the steps."

"Shouldn't you take a rest?"

"What are you, my doctor?"

Choking herself into silence, Judith brought her husband the open sack of seed.

"Hold it," he told her. "At least you can do that."

Judith followed him as he took handfuls and scattered the pale seed across the dry brown soil. The directions, which she had read, specified even distribution, but the light breeze and the curving motion of Ben's hand had made the seed drop in curves, which he didn't seem to notice. Judith waited until he had crossed the entire space before she spoke, "The seed is not even."

"What?"

"You didn't do it correctly." She pointed.

"You're an expert?"

"No one's perfect."

"Perfect?"

"You said you want it right." She had him.

Ben went back again. He corrected, until the grass seed looked like evenly distributed salt. Salt that would sprout into perfect green.

He sent Judith to turn on the faucet, while he held the hose and examined his work, searching for spots he might have missed. The hose stiffened; water shot out, splashing his feet. "Less, less," Ben shouted, putting his thumb over the opening of the hose, reducing the stream to a fine spray. "Here, you do something."

"I have been doing something."

"Do it right." He showed her how, his thumb narrowing the opening. He handed the hose to Judith.

She tried to regulate the spray but her fingers slipped, and a heavy stream of water dented the soil, forming a puddle.

"Watch what you're doing, you'll ruin it," he shouted. Ben turned off the water. "You don't know how to do anything." That's what he had her for, to do things, but she wouldn't listen.

"You don't have any patience."

"Me? You. You don't know what you're doing."

"You should have found the nozzle. It came with a spray."

"I did it without the spray." He tried to stop himself but he couldn't. "I did the work and you ruined it. What good are you?"

"I scrub this house. I clean up after your daughter."

"That's all you're good for. A scrub woman."

She didn't answer him.

"Go, go ahead, pick up more stones, by the steps," he said.

Her hands on her hips, her fists balled up, her face twisted in anger: she looked like an old woman. She turned her back on him, the muscles in her back swelling through the thin cotton of her blouse.

Judith crouched down, dug her nails into the dirt. Blindly she stubbed her fingertips against cold, unyielding stone. Pain cramped her fingers, but she went on digging, scratching under the rock until she pried it loose. The stone was large as a baseball, solid in Judith's sore dirty hand.

Now Susan came out, barefoot, in shorts, her slim legs pale. It was too cold for shorts, Ben was about to say as he watched his daughter tiptoe toward Judith's turned back, bend down and swoop close, her arms raised.

At the sudden sound of a footstep, Judith hunched her shoulders and swung to her left with all her force. "Oh," she screamed, unable to stop her furious hand. The rock grazed Susan's hair before Judith drove it into the ground.

Ben ran toward them as Susan pitched backward onto the seeded dirt. "Don't put a finger on her."

Judith gripped the stone in her tight fist to keep herself from falling. "I thought it was you." The strength had drained from her legs.

"Me?" Ben asked. "What did I do to you?" That crease between her eyebrows like somebody stuck a knife in her.

"You son of a bitch," Judith said.

"Not in front of the child."

"She's not a child," Judith said.

"Daddy, what's wrong?" Susan shook, goose bumps all along her bare legs in the dirt.

"Nothing. Don't worry. Nothing happened, you're all right," Ben said. He reached out to touch her and stopped just short of her face.

"She *is* all right," Judith said as she stared through Ben's dirty hands framing Susan's face. His beloved—he kept his dirty fingers away from Susan's fine skin, tenderly stroked the air rather than touch her. "Your father wants things to be just so."

"My father, the Designer." That's what Tess had called him.

"He *is* a true designer," Judith said.

A sudden heat stung Ben's chest as he looked again at his daughter's white face. He couldn't help himself, "You're like your mother."

"Don't," Judith whispered.

Susan didn't look back at him: what was she staring at, her dark eyes wet and swelling? Susan pushed herself up, leaving the print of her body in the dirt. Tears filled the lower lids, tears caught in the lashes, overflowed.

"Stop it. What are you crying for?" Ben asked.

Judith let go of the rock. "I'm sorry. I didn't mean it," she said to Susan.

"Please, be a good girl, help us," Ben said to his daughter.

"I can't help you," Susan said.

"Come, we'll put things away." Ben handed Susan the rake, which she took, turning her back on them as she walked away.

There was still so much leftover grass seed. He held out the sack to Judith: "I'm so tired."

"I'll put it away." Judith took the weight from his hands.

Ben had nothing to say to her.

Dizzy, Judith spun in the empty silence, the burlap sack rough against her arms as she walked into the garage that still smelled of fresh concrete. Squeezing herself into the narrow space between the car and the wall, she lifted the sack to the raw pine shelf that held Ben's gardening tools. They seemed child-sized—a pointed shovel for planting; a cultivator with small teeth—new, unused. Pity caught her unaware as she remembered his bringing them home. "I'm going to plant flowers," he had told her as he took the tools from the bag, his face open, hopeful. "I'm going to have roses." She hadn't told him what she had learned about roses: they were a difficult flower to grow.

Alone, Ben looked toward the street. A mild breeze blew up from the river; there was still light in the sky, not too late for a walk. But he turned to the three boxes Judith had filled with stones. Those he would take. Struggling, he lifted the boxes one by one and carried them around the house, down through the backyard that was filled with weeds. Working in the growing dark, he placed the stones at the far end of the property where they were hidden by the weeds.

FOR WEEKS SUSAN BARELY SPOKE TO BEN AND JUDITH. EACH NIGHT after supper, which she picked at, swallowing only a mouthful, she would go to her room and close the door. When Ben would bring her to Brona's for the weekend, she would run to her grandmother's arms and not let go of her, pressing against her, her head against Brona's chest. His mother would hold Susan the way he could not. And he was afraid—sometimes Susan was like a little girl again, a baby. He tried to reach her by buying presents—paints, a sketch pad, a full set of pastels in a wooden box—but still she ignored him. "She holds a grudge," he said to Judith one night as they sat at the table, the chicken Judith had roasted and sliced served cold on their plates.

"She will get over it. We just have to keep calm."

"What do you mean? I'm not calm? It was you—you couldn't keep your hands to yourself."

Judith took Susan's plate; the thinly sliced breast meat lay untouched in a pattern of overlapping scallops.

"She didn't eat," Ben said.

"She will." Judith drew out a length of waxed paper, tore it off against the serrated carton lid and, with one hand flattening the slippery curling paper, placed the chicken on the opaque surface.

"All she wants to do is draw and read," Ben said.

"Those are not bad things," Judith said.

She folded the edges of the paper into a neat seam and tucked the ends under the small package, which she put in the refrigerator. Tomorrow she would set the table for Susan's lunch and put the plate of chicken in front of her. She would concentrate—one thing after another. "If you stay calm," her mother had told her, "you will win in the end."

A few weeks later, when Ben told Judith that Brona had suggested he take Susan to the Bronx Zoo, Judith did not object, though earlier both of them had refused Susan's pleas. There was polio, "infantile paralysis"; the spring weather had been unseasonably hot, and the doctors were warning parents to keep their children away from crowds. Roosevelt had recovered from the disease; at least he could walk, not like those children paralyzed inside iron lungs. Judith advised him to take Susan on a weekday, when there would be fewer people.

"You should take her. I have to work," Ben said.

"She doesn't want me," Judith answered.

"She should: you're young."

When he promised Susan he would take her to the zoo, "just you and me," she still looked at him with that mad face on her, but little by little he won her over. He would put aside a whole day for her, a weekday, as Judith had suggested, when there would be fewer people. At last Susan smiled at him and, as the day got closer, became more and more excited, pestering him, slamming around the house like a crazy one. She wanted to see this Alice, an elephant; she wanted to see the panda. Though he was relieved she was talking again, he wished he had not told her so far in advance.

He got the route from Nat. It cost Ben something: he didn't want to drive, but he would do it for Susan. Taking a sweater for her, yellow to match her yellow dress, Ben drove down Route 46, past Lodi, past Little Ferry, through Ridgefield Park, past the new frame houses for the commuters to New York.

The approach to the bridge was a narrow passage that hid the view. They were on the Palisades, but Susan didn't know how high they were. "Where *is* the bridge?" she asked.

"Wait, it's coming. Here, I have a job for you—concentrate." He handed her fifty cents for the toll. "They charge—a bridge for the people: it cost a fortune to build. Don't drop the money."

She held a quarter in each hand. "Now?" she asked as they approached the toll booth, but she still couldn't see as he took her through.

"Patience. You have to learn. You're a Shein. Miss Susan Shein."

"I know who I am."

"OK, you know."

At last their car rose onto the bridge. She pressed her head against the window. There was New York. He pointed to the skyscrapers. He concentrated on the cables, the giant steel ropes that would not break, would not let them go plunging down into the Hudson. He looked straight ahead. He didn't want to see how high they were. "You like it?" he asked her.

"It's huge."

"You don't like it?"

"Daddy, it's fine."

"You're sure?"

She nodded and looked out the window. "This is the Hudson, named for the explorer Henry Hudson. I can't see the end," she said.

"You don't have to."

She started again on the panda. "Pandora." She had a panda doll from Nat, from the World's Fair. She had kissed him for that doll. Whatever Nat told her she got excited about. She started again on the elephant, Alice. She knew about Alice from the zoo show on the radio. "Alice answers the phone. Alice of India and Coney Island—she learned in the circus. She can't *know* it's a phone. Maybe she believes it's a carrot. Do elephants eat carrots?"

"Do angels have stomachs?"

Susan stopped. Her face was serious: she was thinking.

"Laugh." Ben reached over and touched her hand. She pulled away from him. By the time they got to the Bronx, she seemed tired.

At the zoo she woke up, racing ahead of him before he could stop her. He looked up at the high Memorial Gateway to the zoo. Its massive iron crossbar communicated its weight to him directly. The curving iron of the swags and filigree confused him. It looked light, but he knew it must be heavy. He looked for an opening and heard Susan's voice: "Not that way, Daddy." She was just ahead on a small rise. Now he saw the path. And he caught up with her. The bow of her sashes had come undone and the ends trailed from her waist. Ben took hold of the sashes and Susan slowed down. He tied the bow as he walked behind her, the yellow cotton of her new spring dress blowing against her thin white legs as she ran in front of him.

Inside the vast park the animals were expected to behave. Inside the stone houses, the living pictures moved, three-dimensional. The wealthy had built the zoological garden for their collections. The curved walks through the sculpted hills led to the animal houses, which— anchored by columns, porticos, pediments—looked like concert halls, museums, libraries: stately, classical, calm. In relief, in sculpture, each house announced the identity of its resident beast: Aquatic Animals, Antelope, Bird, Buffalo, Elephant, Elk, Great Apes, Lion, Monkey, Small Mammal, Reptile, Zebra. The Bird House had a flying cage. In the Lion House there had once been an Animal Studio, where, it had been planned, artists would draw and sculpt the most magnificent of the game animals. Locked in the modeling cage, the living trophies slumped into torpor. The artists complained the light wasn't right, the smell intolerable. The

Reptile House, with its captives as still as pictures behind sealed glass, did not smell. Some of the artists took to painting snakes. The Animal Studio fell into disuse, and by the 1940s few people knew it had ever existed.

The beautiful birds and beasts ate and defecated, and they and their cages were cleaned. They ate gargantuan amounts—an elephant alone ate two hundred pounds of hay a day. The beasts ate everything: fruit flies, spiders, grasshoppers, cockroaches, rabbits, the best fruit—figs, wild strawberries. The vampire bats from Trinidad fed on fresh blood from the slaughterhouses. Pandora, the giant panda, did not thrive. When she died in captivity, Madame Chiang Kai-shek sent two new pandas, sisters. Their voyage from China lasted four months. They were at sea when the Japanese bombed Pearl Harbor.

"Slow down," Ben called. He was short of breath.

"Miss Moore said it was *immense,* and it is." Susan waited for him.

"So why run?" Ben took her hand, and together they walked up the ramp, past the elephant head carved in stone, through the arched door-way, into the Elephant House. The smell hit him, making him gasp, like the stink of the manure-spread fields in Brona's mother's village in Poland, where the Sheins would visit. His nostrils stinging, he covered his nose and mouth with his handkerchief.

Susan ran to the bars. She stood alone, a small figure under the high vaulted roof.

The stone floor sloped under Ben's feet. The dull yellow tile walls gave off a cool dampness. He looked down the great hall lined with immense, high-arched dens. Seen from this angle, the double bars of the cages obscured the view like partially closed shutters. Ben went closer.

Susan had found Alice. Ben held on to Susan's hand as he pressed against the railing. Alice from India was eating. She lifted small bunches of hay with her rippling trunk and brought the hay to her mouth. The sweet smell of the fresh hay mingled with the stench. Some of the hay had gone to flower and Ben could see the small silvery blossoms. Alice's mouth looked soft. The loose skin of her legs slipped over her knees.

Alice stopped chewing and swayed toward the bars. The tip of her trunk moved over the floor of the cage, sensitive, alive. How could she lift her big feet?

Ben looked up again to the enormous powerful shoulders. The elephant was close. There was so much skin—like the skin of a human being, but dry, every line big, as if seen under a microscope. What did they make from those hides? Suitcases, Ben remembered. He had seen Eli Shein's white shirts arranged inside the black-dyed skin of an elephant stretched across a frame and fitted with brass. The enormous hides were sliced and sliced—they got a lot of pieces, the great beast cut up for us. The flaps of Alice's ears lay against her enormous head. Deep scars cut through the top of the huge, broken ears. Someone had broken them. What had they used to do it? Ben looked into the elephant's eye, which seemed too small for that head, yet full, deep. The eye seemed to know him; the eye was tired, tired to death. What kind of thing was that for a child to see? "Susala, don't look so hard."

"I want to."

"What a belly on her. She can eat," Ben said. For the first time in a long time, Susan leaned her head against him. He put his arm around her—she was skin and bones, her waist so small.

It was a long way to the panda den, the sun hot through the bare spring trees, but she wouldn't give up. When they got there, dry leaves blew against the boarded-up enclosure. The panda was gone. Susan wouldn't believe it. She pulled on his arm, her eyes big, "Uncle Nat said." One minute she talked like a smart little lady, the next minute she was ready to cry like a baby.

"Maybe Pandora had to take a rest." She would see it next time, he promised her.

"But I wanted to."

Her eyes were wet.

"Don't cry. I told you: we will come back."

"Daddy, please. I'll never be here again."

He looked into her eyes and saw a flicker, like a bird passing. The tiny bird was gone, and Ben looked away. "This is not a tragedy. Come on, I'll take you. We'll see the lions."

His hand on her shoulder, they went up a curving path bordered by a low stone wall. Below them, green after the soaking spring rains, were the African plains: Africa in the Bronx. The great cats were out of their cages, loose on Lion Island.

Ben pointed. In the distance, across water, beyond antelopes drinking, beyond zebras grazing, across more water, on elevated flat stones arranged to look natural, the lions sunned themselves. The path was crowded with people looking across the "plains," shielding their eyes with their hands.

Susan rested her hands on the stone wall, and Ben looked over her head. He saw the lions leap. What did they feed them out there? The butcher must cut them raw meat.

Susan spun around, her face white. "Daddy? Why did you marry her?"

"For you."

"For me? She hates me."

"No, no, don't say that."

"She's not my mother."

"She tries." Ben shrugged his shoulders. "You have to try. It's not easy." There would never be a Tess, never again. He looked up: a lion's mane flashed in the sun. An expression he had heard all of his life came into his mouth: "As God is my witness. I'll make it better. I promise you."

Judith Karger's mother had cautioned her, "Look away. You mustn't let things bother you." When Ben came home with Susan, Judith did look away—literally—avoiding their eyes. The table was ready for them, set with spoons for a dairy meal. "You must be hungry."

"I am. It's been a long day. We'll both eat," Ben told her as he pulled out a chair for Susan, who hung her sweater on the corner of the chair back so that the sleeves dragged on the floor.

Still averting her eyes, Judith served them first—cold sugared strawberries and sour cream. By the time she brought her own bowl to the table, the red berries seeping dark juice under the large spoonful of sour cream, Ben and Susan were almost finished. Judith ran her spoon against the inside of the bowl, then slowly narrowed the circumference of her circles, swirling red into the cream until the red turned pink.

"I've got work to do," Susan announced as she tried to push her chair back against the impeding sweater.

"You should rest," Ben said.

"Daddy, I will."

"Your father wants only the best for you," Judith said.

Susan tilted back the chair and stood, yanking the sweater loose.

"You'll stretch the sleeve. Grandma's friend knitted that sweater for you," Ben said.

"Daddy," Susan drawled, "I know."

This time Judith kept quiet.

"Good night, stepmother. Thank you so much for the supper." Susan pranced away, curtseyed in the doorway, holding out her skirt.

Ben couldn't help laughing. "Don't pay attention," he said when Susan was gone.

"I'm not," Judith said.

"She thinks she's an artist."

"Your daughter has talents."

"That's what my mother says. She wants her to continue with her lessons."

"She should."

"Maybe she should have acting lessons, too."

Judith smiled as she took a spoonful of berries from the serving bowl on the counter. The raw, sweet syrup hit the back of her throat, choking her. She swallowed hard, her eyes stinging.

"Thank you. The berries were good." Ben's light fingers were on her shoulder.

IN THE COUNTRY QUIET OF GREEN POND, WHERE BEN TOOK JUDITH for the weekend, he tried to be kind to her. He didn't trust himself to say the right thing, so he said very little. They would walk together on the path that circled the pond. It was still too cold to swim; the trees were bare, and the bright sunlight hammered down on the path, which in summer would be deeply shaded.

The windows of their cold room rattled in the wind that came off the pond. "It's bracing," Judith called out, happy to be away.

"We should have gone to New York," Ben complained. "I should have brought a heavier sweater."

"You could wear one of mine."

"No, I don't need that."

"You could put it on under your shirt, like long underwear."

She held out her white cashmere pullover: "It's soft; it will stretch." Single ply, not full-fashioned, it wasn't one of her best.

For once, he gave in to her. Stripping, he gave her his jacket, then his shirt and undershirt. She held them in her hands like a salesgirl as he pulled the sweater over his head. The soft yarn yielded, giving off the scent of lavender; the neck stretched, the sleeves tight, binding him under the arms, but he kept the sweater on: it was warm. "I hope I don't ruin it. Thank you."

"You look better already," she laughed easily. He rarely thanked her for anything. Peeling his clothes, piece by piece, from her arm, she handed them to him, watching him dress as she talked about their new house, about the roses resistant to black spot she would help him plant. When he told her Nat would take Susan to Passaic for art lessons, she was careful to praise Nat's skillful driving.

In bed, they shivered in thin pajamas. "I'm freezing," Judith said, reaching out. Ben took her in his arms, for the first time in a long time.

"You've lost weight," he said. Her skin felt strange.

She shivered in his arms.

"You should put on that sweater," he told her. He touched her back, her breasts. "It's not good to be fat, but you could use a little fat, here, there." He held her.

And she was grateful. "Not me." She kissed his cheek, warmer than hers.

Her mouth was closed, like a child's, her lips soft. Ben rubbed where she had kissed. He had forgotten to shave.

He was patient with her, forcing himself to rub her back. "Relax," he kept saying. "You don't have to do anything. I promise."

He kept his word. They were like friends, Judith thought, as she let go, letting sleep, for the first time, take her, cover her with darkness in Ben's arms.

Ben felt her long body go slack, heard her even breathing, and was relieved. He woke before Judith. When he came out of the bathroom, she was still sleeping, on her side, her knees drawn up, her hands tight against her chest, against the cold. Her mouth was open, her smooth face distant, separate. Her scent was in the room, sweet, cloying. Ben breathed in and swallowed, the scent filling his mouth and nose, like water. His lungs tightened and he coughed. Judith rolled to her back, but did not wake up. He stared at her chest rising and falling. He knew he should pull the blanket over her, but he stepped back, away from the smell of her.

Leaving Judith's white sweater folded on a chair, he went down to breakfast by himself. A solitary man sat near the window reading the paper, his head down, his back to the view. He wore an overcoat; a cap covered his head—Joe Mavet? Could it be? Ben readied himself for Joe's wild laugh. The man lifted his head, and Ben saw it wasn't Joe. The man turned the page of his paper, his mouth sunken in. He was toothless. "It's cold," Ben said. The man nodded and looked down, covering his mouth with his hand, as if he were trying to shut in his words.

Beyond the windows, the morning light looked as if it might be warm, but a cold wind blew off the pond. I should have brought heavier clothes, Ben thought again. He felt nauseous with hunger. "I better eat," he told himself. "I should know how to take care of myself." His stomach tightened and he felt faint. He put his hand to his cheek and remembered Tess. She had stroked his face as she lay dying. Ben looked out at the bare trees. "I have no one," he moaned. The man sitting near the window turned his face away.

IN PATERSON, BUSINESS WAS SO GOOD BEN ASKED NAT TO PUT IN MORE time. Though Ben pleaded, Nat would give him only forty hours. "I need you," Ben said. "I need my family."

"I have to live," Nat said.

"You live. What do you mean?"

Nat didn't yet know what he meant. "I have to work out. At the track I have to sweat it out."

Ben hired extra help, a part-time person to drive the truck and an assistant for Moe Black. With the new driver to relieve him, Nat took off so much time Ben didn't see him for days.

Though he had all the help he needed, Ben begged Judith to work in the shop one day a week. A wife should help a husband. "Please," he would say, "I need you." She kept putting him off. She was busy. She had to take care of her mother. She had to make lunch for Susan. "You'll come in the afternoon," he would say. He kept after her.

On a Sunday, with Susan gone to Brona's, they sat across the table from each other at breakfast, in front of them the black bread and sweet butter, the cream cheese, lox, and bagels Judith had bought to please him. Her soft-boiled egg in front of her, Judith reached across the table. "We should go away again, a weekend in the City, the way you wanted." At the touch of her fingers on the back of his hand, Ben pulled away.

"You'll come to the store. What do you have to do here all day by yourself? Nothing."

"Ben, are you being fair?" She stole her mother's reasonable tone.

"Fair? You do nothing. I need you."

"You don't. I don't know anything about the fur business. You have skilled help."

"So what. You're my wife."

"Yes."

"Some wives help."

"What do you want from me?" she cried.

"Nothing. You're good for nothing."

Judith picked up her cup of tea and flung it against the wall.

"That's what you know how to do," Ben shouted. "Break things."

"I'm sorry."

"Be sorry."

He kept nagging until she gave in.

When she agreed, he touched her hair, then her hands, "You'll learn," he said. "You'll see. I'm not kidding you."

Judith tried to please him, but the work exhausted her. Again she suggested that Ben add a line of accessories, tasteful little things, but he wouldn't listen to her, even though, to her surprise, Nat had defended her. "Leave your wife alone; maybe she has a good idea," he had told Ben.

Against all reason Ben wanted her to be Tess. He wanted her to charm the customers. She was stiff with them. He wanted her to glaze—to wet down the fur with a brush dipped in water and stroke firmly against the flow of the hair with a furrier's comb until the coat glistened like a living animal. She told him the coats were too heavy. "That's what the Sheins do," he answered, "we learned from when we got to Europe. The goyim trap and kill for us—it's not always fun, not for any of us. We work under the weight."

He wanted her to finish—to sew in the lining by hand so it hung without a wrinkle like a new skin. When she did, her ring would catch on the satin and ruin the job. "Try again," he would tell her. He wanted her to do the final job of the finisher: with zigzag silken strokes to stitch in the black and white label, "Ben Shein."

But they could not work together. Their best moments were silent: Ben would force himself to hold his tongue; Judith would steel herself against her husband's next attack. Hungry for a tender caress, they did not touch. Starved for a light-hearted word, they barely spoke. They lived in the same house, ate at the same table, slept in the same bed, more and more alone.

PART THREE

en walked in on his mother and Nat drinking tea in the back room of Tess's fabric and notions shop. Their heads together, the two of them sat at the table in a small space surrounded by piled-up cartons and boxes. The early spring day was cold, and they warmed their hands against the steaming cups. The overhead light was off, the green shade of the high window facing the alley rolled up all the way, letting in just enough light to see.

Brona put her hand on Nat's arm and turned her face to him as if he were a tiny boy and she was about to take him in her arms. With her eyes still on Nat she spoke to Ben, drawing him to the object of her benevolent gaze: "Your brother wants money." That's how Ben heard the news.

"What do you need money for? I give you money," Ben said to his brother.

"That's it. You give me."

"What are you talking about? I'm your brother."

"I want my own."

"You're in trouble."

Nat pushed the table away and jumped out of his chair. "I want it for myself."

"*Who* wants the money?" Ben asked. Nat must have gambled and borrowed. It was an old story. But Ben would help him.

"Who?" Nat jabbed his finger into his own chest. "Me. I want it."

"It's all yours already." Ben spread his arms.

Nat shook his head, "You can buy me out. My share of the business and the building on Broadway."

"But you get from those rents."

"I don't want it anymore."

If Nat hadn't sighed, Ben would have believed that his brother hated him. "What did I do to you?" Ben asked and went toward him.

Nat raised his hands, palms out. He pushed.

Ben stopped. "What are you going to do with it?"

"Put it in the bank," Nat said.

"You'll run out and buy a car."

"So what? What do I own? Nothing. The truck belongs to you."

Brona finally said something: "To the business. To the Sheins."

"Ben Shein. The fur business: I want something else," Nat said. The weight of the fur had been on Nat's back since he was a boy.

"You have the strength," Ben said.

"Ma, he thinks I'm in shape," Nat told his mother.

"Please," Brona said.

"Ben, I don't want to be a schnorrer."

"You? You're not like Judith—you work."

"Maybe you should listen to that wife of yours; she's not cut out for it."

"You're taking her side? I don't believe it."

"People are what they are. You wanted a young one. Let her be young, let the girl play," Nat said.

"She's healthy. There's nothing wrong with her. Hard work never killed anyone," Ben said.

"You're too smart to believe that," Nat said.

"Listen to me," Ben said. "You're not a leech, I need you. We've always worked in fur."

"In the desert, in the promised land?" Nat said.

"Camel hair—it's making up beautiful for you, Miss," Ben said.

"And from donkeys," Brona said.

"You know what I mean. Grandfather told me: we walked out of there, we got to Europe, we got here, but is this all there is? What do you think I'm going to do in Paterson?" Nat asked.

"We have to make a living," Ben said.

"We make and we make and we make." Nat pointed backward over his own shoulder, jabbing the air to the rhythm of his words, as if he could punch through to past millenniums, where all the Nat Sheins of blessed memory had ever lifted heavy weights onto their backs—tents, wagons mired in oceans of mud, pelts, pots, pans, featherbeds, candlesticks, sacks of grain, bolts of cloth, stones, bricks . . . as if he, who was no schlep, had carried, down through the ages, all the Jews who could not walk. "I'm not going to lug for the rest of my life," he said.

What could he do but lug? Ben sat down. "What kind of way is this to tell me?"

"Tell you what? I'm not going to Europe. I'm too old for this war," Nat said.

"What war? It won't happen," Ben said.

"That's what you think. *Mam-my, I'd walk a million miles for one of your smiles,*" Nat sang at Brona, digging his thumb into his chest. "We're the schvartzes *and* the Christ-killers: They'll crucify us. Bar mitzvah boy, you read but you don't want to know. Jews can't get out, but this boy will be right here in America."

"You feel all right?" Ben asked.

"I'm not going to drop dead," Nat said.

Or die, like Tess. Maybe Nat was sick, but he didn't look sick. His color was good—but then Tess had looked good, too, for a while. A person doesn't know what he has growing inside of him. "Don't talk like that," Ben said.

"I can't make a joke? What's the big deal? I'm not walking out on you. I'll take my time. I'll decide what I want to do." Nat relented. "I'll work three days a week. I'll think."

Nat was going to *think*?

"What's the look for?" Nat yelled.

Ben covered his mouth with his hand and looked down to hide his eyes.

Nat leaned over his brother. "I want what belongs to me—my share." He clenched his fists and pushed his knuckles into the table; his big chest swelled in the space in front of Ben.

Ben leaned back. He couldn't breathe.

Brona put her hand on Ben's arm. "Listen to him," she said as she pulled out a chair for Nat. "He's your brother." In Brona's words, Ben heard what he believed she wanted him to hear: Nat loved him; Nat would always love him; Nat would never leave him.

For a moment the Sheins were quiet. The dim light came into the store-room. "Don't worry," she said to Ben. "Your brother will still help you."

"He will?" Ben heard his own voice, thin, like a child's. He looked at his mother's face, tired at the end of the day, tired in the weak light. She and Nat were letting go of him. Ben felt the muscles in his back tighten, opened his mouth, drew in a long breath, expecting to smile—but he gasped, his eyes burning, as if a salty wave had hit him head on. He rubbed his fists into his eyes. "Anything, anything you want. I don't have to buy you out. You'll keep those rents, and you'll keep your share in the business," he said to his brother.

"We'll each keep our third, the three of us," Brona said.

"You can have whatever you want. It's yours. Cash. Just give me time. Not long. A month or two. And Monday, you'll be in on Monday. I need you," Ben said. If Nat had touched him, he would have cried.

On a Friday in May, Nat was on his way home from New York when he noticed the new spring light over the Meadowlands. The sky was clear blue, and the bottoms of the high white clouds were violet. On impulse, he turned south on a full tank of gas, a hundred dollars in his pocket; in the back of the truck, the bag he had packed for the gym. He drove away from Paterson to the southern tip of New Jersey, where the land narrows to a point and the east is all ocean: Cape May.

Nat found a rooming house on a back street and lay down to rest, expecting to go out to dinner, but he fell asleep in his clothes, stretched out on the spread with his shoes on. He woke just before dawn, thinking he was back in his old room in Paterson, the brother whom he had never refused waiting for him, as it seemed Ben had always waited. But when Nat smelled the ocean, he knew where he was. His ankles sore from his shoes, his back and legs stiff, as they never had been when he was younger, he stretched, drawing up his knees, his arms over his head. He laughed to himself: "What the hell, a Shein could get out of Paterson."

On the way to the beach he found an open grocery store. The boy behind the counter did not seem to see him, his eyes still fogged with sleep—his firm mouth like the skin of an apple. So young—Nat wasn't going to rush him: the kid would have his whole life to work. "Milk," Nat finally said, putting a dollar on the counter. Dreaming, the boy lifted a bottle from the case, looked toward the window and stopped. Nat turned to see: beyond the glass, the sky over the rooftops had lightened, but not enough to wipe out the stars. Nat stepped out into the blue light.

Drinking from the bottle, he walked on until he came to the water. The walk had warmed him, and his muscles did not resist as he stretched out—calves, thighs, groin, ankles. He was going to take care of himself, knock off the booze. His lungs were good: he had never smoked.

Nat ran barefoot on sloping, firm, wet sand. The early morning tide was going out, and the sand was cold. Occasionally a wave broke above the retreating line and washed over his feet. He ran slowly, breathing easily, adjusting to the pull of the sand that slowed him. The houses on the shore were still dark. Nat sensed the sleepers. They were like passengers in a line of ships stranded at low tide. Though the houses with their dark, blank windows looked empty, he felt their fullness. He was one of many. He had come out early, another breather in the dark, expectant. The tide would come in. His life was ahead of him. For a moment everything mattered. But everything was passing, alive and dying. Morning light colored the beach while the houses kept their darkness. Along the shore the waves beat in, played themselves out.

Nat faced the rising sun, alone on the curving beach except for a person walking toward him in the distance, face dark, as if someone had cut a hole in the air. As they came abreast, he realized the figure was a woman.

Not until he saw her again that night in the rooming house did he realize how much he remembered. The long legs, the high waist, the huge honey eyes, the round-tipped clown's nose.

"Didn't I see you on the beach?" he asked her.

"Brilliant." Her sarcastic laugh rang out. "Must have. There was nobody else."

"There was me, Nat Shein."

"You."

You, I want, Nat thought. Beneath her mordant tone, he sensed innocence.

Her name was Renee Goldring.

"I'm a truck farmer," she told him.

"Does a person have to be one thing?" he asked.

"Not even a human being?"

"That's a question."

Renee's socialist grandparents, with a vision of a New Zion in south Jersey, had bought the land and moved out of Paterson to grow sweet corn and tomatoes. In their descendants, the vision was slowly undergoing a metamorphosis. It still wasn't clear what the final shape would be. Except for Renee's younger brother and sister—twins who lived together and studied music in New York—the three generations of Goldrings were still on the land.

Renee managed the accounts, ran the farm stand in the black on cash crops. The weekend she met Nat she had driven to Cape May with the twins in the farm truck. "Go," her grandmother had told her, "I order you," as if she could. "You'll end up a hunchback, a ghost, bending over those books." Renee would say, "The sun hurts my eyes." She would read all night, gorging herself on print, sleeping late, the shades of her room pulled down.

"Give me your number," Nat told her. "I'll call you."

"Don't do me any favors."

"I mean it. I want to see you."

They would meet on the road, halfway between Paterson and the Goldring farm. Often when Nat drove to see her, memories of his cruel pleasures with other women would flash at the edge of his vision—his feet raking the floor like claws, his wild cries, his teeth breaking skin—and he would flick his head back to get rid of them. Instead he felt heat between his legs. His cock ached. The scar high up near his hairline would throb, and he'd touch it to soothe himself, but his fingers made it worse. "I can't win," he would say to himself. Sometimes he would stop by the side of the road and come into his own hand for relief.

When he met Renee, he would buy her coffee at a diner. They would sit in his truck or hers and talk. He told her about his life, his failures—all the way back to his boyhood, when the Hebrew teacher had screamed at him, called him a bulvon. He had never gone back. When he was supposed to be at his lessons, he had wandered the streets alone, sometimes finding his way to the river. He told Renee how he would hurl a rock into the sky until he couldn't see it. His cap off, he would whirl and wait to hear the rock hit. He told her about his bootlegging days. "You should get away from that town," she would answer.

Before the Sheins had reached Paterson, they *had* gotten out—who knows how many times, from how many places? Maybe a Shein could get out of Paterson, away from the fur; maybe a city person could grow corn; maybe a man could be as tender as a woman. He went slow with her; when he did touch her, he was careful, soft kisses—no teeth. He was afraid he would scare her away. He was afraid of himself.

She read poetry to him:

> Once out of nature I shall never take
> My bodily form from any natural thing,
> But such a form as Grecian goldsmiths make
> Of hammered gold and gold enamelling . . .

"Where is out of nature? Where does he think the gold comes from?" Nat asked. "From the air?" Then he thought of his own body—it led him, it drove him, it beat him. He beat it.

She gave him books. He liked *The Brothers Karamazov.* "These characters are really all one man," he said. He found *Crime and Punishment* all wet. Nat Shein disagreed with Dostoyevsky. "Don't tell me that you first have to kill somebody to know that a human being does not kill because of an idea. I don't believe it. How could he not know he hated that old woman? You have to hate to crack a person's skull open with an ax. Even to plan it. Murder? You have to hit hard. He hated her to death. What's-his-name?"

"Raskolnikov." Renee had her eyes on his bare forearms. "You may have something there." Her frightened look slid away from his arms.

"What's the matter?"

"When you were in the rackets, did you ever . . . ?"

"Not a chance," Nat laughed. He had watched Bum Greenberg and Ziggy Fleishman, the loan shark's goons, beat up a man who was behind in his payments, a small man. The man had begged. He had fallen to his knees on the rain-slicked street. Blood ran from his cut mouth. Nat still remembered the victim's high, choked voice. "Lay off," Nat had said. He had turned his back, crouched behind a car, and thrown up. "Too soft." He looked at her closed mouth and knew she didn't believe him.

Renee had a secret: she was still seeing her old boyfriend, her first boyfriend. She couldn't break with him—a boy really, a sensitive boy, who studied accounting at night. Edward was a poet, his desk filled with unpublished poems.

"A fine young man, not like Nat Shein," Renee's mother, Rose, said. "What are you doing with that roughneck? Watch out, he'll get you pregnant. That will be the end of you."

"It's not serious."

"He can't support you. What does he do anyway?"

"He works for his family. And he could work here with me."

"You said it wasn't serious."

"Why do you hate him?"

"I don't."

"He could help us, bring in some money."

"Who wants that kind of money? From fur. They murder the beasts without a prayer. Who knows from where else he gets his money?" Rose had made calls to friends in Paterson. She had found out about Nat Shein—a lugger, a fancy man, a former bootlegger. "The Goldrings don't take money from gigolos."

"You want to save the world but you can't redeem a Shein?" Renee said.

"I don't need your fancy words," Rose answered.

"You want only good socialists. He's a human being."

"Let him cut up animals for rich women, he and his brother."

"He doesn't do that."

"He's a Shein."

"He's a man."

"Another big mensch who stands up to pee." Rose laughed, holding her hand in front of her crotch as if she were holding a penis. "You can have him."

Rose continued to nag, getting to her daughter. Beside herself with worry, she called Renee's old boyfriend, Renee's first love, the accountant who wrote poetry. "Fight for her," Rose told him, as if she were a mythical goddess with the power to control the battlefield, breathe valor into faltering youth. At least Rose knew there was a battle: when Nat called, she told him Renee was out with another man.

On a chilly night in May, Nat waited for Renee until, worn out, he fell asleep in the back of the truck on the side of the road. In the morning, his head and knees aching, no water in the truck, he chewed on aspirins. The taste was still in his mouth when he called her from a diner, his hands shaking, as she told him she was sick. He knew she was lying, but he didn't fight her. He'd let her get a good taste of this other man. One week, two weeks—then he packed a small bag, drove to the farm early on a Saturday morning while it was still dark, parked on the road, and waited.

When the sun came up, he went to the grandparents' cottage, where he found them in the kitchen, dressed for the city they would not visit: Sigmund Goldring at the wooden kitchen table, drinking tea, reading the newspaper from the day before, a gray suit vest over a white shirt with French cuffs fastened by gold links, his white beard closely trimmed; Amelia Goldring ready for her morning walk, a pocketbook in her hand, silk stockings pulled up tight, feet fitted into neat, polished shoes, her tailor-made suit buttoned over a clean white blouse, opal studs in her plump earlobes.

"As you can see, Mr. Shein, we've returned to the land." Sigmund gesticulated like a master of ceremonies, his hand opening toward his wife. "Our family hasn't been on the land for thousands of years. Some return. But I don't think they'll steal the farm from us." He shook the paper: "Not like in Europe."

"I've got to see her." Nat grabbed the old woman by her knobby wrists, his hands burning.

"I'll get her. Don't worry," she said.

"Mr. Shein," the old man said, "she's got a boy, a pisher. I shouldn't tell you, but I'll tell you: from him she gets no pleasure."

When Amelia Goldring came back with Renee, the old man sat there watching. "Come on," Amelia said. "They don't need us here."

"What's wrong?" Renee wanted to know, her face swollen, shut, sleepy.

"You tell me," Nat said.

She had nothing to say.

"Come on, we'll go out, we'll eat together. I've got things to tell you." His voice was so low she had to come close to hear him. He wanted to grab her, but he stood very still, his hands at his sides, disarmed. He couldn't force her. He wouldn't force her. He was done with all that.

She made him wait, but finally she came with him. He took her to Atlantic City. May: the sun had heat, yellow on the thick waves.

She didn't want to go into the hotel in slacks, but he persuaded her to put on a pair of sunglasses and a cheap scarf, which he bought from the hotel drugstore, and come in with him. "You look good," he said as she put on the dark glasses.

"You're biased." She tucked in her shirt, covered her wild, springy hair with the scarf—a bow under her chin—and went into the dining room with Nat, who smooth-talked the maître d'. "The lady," he said, taking the man off to the side, "is in a tight spot. Had to get away. Just give us a quiet table. No one will notice the slacks."

He fed her rare lamb chops; he gave her champagne. He kept waiting on her so she wouldn't talk. Normally he would have taken her hand, but he didn't touch her. Instead he poured more wine, slowly. He saw her watching him. He let her see more—the fine bones moving in his wrist as he poured the wine, twisting the bottle, not spilling a drop. He let her see his chest rise as he breathed. He let her see the dark flush that warmed his neck above the white shirt. He let her see his lips on the glass. He showed himself, the way a woman would show herself. He knew how; he didn't have to unbutton a button.

"I want you to see the view," he said to her in the lobby. She went up with him to the roof garden, where he gave her a brandy but no coffee. They could see down the wide beach to the wild surf. The wind picked up. Nat listened to the roar of the waves beating in, retreating. He felt small, he faltered. Then he looked straight into Renee's face—as he had the first time he saw her. She was paler than usual, her mouth tight, her honey-colored eyes vague. He touched her hand and she jumped, afraid. He could feel it. "Don't, don't. I won't hurt you." He took her hand, cold in his hot hand. So who was he? He knew now: life, heat. Things were mixed up in a person. Chance could shake things up and mix them again. On the way down, he told her they had to talk. "I booked a room."

"Just today," she told him.

"Why look ahead?"

The drapes were half drawn. The light was right, not too much, not too little. He had her by the arm. Her shoulders hunched up, and he saw fear in her eyes. "All that wine," Nat lied. He had drunk very little. "I've got to go." He went into the bathroom and put on his robe. Silk, a red so dark it looked black. His cock was hard, like a stick, hard enough to hurt her, but he wouldn't hurt her.

When he came out, Renee got angry. "This is talking?"

"My kind of talk. Now, the last time."

"You mean the first time."

"Not for either of us." He came close to her and reached out his hand. He ran his thumb lightly across her closed mouth, his other fingers under her chin. He found an opening and slipped his thumb over her bottom teeth, over the sharp pointed one. She lost her balance. He caught her. She was drunk. Good. "Come on, I want to show you something."

He unbuttoned her blouse, her pants. He put his mouth against her ear, his tongue deep in her ear as he pulled her down on her knees on the floor, both of them kneeling. A little cry came out of her, low. He knew he had her, but he didn't need to have anything. He was done with having. He took her hand and ran his thumb over her fingers. "I want you to do something for me." Now he bent to kiss her. Teasing her, his tongue in her ear again, his hand inside her bra, he caressed her nipple. "You'll be good at it," he told her, taking her hand again. "You're going to fuck me."

Renee pulled away. "This is what you want to tell me?"

He held her by the wrist. He kissed her. "Please," he said, "fuck me." He drew her toward him as he lay on his back. "Come on."

She drew down her pants and took off her blouse.

Staggering, she kneeled over him, her full swelling breasts, pink tipped, gold-skinned. "I'm dizzy—the wine," she said.

He pulled up his robe and showed her what he had. He opened his arms and she came into them, shivering. Nat rubbed his hands down her back, stroke after stroke. She sighed and he drew her closer, kissing her warm open mouth. "You do it," he moaned, easing her away from him until she sat upright. His hands on her hips, he guided her, went into her, into the heat. Her skin was moist under his hand on the small of her back. He didn't move. "Fuck me," he said. "Don't be afraid. I want you to."

She moved above him and he went higher into the soft, yielding part of her. "Do it more," he begged her, opening his mouth on her free hand, his lips against her warm palm. Again and again she moved against him, calling out in her pleasure. The muscles in her arms stood out, her chest full, her neck rosy. He wanted to move but he kept himself still. He grabbed her hips, "Stop. Please," he begged. He didn't want to come.

Renee let herself down on Nat's chest, and he stroked her back again. Holding her around the waist, he rolled over until he was on top of her. He opened her little hidden lips and licked her. He went into her so easily now, again and again until he felt her let go, felt her breath on him as she moaned into his mouth. "Come on," he called to her, and she did. He felt her legs shake as she arched her back to meet him.

When they woke, Nat was still inside her, soft. His mouth was soft against her hair.

"You're going to marry me," he said.

She laughed. "Just because I came?"

"Just that?"

"No." She held on to him.

"I'm not going anywhere."

They made plans. There was a piece of land adjoining the Goldrings' farm Nat wanted to buy for Renee, for himself. He wanted to join the Goldrings; though they had found this place, it could be his, too. They told no one what they were going to do.

When they married in secret, a month later, in the house of a justice of the peace in Point Pleasant, Renee was pregnant. From the afternoon in Atlantic City when she had planned to leave Nat, when instead they had become lovers, both of them surrendering and winning, in pleasure.

AT THE END OF MAY, BEN TOLD HIS MOTHER HE WAS GOING TO GIVE NAT the money. He would do it her way, the Shein way, without a check, without a bank. "We're going to take care of the money," was all Ben had told his brother when he asked Nat to meet him at the back of the shop. Ben was waiting as Nat pulled up in the truck, his gym bag on the seat next to him. Ben's slimness was made angular by the cut of his double-breasted jacket. Nat, his broad chest and shoulders thinly covered by a short-sleeved summer shirt, looked like a boxer, still in the game, but aging.

"What are you going to do, knock off the shop?" Nat asked as he followed Ben through the back door. It was a job Nat had done—one partner stealing cash from the business or an owner faking a robbery for insurance, hiring Nat to make it seem like an outside job.

"The Shein bank—it's right here. Ma knows to the penny; she has her third. I'm not stealing from her. Do I look like a crook?" Ben asked.

"What does a crook look like?"

"It's legit—we even paid taxes. Ma talked me into it, 'Because of everything going on in Europe,' she told me. You think she doesn't listen to you, but she does: she wants some money in the vault where we can get our hands on it. Maybe you're both right. 'Who knows what will happen?' she told me. 'Wake up one morning and not get your money out from the bank because you're a Jew.' Why do they hate us?" Ben asked.

"You want an answer?" Nat said.

Ben drew back the heavy blue velvet drape that covered the door to the vault.

"In here?" Nat asked. He grabbed his mother's red wool shawl from the hook behind the drape and threw it over his shoulders.

Reaching into his breast pocket Ben took out a slim leather case, which he unsnapped, shaking out his keys. He unlocked the gate, and Nat pulled open the steel door, stepping back as Ben spun the wheel and opened the hatch. The brothers breathed in cold air mixed with the smell of perfume that lingered in the linings of the fur coats in storage.

Nat shivered in his thin shirt and drew his mother's shawl closer.

Ben led him to the back of the vault and, watching his brother's face, opened a false panel, drew out a dented brown cardboard box, and pried open the flaps that had been crisscrossed over each other. The Shein box was full of money—new bills, old bills, stacks of money tied with colored string, and on the top, on violet-colored paper, Brona's dated accounting; the last entry, eighty thousand dollars.

"You're crazy," Nat said, as a wild laugh broke out of him.

"Not so crazy."

"A jackpot."

"From the Shein Bank, any size you want."

"This is not since the Germans. There's too much," Nat said.

"From before, from when Pa died. Ma never trusted the banks, but she would never steal from us." He handed Nat a stack of bills.

"You didn't tell me."

"You were with bad people."

"Not for years." Nat's large head swayed back and forth. "Nice people, the two of you." The truth had made him happy. "What else don't I know?"

"Nothing, believe me. Take it."

"It *is* my share. I worked like a donkey." Ben wasn't buying him.

"We're all even," Ben said.

"I'll give us that much," Nat said.

They sat on the floor of the vault like two children playing in a closet, their legs crossed, their heads together, Nat draped in his mother's red shawl. Even in the cold air of the vault, their faces were flushed and warm as Ben lifted out a stack of bills. "Tell me how much."

"I want big. Ten thousand."

"Piker."

"But I told Ma ten."

"She thinks you need twenty. She wants you to have."

"What about Susan?"

"In the end she'll get, from the bank, too. I went to a lawyer."

"Your wife?"

"Nothing."

"You don't mean it."

"I'll decide." Ben waved at the money. "Judith doesn't know. I give her by the week for the groceries." The money was a Shein secret. Judith wasn't a Shein. "All she's good for is to clean."

"Why?"

"Why what?" Ben didn't want to talk about it. Besides he didn't have an answer. Maybe there were no answers.

"You know?" Ben said as they carried the money out to the truck. "Maybe we *should* put it in a safety deposit box with all of our names on it. Maybe Ma's wrong. We got a lot."

"What are you talking about? You forgot what happened?" Nat asked his brother.

"The thieves got in," Ben said.

"They stole. On the Fourth of July, while the parade went by and the drums went boom, they drilled into the vault, into the safety deposit boxes," Nat said.

"Uncle Sam Savings Bank. It won't happen again," Ben said.

"That's what you think. The gonnifs know what's in those boxes. They know how much. Ma was right. Keep it where you can get your hands on it. But nothing's really safe. You think Moe doesn't know about this? He knows, but he doesn't tell. Gold melts. Every dam breaks, every wall," Nat said.

"Some things are safe," Ben said.

"Tell that to King Tut." Nat threw the bags he was carrying into the front seat. He put his hand on the back of his brother's neck, pulled Ben toward him, kissed him. His face was warm, flushed, as if he had just gotten out of their warm bed, as he had years ago. "Did Ma tell you?"

"What?"

"I found someone."

"What are you talking about?"

"I told Ma last night. I got married." A big smile parted Nat's lips.

Ben loosened his grip; the bags of money fell to the ground. He slumped to his knees, his head down. Black ants crept in a line in the cracks of the pavement. An unbearable pain shot into his chest as it had when he was a boy and Nat had punched him. Now he wanted to bang his fists against his brother's face, but he couldn't: Nat would hold him down—as in the past—while Ben screamed, locked in Nat's grip, unable to move.

"I'll help you," Nat kneeled down and picked up the money.

They stood, both of them with the money in their hands. "I don't believe it," Ben said.

"What did you think? I'm going to be here for the rest of my life?"

"But you told me . . ."

"What did I tell you? I didn't know her then. It's Shein and Goldring. You'll come around. Her family does OK. They have a farm, in south Jersey." With that big smile on his face, he kept talking about the farm.

"You don't know anything about this kind of work. What will you do there?" Ben asked.

"I lug here. I'll lug there. A new place." Laughing, he kissed Ben's cheek. "Did you hear about Joe Mavet?" he asked as he got into the truck.

"What?" Ben didn't want any more news. He shoved the rest of the money through the open window.

"They finally put Joe away. In Greystone."

"What for?" Ben couldn't believe it.

"To lock him up. He got worse. Screaming. I told you: Let him scream in the cemetery. He said he was going to kill his sister. Yetta couldn't take it anymore. 'It's him or me,' she told Ma. People don't get better there, but she called the cops anyway; the sister did it. 'I'll be the one to end up in Greystone.' She said that. Ask Ma."

"Why didn't she come to me? Joe Mavet wouldn't hurt anyone."

"How do you know? People go crazy."

"But a sister?"

"Yes, even better, a wife or a child. They have to take it out on someone. Who else do they see? Ma said in her mother's village a woman . . . ," Nat began.

"What does she know? It's 1941. We're not in Poland. Yetta should have come to me. I would have got someone," Ben said.

"For what?"

"To take care of him. Tess used to give the sister extra money when the woman worked for us. Tess called it a bonus, used to put it in a special envelope, gave her clothes. 'Better than giving to the synagogue,' she used to say. The woman never let us down, came to work sick, and Tess would send her home. A sister should help out, a *brother* should."

"Joe Mavet is not family," Nat said, looking past him.

"His sister worked for us."

"This is different."

"He's all alone there. I could take care of him," Ben said.

"You? *You're* going to take care of him?"

"I'll visit, I'll bring him something."

"He's a dangerous man—if he is a man," Nat said, starting the motor.

"Where are you running to?"

Nat smiled, shrugged, quickly dropped his shoulders, that smile still on his face. Ben stood there, watching as Nat pulled away. Gray exhaust came out of the tailpipe, covering Ben's legs as if he were standing knee-deep in a misty pond, his feet sinking toward the bottom he couldn't see. He coughed as the truck disappeared.

Soon after he had heard the news about Joe Mavet, Ben called Yetta, who cried to him. "I'm an old woman, not like when I worked for your wife, may she rest in peace. I can't go there to the hospital. I'm finished, I'm on the way out, I'm telling you the truth. You have to schmear the attendants; if you give them a tip, they'll watch out for him."

"Maybe I'll go see him," Ben answered.

On a Sunday in June, Ben drove to Greystone. He rubbed his fingers down his thigh, feeling for the small wad of bills in his trouser pocket— Joe's portion. Ben carried the rest of his money in a wallet in his breast pocket. In the back seat of the car was a box of chocolates, his gift for Joe, assurance to himself that Joe was somehow—though at the farthest edge of the circle—still in the realm of the normal and that Ben Shein himself was all right, a friend, a good man who did not forget the people who had once worked for him and Tessie.

As he drove west through Pine Brook, he could see from the highway the town's two businesses—a grocery store and a gas station—and he imagined himself living alone in such a place, without his family. He couldn't breathe with them. Who needed them? Nat was gone, a farmer—let's see how long he would last there. What good was Judith to him? Maybe someday, when Susan was older, he would leave his wife. He could lose himself in a place where no one knew who Ben Shein was. He could open a little shop in one of these towns, a variety store with a little of everything—newspapers, cigarettes, gum, candy. As he daydreamed, he could smell the shop—the tobacco, the malt for the sweet drinks. He saw himself behind the counter, counting out small change. He saw himself look out the shop's one window, out to the quiet street. I'd get along, he thought. Nobody would bother me.

Ben made the turn. The steering wheel spun back in his hands.

The approach to Greystone, once a wide carriage drive, rose from green slopes to a ledge. On either side of the long drive were double rows of maples and oaks planted at the end of the nineteenth century to mark the ascent through the four hundred fifty acres of the estate that was home to the mad. This country seat, with its own post office, police department, greenhouses, piggery, farrowing house, hog feeding pens, chicken house, dairy farm, horse barn, reservoir, garden shed, steam plant, print shop, tailor shop, and cottages, had been named and repeatedly renamed: New Jersey State Lunatic Asylum, New Jersey State Insane Asylum, New Jersey State Hospital for the Insane, New Jersey Hospital for the Mentally Ill, and, finally, Greystone Park.

This last name, scoured of any reference to people or madness, exactly fit the architect's pen and ink drawing: the place was grand and looked empty. Yet there were seven thousand people locked up inside Greystone.

Beyond the trees were the empty lawns—glowing green, rolled, cut to a uniform height, lush from spring rain. Precise gravel paths swept clean of stray leaves crisscrossed the green expanse.

At the end of the rising drive, on the highest ridge, the main house, with its enormous wings, looked down to the park and the surrounding hills. The gray stone that formed the walls had been quarried on site. The plutonic rock glinted in the June sun.

Ben got out of his car, locking the door behind him, the sound of the key in the lock, loud in the quiet of Greystone. A silver and blue bus stopped across the drive, its motor running, as one by one each passenger got off without speaking. Ben turned for a moment to make sure he had locked all the doors. When he turned back, the silent people and the bus were gone, the park empty again. A breeze stirred the maple trees, lifting the leaves that were still again as the breeze dropped. The air was cool, the sun bright on the vast, green lawns.

Carrying the box of chocolates, Ben walked up the drive. At the angle formed between the center building and the north wing was a grassy courtyard secured by high iron bars. Ben looked up, kept looking, his neck stiffening. There were hundreds of windows, the ones on the top floor smaller, jammed under the eaves. Puzzled by the windows' dull blankness, he stared, until he realized every window was barred.

He climbed the stone steps to the main entrance; high over his head the flag of the state of New Jersey hung limp in the still air. He turned and looked back down the drive: there was no one there. The narrow landing brought him to two narrow wooden doors that were so high they could have admitted a giraffe.

Ben walked through. Ahead of him stretched a long, nearly empty corridor whose end he could not see. Here, too, it was quiet, but he sensed the life behind the thick, green-painted walls. There was a dense, steamy smell of cooked food. Ben gagged, tasted bile, and swallowed.

When he told the young woman at the desk he was there to see Joe Mavet, his voice was hoarse. He coughed and spoke again. As the nurse wrote up Ben's pass, she told him he was allowed to give Joe the chocolates but nothing else. "Nothing."

"But I have money for him," Ben explained. "So he can buy things."

"He doesn't have buying privileges. Patients on his ward aren't allowed to keep money. You'll find him, just go down the hall."

He could tell she had made this speech before and did not care for him, for Joe, for anyone. Ben's throat burned as he looked to his left down the long corridor. He felt his blood as a flutter beating in his head, behind his ears, and he was afraid. But he went ahead, past thickly paneled closed doors until he reached the end of the corridor, where he turned left and passed through swinging doors into a narrow hall of closed doors. He tried a door. It was locked. He opened another door and stumbled into a janitor's closet. The deep white enamel sink was splashed with dark brown liquid. Choking on the close smell of mildew from the gray, clotted mops, Ben rocked backward, his heart thudding. Panicking, he ran back through the swinging doors, afraid he would never find his way out. He was about to yell for help when he turned right and found the visitors' room.

At first he thought the room was empty, but when he looked more closely he saw a woman and a young man sitting side by side. The woman, who wore a pink flowered dress with a white collar, held the young man's hand. Ben assumed he was her son. The young man was thin, long-necked, his dark eyes huge in the gray light of the room.

Ben waited, the box of chocolates in his lap, his head down. When he heard the sound of shuffling footsteps, he raised his head and saw Joe walking in front of an attendant. It was clear someone had dressed Joe— his shirt was buttoned to the collar and tightly tucked in. But the trousers had slipped down to his hips: Joe wore no belt. His face was scraped raw; his head, shaved some time before, was gray with the shadow of returning hair. Ben noticed first the blue-red healing seam of a deep cut that crossed the scalp line and marked the top of Joe's skull. The right side of his face was bruised blue. His eyes were blank.

"Do you know who he is?" the attendant asked Joe, pointing toward Ben.

A look of scorn passed across Joe's battered face and his eyes sparked.

"Of course I know. He's me." Joe reached out his hands and held them over Ben's head as if he were blessing him. "How are you Ben?"

Ben felt the shadowy weight of Joe's hands, though Joe did not touch him. Ben nodded.

"You can sit down." The attendant pointed.

"I can fly," Joe said and remained standing. He pursed his lips and giggled.

"What happened to him?" Ben asked the attendant.

"They get into fights." The attendant stood there, his oiled hair waved flat to his head, shining, even in the gray light. His face was old. He must have been sixty. "Joe, your visitor wants you to sit down. You can do that."

"I know more than you do, I know, I know, I know," Joe said.

"Maybe you do," the attendant murmured.

"Who lives and dies."

"That's everybody," Ben shrugged, his right shoulder lifting, his head tilting right, his mouth twitching.

"I got news for you, Ben Shein: the schvartze believes me. You know why? Because I'm black on the inside, like the grave, my mouth is black."

"He didn't mean anything," Ben said.

"I pay him no mind," the attendant said.

"I'm ready," Joe said as he sat down, keeping his eyes on Ben, waving off the attendant, who took a seat near the door.

"I brought you chocolates," Ben said.

Joe blew though his lips, as if he were trying to blow out candles that would not go out.

"I want to give you money, but they won't let me."

Joe brought his face close to Ben's. Joe's already swollen features were exaggerated by the lack of hair, his face exposed, naked. "Ben, I want to go home. Take me home."

"They won't let me," Ben said.

Joe rolled his head from side to side.

"I'll ask," Ben said.

"They put me in water," Joe said.

He looks clean, Ben thought.

"This water is poisoned. The general tells them to put poison in the water. I can see it. There's poison in the stinking food. They are putting cock in my mouth," Joe said.

"What?"

"You heard me. You can hear me. I can hear them. You see that one there?" Joe said, pointing to the attendant at the door, the middle joint of his index finger red and blue, swollen. "He's talking. He's listening to orders. They are planning."

As Ben untied the red ribbon that bound the box of chocolates, the attendant rose from his chair and walked toward him.

"I'll have to take that."

Ben handed him the ribbon and the man carefully wound it. He reached into his pocket and took out an elastic band, which he wrapped around the ribbon.

"Have some chocolate," Ben said to the attendant, as he lifted the lid.

"No, not for me," the man answered. "I'm full up. Give him some. Maybe he'll like it. Maybe he'll eat. That patient is pitiful. Thin." He went back to his seat. His hair looked like a boy's but his walk was slow as an old man's. He had to witness scenes like this every day.

Ben held out the box to Joe.

He ran his fingers over the tops of the chocolate. "They've injected them. I can feel it."

"Come on, I bought them special at Park."

"I'm telling you." Joe's voice rose. "Believe me. I've been telling you. If I tell them, they will never let me out from here. And listen—more I got for you. From a Jew they are taking it. The doctors found a Jew. Dr. Catman from the Rockefeller Institute. Pure. We're a mongrel scum race of the world, but we're beautifying it. The Jews are purifying it. From one Jew they are taking pure seed. We will purify the world. Then they'll let us live, only then. Then I can sleep. Ben, I don't sleep. God in heaven, a Jew gives them pure seed. A Jew gives pure breed to animals."

"What kind of animals? What do you know about animals?" Ben asked.

"Cats, dogs. Everything. From Mrs. Rockefeller. They come. Pure breed. She's got between her legs." Here Joe Mavet lifted his hands, his fingers curled, as if around a ball. He stuck his tongue out. He licked his lips. "White cats. From a Jew. From his wife, Mrs. Rockefeller. Boys, girls. She drowns the weak ones, but the strong ones live; no one knows they are Jews. What about your wife? The one with the knife. She's a strong one. Is she as rich as Mrs. Rockefeller?" Joe asked.

Ben sprang out of his seat and rushed toward the woman and young man. His right leg cramped; a sharp pain shot through his calf muscle. He straightened his leg, and the pain lessened. He held out the box of candy with both hands. "Please," he said. "Take. Chocolate. Please." The woman, her face tranquil, took one of the dark, domed candies and, with a quick thank you, brought it to her lips. The young man did not move. His feet were on his chair, his knees drawn up, his head bent to his knees, his face hidden, as if he were locked in a box.

Joe rocked from side to side. The chair rocked with him. He moaned, "See. See." He held his head. "A cemetery—the whole world; it's raining."

"Shah, shah," Ben soothed as he returned to Joe and sat down.

"Nobody wants to listen to me. Believe me I know what I'm talking about," Joe said. He jabbed his finger toward Ben. "You got two eyes, from two different heads. You're cock-eyed. You're finished. I'm singing to you, why don't you listen?"

"Don't worry."

Joe put his hand up to his own mouth. He sucked his fingers. He looked at the attendant. Joe coughed, rubbing his hand across his mouth. "I have something for you," he said to Ben.

Ben didn't believe him. "I don't need a thing."

"Here. You'll have it." Joe took Ben's right hand as if he were going to shake it. "For your daughter, the little kitten." With his other hand, Joe drew his finger across his throat.

"Stop it, stop it. Nobody will hurt you," Ben said. He felt something wet, hot, hard. A ball of snarled thread lay in his palm. He squeezed the rough wad, Joe's gift. He must have pulled the threads from his clothes and wrapped them into this tough, hard ball. He had found something to keep himself busy.

"I saved it for you," Joe whispered.

"Thank you."

"My pleasure, Ben Shein."

Maybe he got this from Mrs. Rockefeller. Ben smiled. What does he expect me to do with it? Sew it into a coat? But he took it. He stuck the spit-soaked ball into his pocket and carried it home, out through the high doors of Greystone.

Ben went back to Paterson and drove aimlessly through the empty Sunday streets. Paterson was never quiet, not even on Sunday. The sound of the Falls was close and loud, the river fed by spring rains and the snow-melt far upstream. Near the side of the road a boy stopped at a puddle, his hands on his hips as he gazed into the water. Deliberately placing one foot in front of the other, he walked in, head down. At the center, he rolled his feet out and balanced on the outside edges of his soles. He was in another world.

Ben parked across the street from his fur salon, turned off the motor, and stared at the shop front shaded by the massive Quackenbush's. He looked at the windows he had decorated. He read the thin and thick letters above the windows, the sign: *Ben Shein Furs*, which had replaced *Eli Shein and Sons*. "Put your name. It's your show," Nat had told Ben.

The business had thrived, but now the evidence of Ben's enterprise had become unreal. He had believed he was making a life of his own—solid, unchanging—but suddenly he felt like a stranger looking into a world that belonged to someone he used to know, the man he once was.

He drove around to the back, let himself in, and climbed the stairs to the workroom. The exterminator had come a few weeks before, and the sweet oily smell of insecticide was still present. Like a stranger, Ben spied on his old life. Standing at his desk, his hands at his sides, he looked at the closed sketchbook, the black metal case that held colored pencils, the pens in the gold and orange cup. He had sanded down the sharp stumps of the broken handle and reclaimed the cup. He had arranged these things, made this order, but he could not find a way in. Like a thief, he studied the closed arrangement. He would have to sneak in—silently slide a pencil from its groove—break in—snatch, grab, pinch—but there was nothing he wanted.

Ben heard a creaking noise and felt a flicker of fear. He didn't want to see Moe Black, who had a key to the shop and sometimes worked weekends to finish an order. He waited, dreading the sound of Moe's inevitable greeting, "What are *you* doing here?" But there was no sound at the door, no sound on the stairs; there was no one there. Moe's work jacket hung from its hook like an empty sack whose heavy contents had broken through the bottom: the lining hung below the body of the jacket, shredded to tatters.

Ben went down the stairs. The afternoon was almost over and the store was dark, but he did not turn on the lights. He wandered around the perimeter of the first floor, hearing the sound of his own footsteps. Drawn to his mother's desk, he stared at the black phone—he would call her, step into Manor Street, see Susan. His hands felt light as he picked up the heavy receiver, held it to his ear, and heard the operator's voice. He pressed down the lever, cutting off the voice, tipped the receiver back into its cradle. He didn't want to see his mother, her face with a question he didn't want to answer.

He wouldn't go home to Fairlawn, to Judith. Yesterday, when they had fought, she had screamed that she wanted him to die.

He drifted like a ghost. As he spun the wheel to the vault and felt its chill, his hackles rose, and, though he wore a jacket, the skin on his forearms contracted in the cold. Deep in, at the back of the vault he found Tess's coat. Keeping his eyes on the fur, wary yet determined, Ben took off his jacket and, holding the coat with the opening facing him, slipped his arms into the cold sleeves, as if the coat, which came down to his thighs, were a straitjacket. The sleeves were so tight he might split them. No, impossible, the fur was strong, the stitching firm. Ben eased his arms out of the sleeves, turned the coat the right way and put it on, tilting and rolling his head to the side so he could feel the collar against his neck, as if the fur were stroking him.

He left the vault, closing the door behind him, and, in the warm narrow space between the gleaming steel and the blue drape, lay down on the bare floor. In his pocket was Joe Mavet's wad of snarled thread—hard, spit-dried, shaped by Joe's teeth and tongue.

Ben ran his hands over his sides, over the fur, as far as he could reach and felt a small bulge in the pocket of Tess's coat. "It couldn't be," he said out loud; the sound of his voice startled him. From the slippery black pocket he drew out a cold metal lipstick case, which he opened, twisting up a small slanting nub. He rubbed his finger over the tip and pressed the reddened finger against his lips, smelling violet scent, his lips red with Tess's old lipstick. His penis stirred, half hard. He shut his eyes and tried to see Tess's face, but he could not find her. His hand streaked with lipstick, he reached inside his jacket, under his shirt, and touched his own breasts, his nipples tightening, as he caressed himself, feeling for Tess. "Ben, Ben." He heard his name inside his own head. Then "Ben" out loud in the silence of the shop. But his name came out of his own mouth, rough, hoarse. No one was there. He couldn't see her. Ben's eyes were open now. "So what?" he asked as if he were facing an interrogator.

He closed his eyes again and drew the coat around him as tightly as he could. His thin wrists stuck out of the sleeves as he curled on his side, his hair damp, disheveled, his lips smeared red. He rested his head on his arm, his cheek against the silky, curled fur that now was warm. His stiff shoes made it hard for him to relax his feet. I'll take them off, he thought, but already he was dozing, about to fall, his shod feet on the edge of a cliff. He jerked to keep himself from falling, but he fell, the sound of the air, as he plummeted, like Susan's voice. He couldn't make out the words.

Late one Friday night, after Ben had dropped Susan off at Manor Street for the weekend, Brona called him at the shop to tell him Susan was sick. Though Brona had bathed Susan in alcohol, the fever would not go down. Now she waited for Doktor to come. He had been delayed—an emergency.

Ben went to Manor Street and found his mother in the kitchen on her hands and knees, pieces of white cloth cut from a sheet spread out in front of her, her large black-handled tailor's shears in her hands. Looking up at him, her eyes hard as coat buttons, she told him she was doing what her grandmother had done in the shtetl, in Rozana, when Brona herself was sick with a fever. Like her grandmother, Brona would trick the Angel of Death, the Malakh ha mavet, who, Brona had been told long ago, could make a mistake, though, in the end—the bottom of that hole in the ground—he brought everyone down, never to rise again. Let Susan wear her shroud now—white, they had to dress her in white, but she had no white gown. Brona would make one without one speck of color. When the Angel of Death came, he would see the girl laid out in white—clean, still, pale—and, believing she was already dead, would leave her alone. Brona had not been ready when the Angel had come for Tess. This time she would fight.

Already Brona was at the sewing machine. Her feet firm on the treadle, she pumped hard as she pushed the material under the needle. In a minute she was done with the little tunic. Lifting the clamping metal foot, she slid the fabric away; the bobbin rattled; the long threads pulled. She cut them away, stood, and shook the white gown over her head as if she were beating off birds. The little shroud flapped.

"Ma, the doctor will take care of her. There's no typhoid here," Ben said.

"You," Brona pointed, "you be quiet. Candles I need. Where are they?" She yanked at the kitchen-table drawer, sending it crashing to the floor. Stuck in back, away from knife tips and fork teeth, was a wrinkled paper bag. On her knees again, Brona felt through the paper: there were candles.

"Ma," Ben kept saying as he followed her up the stairs.

Susan lay on the bed under the yellow blanket, her cheeks red, her eyes closed. When Ben called her name, Susan whimpered, "Mommy, Mommy."

"It's me, Daddy."

"Mommy," Susan repeated, grabbing onto his hand, panting as if she had been running.

Brona ran for alcohol and tepid water, soaked a face cloth in the mixture, and, without removing Susan's pajamas, bathed her, reaching under, easing down—chest, back, stomach—turning her, pressing the cloth against the hot soles of her feet, against her hands, wetting each finger before she soaked the cloth again, wringing it out more firmly so that it would not drip when she lay the cloth across Susan's forehead. Susan's breathing slowed and Brona sighed.

Ben lifted the cloth and saw through the red fever flush to a blue whiteness that gleamed like a candle flame about to go out. His ears began to hum, deep inside. The buzz grew louder. At Tess's funeral, bees had hummed in the pink spreading graveyard sedums. The rabbi had grabbed Ben's black tie, pulled it straight out and with one quick motion slashed it straight through—the rending sound. The mutilated tie had hung from his neck.

Susan whimpered again.

"Shah, shah," Ben touched her hand. It was burning.

Brona stripped away the blanket, threw it into the hall, ran to the linen closet, returning with a clean white sheet. Now she undressed Susan down to the skin, white skin, at the nipples a swelling—so soon. And below there was hair.

She pulled the new white gown over Susan's head, and then the sheet, covering her. At last he wouldn't have to see.

As Ben patted Susan's face with the wet cloth, she called out, sat up, and pointed to the corner of the room. "Mommy, there's something there."

"No, no." Ben held her, his knee on the bed.

"I can see her. With big teeth. Make her go away. And him." Susan screamed.

"What is it?" Ben asked her.

"A big red tongue."

"Nothing is there," he said.

"I can see them. I can see his tongue." Susan shrieked, "His black mouth."

"No, you have a fever. You have to sleep."

"He's laughing. He's laughing." Susan screamed like Joe Mavet.

"Wait," Brona called out. "Turn her, turn her—her head, her head must point to the door."

"Ma."

"Listen to me."

Ben stroked his screaming daughter's face.

"This way, this way." Brona tugged at Susan's feet. "This is the way—out from the door, they carry the dead."

"Ma, I beg you."

"Listen," his mother said.

He did, his hands under Susan's arms, turning her, until her head pointed toward the door. Finally her screams diminished, and she lay down and closed her eyes, quiet at last. Ben slumped, his ears stinging.

Brona smoothed the white sheet over Susan's still body, took a saucer full of strawberry hulls from the table near the bed and threw them into the wastebasket. Kneeling at the foot of Susan's bed, she struck a match and held it to the bottom of a candle until the wax began to drip clear drops onto the saucer. She pressed the candle into the liquid and watched the wax turn white as it hardened. When she took her hand away, the candle stayed upright, ready for her match. She struck; the flame blazed up; the wick took fire, and Brona turned off the lights. When the Angel of Death came, he would see the white flame, the open door, and believe Susan, dressed in white, laid out, her head pointing to the beyond, was already dead, and he would leave her alone.

Brona sat down in the chair close to the bed, her knees pressed against the mattress. Swaying, she slumped forward, her head near the pillow, her face turned toward Susan, her hands in her lap.

Covering his mother's back with a blanket, Ben stretched out on the floor. The candle burned on the table under one of Susan's pictures: the purple road flared at its edges into paler purple that flared into white, but still the road kept its shape through the blue-green around it. Was the green a meadow or was it water? The road was seen from above. Ben remembered: Susan had told him it was not just a road. She had drawn her initials, elongated them, turned them on their sides, and connected them.

At dawn when the sky turned pale and the moon was fading, Susan woke.

Ben felt her head. She was cool.

She sat up. "Daddy." She put her arms around his neck. "You're here."

"Grandma called me."

She had her lips right against his ear. "Daddy, let me stay here. Don't make me go back."

"You had a fever. You had a bad dream. Everything will be all right," he said. Susan would go home with him to Fairlawn—the school was better, the air cleaner. She would have her art lessons, her weekends with her grandmother. Brona would take good care of her, the best. In a few weeks school would end, summer would come, and she and Brona would go to the mountains. Ben could already see them together, high up, under the pine trees in the fresh, clean air.

"I'M KNOCKED OUT," BEN TOLD JUDITH AS HE LEFT HER IN THE KITCHEN and went to bed. He slept hard and woke before six, so tired he could not imagine ever lifting a piece of fur again. Instead of immediately getting out of bed as he usually did, he closed his eyes, his legs and arms heavy, aching. "I'll get up in a minute," he told himself, but he kept waking and dozing off. At eight o'clock, Ben woke to the sound of Judith's voice coming from the kitchen, the bang of the back door. He was not used to being home at this hour and felt as if he were in a dream, in a strange house.

Gathering his clothes and shoes, Ben went barefoot into the bathroom. A cramp gripped the toes of one foot, and he stood still until the muscles loosened. Barely awake, he held his shaving brush under the hot water, shook it out, and worked the brush into his shaving soap. Stroke by stroke, he scraped off the dark bristle, avoiding looking into his eyes in the mirror. He could hear Judith moving around in the kitchen and took his time dressing, hoping she would go out into the yard.

He listened at the door: the house was still. Cautiously he went into the hall and found the bedroom door open, the room empty. His topcoat over his arm, Ben stepped into the kitchen. Judith sat at the kitchen table, her back to him, the paper propped up on the fruit bowl, a bowl of corn flakes in front of her. He took a step and knew from the hunch of her shoulders she had heard him.

"I'm going," he said and walked closer.

"Good morning." Judith waited. Sometimes Ben would return her greeting.

"Did Susan eat?"

"I prepared her breakfast." Judith had set the table—a blue glass plate on a pink placemat; on the left, a fork next to a napkin folded in a triangle; on the right, two spoons. She had sliced the banana, poured juice and milk, offered Susan a choice of three cereals, offered to cook eggs—but Susan would not sit down. Her hair falling over her face, her books in one arm against her chest, she had danced from side to side as she gulped milk, spilling it down the front of the blouse Judith had ironed. She had crammed the banana into her mouth, so that her cheeks bulged, snatched an apple from the fruit bowl, and had run out the door without speaking.

"You prepared it?" he asked her.

"She took some."

"The child has to eat. We have to build her up—eggnogs."

"She is better—her color . . . ," Judith paused.

"Color?"

Judith folded her hands on the paper and closed her eyes. Without moving her lips, she counted, concentrating on the numbers—a routine, which, while it held her in check, offered no solace. She reached ten, went back to one. She was empty, the numbers hard as stale bread.

Ben stood at the edge of the table. "I asked you something."

"Sometimes color . . ."

"What?"

Judith glanced at him. "There's coffee."

"I'll eat downtown. Sophie Winik knows what to give me. She knows quality."

"Ben, I haven't eaten." The corn flakes were dry in the bowl, the pitcher of milk ready and the sugar bowl full.

"You have all morning to eat."

"Yes," she said, looking away, as her mother had told her to do—but what was there to look to? Judith tried to find a dream that would lift her from this room, but her eyes, locked on the sink, the gleaming new faucet, held her exactly where she was.

"I'm tired. I'm a tired man."

She tried to reach him. "You don't have to apologize. Everyone gets tired," she said.

"Even Ben Shein?" He laughed, waiting for a tender word.

"Even the *great* Ben Shein." She had tried for a light tone and failed.

"What's so special about Ben Shein? That's what you think?" he asked.

"No."

"No?"

"What do you want from me?" she asked.

"Nothing. You're good for nothing."

Judith jumped out of her seat, lost her balance, and rocked against the table, spilling the milk. "Leave me alone," she screamed.

Ben stepped back. In a second he was out the door.

LATE ONE AFTERNOON, WHEN NAT COULD NOT GET AWAY, BEN DROVE out of Paterson to bring Susan home from her art lesson with Miss Moore. He had never met the teacher, having left the arrangements to Brona, who had convinced him the teacher knew her business. Into Passaic, down Main Avenue: one straight line parallel to the Erie Railroad tracks that cut Passaic in two. The buildings facing the tracks were smoke-blackened—the black like shadows, where, on this bright morning, no shadows should be. At Main Avenue and Monroe Street a train slowed as it approached the station. The engine barely outran the great cloud of smoke that poured from its stack, the iron wheels locked to the pistons. At the crossing, people in light summer dress waited in the smoke, in the roar that filled the downtown.

Ben had the windows closed, the vent open. When he was forced to slow down at Main and Henry, he began to sweat, but still he shut the vent, cutting off the air, locking out the smoke. His jacket would hide his damp shirt. The line of cars began to move and he went on. At Passaic Avenue, he turned, shifting down for the hill that rose to a fountain, where a single jet of water shot up from the center of the round basin. The air cleared, and Ben opened the vent.

Following the directions Nat had written in his large childish hand, Ben passed the cross streets—Gregory, Paulison, Boulevard—and drove under the railroad trestle. A right turn took him through the park to the edge of Willow Brook Pond, where a man held the hand of a little girl as she threw bread to the mallards. A trio of willow trees slanted toward the water, their branches dragging. Ben rolled down the window and leaned into the draft.

In a moment he was on the Circle. The big houses set on deep lawns surprised him, bigger than on Manor Street—with a pond to look at. Ben had no trouble finding the art teacher's house. "Plain," Nat had called it. But still Ben was astonished: *plain*? The house was bare, except for metal work above the door, like a grate. The metal seemed to move. Wings? Birds? Who knew? The windows were bent around soft corners, while the lines of the front were straight.

Ben pulled up to the concrete path that led to the front door—but was it the front door? Before he could ring, the door opened, and Miss Moore stepped toward him, her arm extended: "How nice to meet you, Mr. Shein."

"Likewise."

"Miss Moore, I told my father your house was Bauhaus." Susan's thin neck stuck out of the men's shirt that served as her smock.

"Bauhaus in Passaic, Mr. Shein." Like Susan, the teacher wore a men's shirt.

Haus he knew. *Bau* he didn't know. Miss Moore laughed as she bent over him, a long drink of water, her face close to his. Ben drew back. The teacher's large violet-blue eyes stared, naked, raw in their softness.

She looked as if she were going to cry, but she had a smile on her face. Her light brown hair was streaked with gray, wound into a loose knot at the back of her head. "Mr. Shein, I have something to show you." She swept her arm toward the house.

Mary Elizabeth Moore's parents had never forgiven her for being clever. They had expected her to play a good hand at bridge. If she insisted on doing good, she could do charity, as long as she didn't bore them with it. At Christmas, at her grandmother's house in Montclair, across the table weighted with silver, service plates breasted with linen, crowned with crystal, her father had called out to her, "Have you taught anything to those kikes and niggers?" In this family, she had become ashamed of having money.

"Come in," Miss Moore said.

Ben hesitated. When Susan ran ahead of him, he had to follow.

"Look," the teacher said. She stood in the center of a large front room that faced the pond and lifted her hand. "Isn't the light wonderful?"

"Yes," Susan answered for her father. She took him by the arm and pulled him to the work on her easel—blue slashes, crimson circles that jumped at him. "It's a mood," she explained, waving her paint-stained hands.

"We'll wash now, Susan." The teacher beckoned, and Susan went to the set tub in the corner and turned on the faucets. When she had scrubbed off most of the paint, she willingly held out her hands for Miss Moore, who covered them together in one clean towel, pressing, blotting, before she let Susan finish the job. Susan smiled at her the way she had smiled for Tess, her face open, flushed with joy. Putting the towel back on its hook, her eyes on Miss Moore, Susan unbuttoned her shirt and tore it off, her shoulders bare in the sundress.

"How lovely. Susan . . . ," Miss Moore began.

"My father made it." Susan took the shirt by the collar and carefully hung it near the sink.

"Mr. Shein, a sun dress is such a good idea."

"She won't get too hot in that dress, sun dress with bolero."

"It's jaunty," Miss Moore said.

"I gave her a pocket, hid it in the seam."

"A Shein creation," Susan said.

When he had cut out the pattern and then the white pique, he had felt Tess with him. She would have liked it—the material held the shape but would not scratch Susan's fine skin. He had fooled the kid. What did she know? She hates starch, throws dresses in the tub after Judith starches and irons, so no starch: pique doesn't need starch. Susan looked good, good enough for anybody. Ben glanced at Miss Moore's drawings on the walls. "Cats," he said. *Goyisheh naches*, he thought, amazed again at what made Gentiles happy. But well drawn; the woman could draw. "You do a good job," he said to her.

Miss Moore moved closer to Susan. "They might make a book—if I can do it."

Ben looked again. A gray cat in a red bed. A blue blanket. A black cat in a pink chair, reading. Yellow book. Yellow room. Through the windows a sky, big bright stars. More pictures. The room darker. The little cat boy asleep. The lamp lit. "Good luck," Ben said.

"Daddy, they're wonderful."

"Everything's wonderful," Ben said.

"Mr. Shein, there's so much to see, to study, to draw. Let me show you more—out back," Miss Moore said.

"You have to see the rabbits!" Susan ran to the back of the house.

"She gets so excited," Ben said.

"I admire that in her." The art teacher rushed after Susan, following her out the back door.

Ben reached out to catch the screen door before it slammed, but missed. Standing there, his face against the screen, he pushed. The door swung, and he went out into the bright light. Near the edge of the driveway, Susan stood with Miss Moore at a row of hutches. Dark rabbit hutches—Ben knew them from the village in Poland. He had seen the dead animals hanging by their ears in the outdoor market. The Polish peasants ate them.

Miss Moore held a brown rabbit by its loose neck flesh, cupping its hind legs with her other hand. "I like to draw animals," she said.

Susan reached out. The teacher had her hand around Susan's hand. "Hold her bottom like this, or else she will scratch," Miss Moore said. The animal was in Susan's arms, against her chest, against the white pique. "Daddy!" She called to him.

"Your dress," Ben said.

"My rabbit is clean," Miss Moore said.

Susan lifted the creature away—not a mark on her sundress—then pressed it to her chest again, its fur against her bare skin, its head against her thin throat. The animal was trembling. "I won't hurt you—no, no, no, I won't," Susan crooned as she stroked the fur. When Ben looked into its eyes, the rabbit did not look back. A blue haze covered its brown eyes.

Susan stroked the rabbit again, this time with only her index finger. "Her heart is beating. Feel."

"I don't have to." Yet Ben put his index finger next to Susan's and felt the heart beat and beat. He moved his finger down next to the ear, down to the bones where the rabbit's ears rooted into the skull. He had to be careful: the bones were so delicate. His fingers brushed his daughter's warm throat. "She's getting used to me. She's so small, there's nothing there." We never used rabbit, Ben thought, relieved the Sheins had refused the common pelts.

Miss Moore bent down to the rabbit's sleek haunches, blew into the fur as if she were blowing into coals to quicken a fire, revealing the pattern, the layers, the white underdown showing in flamey points deep under the dark brown top coat.

The pelage. Ben remembered: his grandfather Jacob had told him—the fur closest to the skin.

"It will get thicker in the winter. I keep all the rabbits outside. They are really very strong," Miss Moore said.

"Strong." Ben murmured to himself. "Until a peasant slits its throat."

Bending her thin neck, Susan put her face close to the rabbit's pulsing flanks and blew into the fur. Her upper lip was damp with sweat. Ben wanted to wipe her face.

"Her name is Billie. She used to be Billy *Boy*, but I was mistaken. It can be difficult to sex a rabbit," Miss Moore said. She lifted Billie from Susan's arms and put her down on the grass.

For a second the rabbit was still; then she burst from a fierce pivot and zigzagged across the fenced garden. She leapt, she danced, she seemed made of air. From furious speed, she came to a sudden still stop. She leapt again, was still again, eating clover from the lawn.

"Some Billie," Ben said.

Miss Moore laughed—a high voice like Mrs. Roosevelt's.

"She loves her cage. She returns at night."

"You got her tamed," Ben said.

Miss Moore lifted the trap door of a big cage, reached in like a peasant, and pulled up another rabbit, letting its hind legs dangle for the briefest second. Before she could bring her hand into position, the animal clawed air, raked for a hold, hung, its hind legs spinning. "He's going to get away," Susan shouted.

"No." Miss Moore fixed him, her big hand under its bottom. The rabbit lay still across her chest, head at her neck, like a fur for a collar, black, white, and gray. "This is Chamberlain in his morning suit, lest we forget." She put him back into the cage.

"Forget what?" Susan asked.

"Never mind," Ben said and raised his hand to the sky. "It's a nice day."

"Daddy."

The teacher looked past Ben to the back door. "Shirley wants us. Please let us give you some tea."

The maid stood at the back door, her white dress clean, her hair neat, oiled, rolled close to her head, her black face calm. Shirley's skin looked hard, carved, but Ben remembered touching his housekeeper Jeannette's bare black arm for the first time: her skin felt like his, like the Sheins'.

"It's ready," Shirley called, her accent Jersey and Mississippi, her tone firm. "I put everything out. You won't need me."

"Thank you," Miss Moore said.

Shirley held the door as they passed into the house. "I am going off duty," she announced. "You serve yourself."

In a room off the kitchen a low table was set with odd pieces of silver and pale yellow dishes; three tall glasses filled with tea stood on a steel tray. While Susan talked, Ben took his tea, still cold from the icebox, sweet and sour, already mixed with lemon and sugar, not too strong. He wouldn't say a word if Susan took a glass. Above the steel mantel was a strange painting, like rooftops, but not rooftops, like pieces of broken glass, white and blue-black. Ben made out the name, Feininger. A name from Europe. Everybody was from somewhere else, Ben thought. He was sweating, but he kept his jacket on.

Miss Moore's hair had come loose and swung close to her face. She could have been a cover girl. She had the bone structure. But not with those eyes. She picked up a plate of strawberries, which still had their dark green hulls, and offered them to Ben. "I picked them myself; washed from the rain, they smell like wine."

He took one and held it, as he kept his eyes on Susan. She helped herself—maybe she'd eat something. Miss Moore held a berry by the hull and pulled the fruit away with her teeth. Copying her teacher's movements, from the exact placement of her fingers to the slow pluck-ing of the fruit, Susan ate half a dozen berries. When Brona made straw-berry jam, cooking the berries down in sugar, it smelled like this. He ate a berry. "Not bad," he said. His eyes were on the painting.

"I love it. So interesting, like a deck broken and sliced into a wild fan of thin cards. There's light in the painting. It never goes off," Miss Moore said.

"Unless you forget to pay the bill," Ben said.

Miss Moore turned red.

Ben wondered what she was ashamed of. "You live by yourself?" he asked.

Miss Moore nodded.

Ben motioned toward the door with his head: "Your," he began. He had been about to say "schvartze," as if he were talking to a Jew. Finally he found the right words, "Your person?"

"Yes, my *person*. What a good word. Better than maid," Miss Moore said.

Better than schvartze, thought Ben.

"She comes to me days."

"What day, if I might ask?"

"Every day."

"Must cost you." Ben was impressed.

The teacher's face became redder: he had mentioned money again, a dirty word. He changed the subject. "You think my daughter can draw?"

"Oh yes, Mr. Shein. I would love to go on working with her."

"I want to." Susan chewed on a cookie. "All summer."

"We'll talk more. Miss Moore, my daughter goes to the mountains with her grandmother in a few weeks."

"But not for the whole summer, Daddy."

"Miss Moore isn't running away," Ben told his daughter.

"Never. And we are all here together now, in this day," Miss Moore said.

Ben stood with Susan on the Circle. She wrapped her arms around his waist, the way she used to do, and he felt her legs press against his legs through the white pique.

"Come, we'll go home." He pulled away—maybe Miss Moore watched from the window. Holding the car door open for his daughter, he looked back at the house.

As soon as he was behind the wheel, she started on him: "Daddy, I want to go on working."

"I told you. We'll see."

"Please."

"Be good. Be a good girl."

"I must work."

"Don't get so excited."

"Miss Moore is everything to me."

"Where do you get such ideas?"

"They're true."

"True?" Maybe you want to *live* here? That's the truth."

"I want to work here."

He looked again at the Bauhaus—the only house on the Circle like that. A single woman—that's where Susan wanted to go. "You're a child." But she was so mixed up—old and young.

IN THE HOUSE IN FAIRLAWN, JUDITH HAD FINISHED IRONING AND placing on hangers the last of her stepdaughter's dresses, a task she could not leave to the maid, who came only every two weeks to do the heavy work. Across the fine skin of Judith's inner arm was a tender burn line, which she avoided touching, using the thumb of one hand as a hook to carry the dresses into Susan's room. With her free hand, she made space in the closet, then, with both hands, held the dresses in a bunch and hooked them all at once onto the bar. The fabric rubbed against the burn; wincing, Judith lifted her arm close to her mouth and blew against her wound. Although she had barely relieved her pain, she now drew in a deeper breath and, forgetting herself, blew softly against her arm from the inside crook of her elbow down to her palm, the mild air down across her fingertips, a virgin caress. She reached for Susan's dresses, sliding them along the bar, smoothing, separating; metal grated on metal. The cotton gave off the smell of hot soap released by the iron. The spring pastels did not brighten the closet—like thin curtains on a black window.

Judith was about to turn away when she noticed the jumbled pile of shoes at the bottom of the closet. Unable to stop herself, she bent to one knee and began to straighten, pulling shoes out by the heel, until she reached the tangled laces, freeing every pair except one. Susan had tied her expensive new oxfords together by the laces, the securing knot hard and tight. Judith slammed the shoes down so hard that pain stung her wrist. Tightening her hands and arms against the pain, she matched the other shoes, lining them up under the dresses so they pointed to the back of the closet.

She reached over the line of shoes, felt in the dark, and found what at first she thought was a rag. In the light she saw it was Susan's balled-up underpants, the yellowed crotch still damp, stinking of urine. I should make her wash her own filthy pants, Judith thought. She wanted to throw them into Ben's face so he could see how badly his daughter behaved. Holding the pants by the waistband, she carried them into the kitchen and dropped them into a bucket of hot water and bleach.

What else was Susan hiding? Judith went back to her stepdaughter's closet and searched the top shelf—nothing. She scanned the room: bare walls, the room's one window closed, not one thing on the white-skirted vanity, and on top of the white chest of drawers only a pink dresser scarf and Susan's comb, black hair stuck in the teeth.

Judith opened the top drawer, slipping her hand down under the neatly folded underclothes, feeling along the bottom of the drawer, which just yesterday she had lined with paper. There was only the smooth, slippery surface under her hand. Searching every drawer, Judith found only the order she herself had created.

On her knees she searched under the bed and found nothing. The bed was a mess, the top sheet pulled out, the blanket pushed up against the headboard, the spread on the floor. Judith had told her stepdaughter to fold the spread and put it on a chair, but Susan wouldn't listen to her. Yanking the bottom sheet tight, Judith tucked in the corners. She straightened the top sheet and blanket, folded the bottom corners and jammed them under the mattress, but still her work was not done: there were black hairs on the pillow. Judith lifted the pillow by the corners, shook it, pounded it with her fists. The black hairs dropped away. As she beat and shook out the pillow again, she sniffed the oily smell of Susan's hair, the stale smell of her saliva. Her stepdaughter breathed through her mouth, chewed with her mouth open, slept with her mouth open, like a dog.

Though she had just changed the bed linen the day before, Judith stripped the pillow again. Taking a fresh pillowcase from the hall closet, she turned it inside out and, with one hand in each corner, matched the case to the pillow—corner to corner. She jerked hard, reversing the case, which slid over the pillow, right side up. With both hands, she punched the soft down until the pillow filled the clean linen case. Finally she could lay out the spread, folding it back to receive the pillow, which she placed precisely above the fold, drawing up the spread so the pillow was held, properly covered—until her stepdaughter tore the bed apart.

Judith had had her breakfast only an hour ago, but she felt empty. "I'll have a cup of tea," she promised herself as she opened the shallow drawer of Susan's vanity to the little row of front compartments, which held barrettes arranged by size, a few bobby pins, nothing else: how little Susan kept here. Judith pulled at the drawer, slamming it against the resisting guard that held it in place, three-quarters open. Filling the entire space at the back, covered in fine gray linen, was Susan's sketchbook. Pausing only for a moment, Judith grasped the book by its bottom and pried it out of the drawer. Once she had it on the vanity top, she spread her hands across the cover, her fingers curling around the edges, but she did not open the sketchbook, unable to go back or forward, fear locking her hands. "I'll put it back," she told herself, but she did not move. "What was the harm of looking at sketches?" Judith's hands unlocked, and she ran her fingers over the book. She felt the pressure of eyes on her back, but when she looked over her shoulder, she saw no one there. Rising from the chair, she closed the bedroom door, turned back, and, standing, opened the book.

Pasted to the inside cover was a clean, uncanceled French postal stamp, which the art teacher must have given to Susan. Ben had never told her how much he paid for those lessons. Within the saw-toothed frame was a brightly lit castle, in the foreground a branch of blooming lilac, a lady alone on a horse. Her long hair bound, her pink mouth bright, her robe dark blue, she rode alone through those violet-shadowed hills. A fairy tale, thought Judith, as she picked at the corner of the stamp. On the page facing the cover, Susan had drawn the castle, enlarged it, drawn it at a crazy angle, made the window holes burn. She had broken the border of the stamp drawing so that the points fell off the right side of the page. Below, in purple ink, Susan had written the date, June 10, 1941, her name, in large letters, and the address—37 Manor Street, Paterson, New Jersey. Brona Shein's house: not this one. I do the work, Judith raged to herself. And she is rude to me, insulting. I can't speak a word to her. If I do, she tells him, and he screams at me. She stared at Susan's letters, a mix of printing and cursive, curve and slant, link and break, a mix-up, but the mix-up flowed.

Judith turned the pages. They were empty. Hungry, tired, lost in loneliness, she went back to the drawing, scratching at the fresh surface to hurt and to steal, as if she could get what was Susan's under her nails.

When she had finished soaking and scrubbing Susan's laundry, Judith worked on her grocery list at the kitchen table. The refrigerator motor went on with a shaking gurgle that flattened to a hum. Starting with dairy, Judith wrote the word *eggs* in pencil. The sound of the motor stopped, and in the amplified silence left in its wake, Judith looked up to the window where Susan had pushed open the curtains. A sparrow with a dark brown patch under its tiny throat came down on the tip of a branch and opened its pale yellow beak. Inside the closed window in the silent kitchen, Judith scrutinized the faint pencil marks spelling out *eggs*. Dissatisfied, she went to the bottom drawer of her own dresser, where, among closed boxes of the little things she saved, she found the pen her father had given her when she entered high school and which she hadn't used for years.

Maneuvering the thin lever, she filled the pen from a bottle of blue Waterman's ink and began to trace the first letter of *eggs*. The dry point scratched, and she had to press down—too hard: ink filled the round opening of the *g*. As she went on, item by item—milk, pot cheese, sweet butter, tuna—the ink flowed and did not leave blots. The upright letters began to take on an angle. Judith did not see what she was doing: the slant was Susan's.

FROM THE DOOR TO THE KITCHEN, JUDITH WATCHED AS SUSAN LAID OUT cards on the kitchen table for a game of solitaire. The room was quiet except for the slippery flick of new cards. Unaware of her stepmother, Susan played, speeded up, bent over the table, her hair wild. She found an opening and raced through the cards.
Judith moved closer.

Susan flinched. "You scared me."

"I'm so sorry."

Without answering, Susan brushed her hair back from her forehead, from her cheeks. She had put on weight at Brona's, and the pointed nipples of her swelling breasts showed through her thin polo shirt. Judith jerked back, as if Susan's new breasts had, like wasps, flown from her chest and stung Judith's eyes.

The chains of black and red cards grew under Susan's quick hands. She put one foot on the rung of the chair next to her and rocked back, spinning the cards. She shifted kings, turned up aces, built rows. "I might be lucky." She raced through the deck and found an ace of hearts. "I could win this one," she said.

"You might." Judith took her wallet from the counter near the back door. "Your father is working late."

"I know."

She knew everything. When Judith told her she was going to the store to buy some things for dinner, Susan ignored her. With her head down close to her game, she flicked a card, bending the corner as she turned it over.

Back from her shopping, a heavy bag of groceries in her arms, Judith stepped through the back door and sniffed the spicy smell of fried food. Her stepdaughter was gone, leaving behind the remains of her dinner. The kitchen table was smeared with mustard, littered with crumbs; in the splattered sink, a greasy frying pan with a piece of hot dog stuck to the bottom, a saucepan caked with tomato soup. The ripped-open package of hot dogs lay next to the dirty dishes piled on the counter, the torn butcher's paper on the floor. Susan had pushed open the window curtains above the table, jamming the curtains against the window frames. The bent rod sagged in the middle, where the two ends barely met across the wide-open window. A fly had come in through a tear in the screen. Across the smeared mustard, the edge already crusting darker brown, across the crumbs stuck to wet circles of milk, the fly buzzed, dived, landed, shot up.

Judith shoved the bag of groceries into the refrigerator and slammed the door so hard the bowl on top of the refrigerator fell to the floor, cracking and splintering, the debris close to her feet. She rushed for a paper bag and began to pick up the larger pieces with her bare hands.

She knew what to do: wrap the large pieces in the bag, sweep up the splinters, and vacuum the floor. Susan's loud voice came from the doorway. "That bowl was my grandmother's."

"It was an accident. No one got hurt."

Judith stood up and dropped a jagged piece of glass into the bag. "I bought food for dinner."

"I'm not hungry." There was a dry streak of tomato soup on Susan's cheek, a half-peeled banana in her hand. Her open mouth full of fruit, she rolled the yellow pulp onto her tongue, pointing the tip at her stepmother through open teeth.

Judith turned her back, looked away, but her breath came so fast that she had to open her mouth for air. "Hot dogs should be steamed, the skin pricked with a fork. You fried them. Greasy hot dogs are not healthy."

"So what. They were good. I'll do what I want."

Whirling, Judith swung her arm just as Susan hopped back.

"Missed," Susan taunted. Crouching, hands on her knees, she danced from foot to foot, stopped and thumbed her nose. Her small breasts shook as she leapt up. Judith looked away.

There was a sound at the door, a muffled fumble—Ben was early, one foot on the threshold, his hand on the knob, his face in shadow— she hadn't put the back light on. For a moment Judith thought he was wearing a hat.

"Why is it so dark out there?" Ben asked.

Now she could see his face, the late afternoon beard bluing his cheeks.

Susan answered, "Because the sun is sinking and night is drawing near."

"Wise guy," he laughed, his eyes on her dirty welcoming face.

Susan wiped her mouth. "Daddy," she called out like a baby.

His eyes swept around the kitchen—the smeared table, the broken glass. "This kitchen is a pig sty."

"I . . ."

He didn't let Judith finish. "Every child needs a mother, a real mother," he said as he removed his jacket and folded it over a chair. "This is the way you're supposed to wash the dishes." He piled the few dishes from the sink onto the counter. "You don't listen." He ran the hot water. "You don't know how to do things for your own good. It only stands to reason." He flung the words at Judith.

"Daddy."

"Go away," Ben said to his daughter.

Susan ran.

"Ben, I know how to clean."

His arm shot out, his pointing finger. "Then why don't you?" He turned on Judith. He instructed; he hocked her; he drilled her.

"Stop it," she finally said.

His voice ripped into her ears: "Stop screaming at me. I'm advising you."

"I'm not screaming," Judith answered.

"You are. You are screaming."

"Please, no more," she said.

Ben could not stop.

Nothing she could say would make him stop. Judith looked toward the window but could not make out the tree. She put her hands to her ears and drew in her head, pressing her chin into her neck. On the kitchen counter a sharp paring knife pulsed and swelled in Judith's vision as Ben drilled on, banging the dishes. Judith imagined the knife in her hand, imagined herself sinking the knife up to the black hilt into Ben's chest, but she did not move.

"I'm being patient. I'm being as patient as I can. You have to do the right thing, take care of things. I'm worried about my daughter. What do you do here all day?" His voice was now low and bitter. "Nothing. We need help and you do nothing. You are good for nothing."

Judith opened her mouth to speak, but no sound came.

As she lay sleepless, Judith could hear Ben's even breathing. All her energy was concentrated in her head, which buzzed and boomed, while the rest of her body seemed barely to exist. She longed to sleep, but she could not keep her eyes shut. She strained to see in the dark. Finally her eyes closed and she lost consciousness—for a moment. Shocked into wakefulness, she cowered: the high dresser loomed as if it would topple and crush her. She heard Ben's drilling voice inside her head—his words came back to her—amplified, sending new shocks along her veins. Her pulse raced with hot, sickening shame.

"Stop," she said to herself, but she couldn't make the words stop. After each repetition, there was a blank pause in which she drew a long, shuddering breath. The words began again. She began to interject her own words, her defense, but this exhausted her more. I'll go, she thought. I will. I'll leave him. But even as she allowed herself this thought, she wondered where she could go. She did not want to go back to her mother's house. Whatever escape she imagined seemed impossible.

On and on, her brain spun out words until the spaces between the words grew and the words stopped. Judith slept, deeper and deeper, washed in the waves of her soundless dreams.

When she woke, the faint gray light of dawn had seeped into the room and she could see her husband sleeping on his back, his defenseless eyelids smooth and pale. A gust of wind blew against the house, catching the few remaining fall leaves that now scraped along the driveway. She pushed herself up on one elbow and drew back from the sleeper, his face unguarded, as her brother's had once been.

Ben turned onto his side, toward Judith, pulling the blanket off his shoulder. Cold air flowed down Ben's neck and across his back. He drew up his legs against the chill, which disturbed his sleep but did not wake him. The cold reached the small of his back, and Ben curled tighter, warmer now, but not for long. The advancing cold spread across his buttocks, down his cramped legs into his feet, and he trembled, rolling back under the blanket.

Judith eased her body to the edge of the bed and slipped to her knees. Ben's forehead gleamed white above the bony ridge of his nose; his breaths came slowly. Never had Judith watched her husband so closely.

Ben was in another country, alone on a road that took him past unpainted wooden fences and one-room peasant houses. The huge, white clouds lay low over the fields. He heard the wild shouts of children lifting him into the clouds. "They are crying," the children called. "The clouds are crying." Suddenly he was back in Fairlawn, in the playground near Susan's school. Two girls pumped in the swings; higher and higher, their skirts flying up, they jumped, the heavy swings just clearing their heads. Something moved above the clipped privet, and Ben shifted his eyes without turning. A doll lay where someone had tossed her onto the top of the shrub, her bloodied head twisted on the thin broken neck, her white dress torn, a tiny, black shoe dangling from one foot; the other, blunt, toeless, bare.

"Oh," Ben moaned as he dreamed, his face turned away from Judith on her knees. He touched the blood. It was as hard and cold as a painted-on fire.

"Ben?"

"Sorry, sorry," he whimpered, as he slept, oblivious of Judith.

Believing he had spoken to her, she took his words as a gift, forgave him in his pitiful weakness. "It's all right," she whispered as she rose from her knees. Ben lay with his legs straight out, as if someone had positioned them. His eyes were sealed, and his white fingertips curled over the blanket edge, his mouth unmoving in its dark stubble. He was sound asleep. Swallowing to keep down the wave of nausea rising to her throat, Judith stood there alone in the fragile light, her feet bare, tender hope choked newborn. "Go, go," she said to herself. Her arms crossed against her chest, she clenched her fists and held herself.

"What are you doing in here?" Ben asked when he found Judith in the living room, huddled at the far end of the couch. She still wore her pajamas, and her hair was uncombed.

He was dressed for work, looking well rested, freshly shaved. "I'm talking to you," he said.

"I'm going to leave you," Judith said.

"That's a joke." His voice rose. "Where would you go? Back to your mother? She loves you so much? She wants you? Back to your lousy job?"

"I liked it. I was the first in sales."

"You? You never were good at anything. You never made a nickel."

"I made what I needed."

"You did work. I admit it. I should have let you stay there." His voice was softer. He paused. "You never loved me."

"And you? What did you ever feel for me? What do you want from me?" Judith shouted.

Ben had no answer. "Susan will hear. Look at you." Ben was frightened. "Calm down. Go fix yourself."

"You fix *your* self. You are the one who is yelling." She smoothed her hair and folded her hands.

"That's better. You can listen to me. I can see that. I have work to do. You have to remember. You have to take care of things. The child has something at school today; in the afternoon she recites from the stage. For that she needs a good dress."

Judith nodded.

"You *do* know. She comes home to change at lunch. You'll help her. It's the least you can do." Ben turned in the doorway and pointed at her, "You'll get it ready. A white dress."

BEN REACHED THE BRIDGE THAT SPANNED THE PASSAIC RIVER, flowing full and fast. Along the swollen greening banks, the silver maples—fresh, red-budded—leaned toward the black water. Sunlight shot through the back window into the rearview mirror. Ben looked away from the glare, his eyes stinging. Let her leave me, he thought. She'll never do it. The thought of divorce was intolerable to him, a shameful sign of failure. As he crossed over into Paterson, the buildings along Broadway cut off the sun; the rearview mirror cleared, revealing the familiar street.

Walking toward him, on the pavement to his left, was an old woman carrying a shopping bag in each hand: Yetta Mavet—he was sure. That round, full, fleshy face. No, it couldn't be. Yetta would never cover herself like an Italian in such deep mourning black—scarf, coat, stockings, shoes: all black. Even the rims of her glasses were black. What did they do about their undergarments? Were they all black, too? And their nightgowns? Did they cover themselves with black when they went to sleep? Stopped at the light, Ben watched as the woman stepped off the curb, her ankles and calves stick-thin beneath her heavy body. Standing a foot from the curb, she looked up and down Broadway. Ben rolled down his window: "It's OK, you have time," he said to her. Wagging her head back and forth with slow, exaggerated motions, she stepped back-ward onto the curb and put down her bundles. With her mouth open, she smiled, her face lightening in generous curves, her eyes lighting up, delirious. She smiled on, wagging her head, now clapping her bare hands together with the same deliberate slowness, as if Ben were a baby she had to amuse. What did she know about Ben Shein? Nothing.

When Ben got to Sophie Winik's, he found her with her son, Theo. Seated, the baker blocked the wall behind him, his torso nearly the length of a full-sized man. On the table in front of him, next to his wide hands, was a camera.

"Coffee you'll have," Sophie said to Ben. "He," she nodded toward her son, "brought already from the bakery rolls and bialy. What?"

"Give me a roll, a little butter."

"I told him to go home," Sophie said and put the plate in front of Ben.

"So?" Ben asked.

Sophie paused and delivered her truth in a clear voice: "He didn't."
The canary sang from the back room.

Theo stood up, the bottoms of his pants dusted with flour. He had
worked all night.

"He takes pictures," Sophie said.

"The baker?"

"Yes, this one," Sophie said.

"You take your mother?" Ben asked.

"Her face . . . I find it unusual," Theo said.

Ben pulled back his shoulders and sat up straight. He hadn't had his
picture taken since his trip to Florida with Judith. "That's a good camera
you got there," he said.

"A Leica."

"German." Ben straightened his tie. "They make the finest."

"May I?" the baker asked, raising his camera.

"Why not? But not for nothing. I'll pay you." The shutter clicked.
"I wasn't ready."

"Make believe I'm not here." The shutter clicked, clicked again. Theo
turned his camera toward his mother coming toward them, bearing the
cup of steaming coffee. "She never spills," Theo said. "Not one little drop,
not one grain of sugar." He drew his words out, making Ben forget himself.

The camera was on Ben, but he did not see it. The shutter clicked.

"Maybe you can take my daughter," Ben said.

"Maybe."

"If I like these."

SOON AFTER BEN HAD LEFT THE HOUSE IN FAIRLAWN, SUSAN GALLOPED
into the kitchen and thumped her books down on the table. She had

on the clothes she had worn the day before, her face oily and her socks dusty. Judith turned her back and tried to keep her eyes on the wall over the sink, but she could see her stepdaughter moving closer. Susan grabbed a banana from the dish on the counter, threw open the refrigerator door, grabbed for more. With the door open, she gulped milk, gasping between long swallows.

"Susan, close the door."

Her stepdaughter took another swallow, spilling milk down the front of her blouse. She pushed the bottle into the refrigerator and stood there.

"Susan, I've spoken to you. The food will spoil."

With slow exaggerated motions, Susan shut the door. Without looking at Judith, she gathered her books from the kitchen table and, holding them against her chest, ran out of the house.

Judith picked up the bowl she had filled with corn flakes for herself—now a soaked slop—lifted it high with both hands and brought it down on the sink edge. The bowl broke cleanly in half with a sharp crack that gave Judith no release. "Fucking bitch, filthy fucking bitch. Son of a bitch," she muttered. She wanted to put her hands around Susan's neck and squeeze until she stopped breathing. Her day stretched out before her, one chore after another. She took hold of her own hair and pulled. Her scalp burned, and, for a moment, the burning relieved her.

All that had happened began again inside her head. She heard, she relived, she rehearsed all the rotten things Ben had ever done to her. Deliberate in the fury of her impotence, she straightened the kitchen.

She jerked open the ironing board and unrolled the towel that held Susan's freshly washed dress, the only white dress that still fit her. The fine cambric Judith had sprinkled was still damp, ready for the iron. Judith spread the width of the bodice on the tightly padded board and, as she had been taught, started with a sleeve. She lifted the iron from its metal rest and dropped it nose-first onto the intricately puffed sleeve. Holding the iron at an angle to avoid pressing in wrinkles—right sleeve, left sleeve—she guided the iron toward the cuff. Now she pulled Susan's dress onto the board: the front of the dress lay flat, the point of the board sticking through the headless neck. The back of the skirt hung loose, grazing the floor. Steam rose from the fine cotton and with it the smell of starch and flowery soap. She had done what Ben told her, a little starch, so Susan wouldn't feel it. She slammed the heavy iron again and again onto the board. She pushed the hard point of the iron into the white lace collar.

When Judith was done, she pulled the dress off the board and smelled the underarms. Mingled with the soap was the smell of Susan's perspiration, but Judith had no time to wash the dress again. She carried it into Susan's room. She had to make the bed before she could lay the dress on the spread. She drew out the sashes so the dress made a spindly-armed cross.

From Susan's chest of drawers, Judith took out clean white socks, white underpants, and a white slip. Susan must wear the slip. She would be on the stage in the school auditorium. People would see her, see through the thin fabric, see everything she had. She would have to cover herself. Judith carried the underwear and socks to the bathroom, hung the slip on a hook on the back of the door, and placed the socks and underpants on the narrow radiator top. She pulled open the shower curtain, knelt down, and felt the bottom of the tub. The porcelain was cool and clean. Not a speck of grit. She put her hands on the edge of the tub and rested her face on her hands. The phone rang and rang in the kitchen, her mother calling, as she did every weekday morning before she went out. Judith let it ring, at first anticipating the next ring, until she no longer heard. The phone stopped.

Mechanically she unwrapped a fresh bar of soap and put it into the soap dish. She felt heavy, the inside of her head one solid mass, her eyes wood, her backbone an iron pole from which her arms and hands lifted and fell. She was all one piece and the piece was hard.

Then she prepared Susan's lunch. Under cold running water she scrubbed the potato with a stiff brown brush, stabbed it with a fork, and locked it inside the top-of-the-stove baker, pushing down hard with both hands on the tight lid. She grabbed the corner of the butcher's paper and jerked the package open until the rib lamb chop flopped on the counter. Taking the chop by the tip of the bone, she held it under the running faucet and pulled her fingers along the slippery chop to squeeze away the water. She dropped the meat onto the broiler tray.

The phone rang again. This time it would be Ben calling to give her instructions, as if she could not remember what to do. He would stand at the phone in the salon; he would worry: was the dress ready, were the shoes polished? She could hear him: it's important. The child, the child, the child. The ringing stopped, and Judith looked out the window to the tip of the maple branch—a sparrow again, the brown mark on its throat. Later she would remember that sparrow—plump, but so light: the branch did not move under its weight. She would tell herself she could have opened the door and gone out to hear it, could have walked to the river, could have let Susan come home to an empty house.

Why didn't she open the door and walk away? Or call a cab? She had enough money in her purse.

Ben can't tell you.

And neither can Susan.

Ask Jacob, Ben's grandfather. He'll smile. He'll say Judith didn't leave because the sparrow couldn't speak to her, couldn't carry her away. And if there had been a great bird with claws strong enough to lift her into the sky, Judith would have escaped, run to the house, locked herself in, and turned off the lights. It happened, Jacob will tell you, because it happened.

IN HER CLASSROOM AT MEMORIAL SCHOOL, SUSAN SAT WITH THREE OF her friends, their desks pushed into a square, where, for most of that spring, they had worked together on their Egyptian project. They had written plays about Queen Nefertiti and King Akhenaton; they had painted murals of the huge radiating sun shining on the temples of Karnak. Susan was the only one who had studied hieroglyphics. She had tried to teach the group the few signs she had learned, but they had become bored. Marley Russoff was more interested in dressing as Cleopatra, her eyes outlined in sweeping black strokes of theatrical makeup her mother had bought—an effect Susan had said was perfect. Now most of the term's work was over, and the girls sat talking.

They all would go home for lunch at eleven, instead of the usual eleven-thirty, and come back dressed in white for the pageant. Susan stopped listening. The girls' voices faded. Exhausted from lack of sleep, she put her head down on her desk and dreamed of running away, down to the river, to the tree near the bridge; of stretching out on her back in the shade and sleeping and sleeping through the afternoon, of never going back to the house in Fairlawn. But then she would miss everything: Miss French had given her a poem to recite for the pageant.

The music teacher was happy that the month of May had passed and with it the lugubrious Memorial Day observances with which the school lived up—"died up," Miss French would say—to its name. Memorial School, a memorial to the fallen soldiers of the First World War. Miss French had surrendered to the school's old guard for whom the first Great War had been the Great Experience. Their young men had died—sweethearts, brothers, cousins, friends. She had led her singing pupils through *It's a long, long trail a-winding into the land of my dreams,* yet she could not bear to see their young faces turn sad as they sang the mournful lyrics. In the lobby of the school on an iron bier was a wooden casket filled with slips of paper, each printed with the name of one of the fallen. Once a year the children were led past the casket. Susan Shein, thought Miss French, had a talent for sadness, which should not be encouraged.

Though Miss French disliked these funereal excesses, she, like all the organizers of celebrations at Memorial School, was not governed by questions of suitability. Her June pageants were strange and wild. There would be dancing. There would be tossed flowers from torn-apart bouquets. There would be songs—not hymns to the Virgin Mary, which is what the girls at St. Agnes School sang when she had been invited to their concert, but songs of love and the season of love. Those songs would make Susan Shein smile.

Miss French entered the classroom, gathering her group of twelve, leading them to the auditorium to rehearse the song that would begin the program, but she discovered she had forgotten her pitch pipe and went to get it, leaving her pupils seated in the front row of the small auditorium.

As soon as the teacher was out of the room, Marley Russoff stood up on the seat and shouted. Susan sprawled in her seat, her blouse pulled out of her skirt, one sock stretched loose around her ankle. She was tired but too excited to rest. Just as the door creaked, Marley slid down into the seat and the students sat still. "Just a moment, just a moment," Miss French chirped. "Now think sweet thoughts and soon you'll be singing."

Susan, who could not sing on key, would recite the song before the little chorus sang it—Ariel's song. She stood with the group behind her on the small stage. Her thin legs stuck out from beneath her dark green skirt. Her face was pale from lack of sleep, and there were blue smudges under her eyes. Miss French led Susan as if Susan were singing. "Don't *pounce* on the rhymes: read on through the end of the line," Miss French had told her. Now Susan followed her teacher's advice. Speaking lightly, she took care not to emphasize the rhyming words:

> Where the bee sucks; there suck I
> In a cowslip's bell I lie;
> There I couch when owls do cry.
> On the bat's back I do fly
> After summer merrily.
> Merrily, merrily shall I live now
> Under the blossom that hangs on the bough.

Upon the instant Susan breathed out "bough," Miss French raised her hands. They began: "Where the bee sucks; there suck I . . ."

Marley swayed. Dennis Fazio rubbed the toe of his shoe against the inside of his ankle. Susan, nervous and excited, wanted to move her hands, to shift her feet. She stopped herself. She held her hands together at her waist and heard Marley's voice above the rest—"Merrily, merrily shall I live now."

"The best yet," Miss French said when they had finished. "You may not sing as well this afternoon. It doesn't matter."

SUSAN AND MARLEY LINGERED AT THE EDGE OF THE PLAYGROUND. IT was a little after eleven. The air was warm, and the sky above the maple trees that bordered the schoolyard was a transparent blue. Thin clouds drifted above the river as if someone were pulling a veil across the sky. The veil kept tangling. Susan took a few steps away from her friend and began to walk down the street that would take her home. She stopped, called Marley's name, and ran back to her. "It'll be OK," said Marley, reaching out her arms. Susan pressed her head against Marley's shoulder. A sob rose in her throat. "Don't," Marley whispered. She held her until Susan pulled away.

"Good bye," Susan called as she ran to get her white dress.

A flock of sparrows pecked in the grass under the tree near the front walk of the house on Fourth Street. At the sound of Susan's step, they flew off.

She walked to the back of the house and into the kitchen, where Judith had set a place for her at the table. There was a napkin on the left, folded in a triangle. The knife and fork, perpendicular to the table edge, marked an empty space. "Don't want it, don't need it," Susan crowed, shaking her head.

Judith turned from the sink, a knife in her hand. The kitchen was hot from the gas broiler, where a chop sizzled as fat dropped into the pan, and from the top-of-the-stove oven that held the potato under its dome.

Susan leaned over the table, upsetting the arrangement as she opened the window. "I'm not hungry."

Judith's face was wet. "You have to eat. I made it. It's ready."

"I have a performance. I can't eat."

"The pageant is later," Judith said. She thrust the knife at Susan. "You will have digested your lunch by then."

"No, I don't want it," Susan said. "I can't eat it. You can't make me." She twirled as she ran out of the kitchen, one sock loose around her ankle, her hair swinging. "Don't want it. Don't need it. Don't need it. Don't want it," she sang in a high, nervous voice.

Judith turned off the broiler; the chop went on sizzling. The spinach was still in the colander. She grabbed the leaves and crushed them. Flinging the spinach into the sink, she slammed down the colander. Her scalp was wet, her face burning hot.

Susan was at the door, in the white dress, her hair loose, her feet bare. Judith could see everything through the thin handkerchief cotton—the pink, swelling nipples, the line of the waistband of Susan's underpants.

"You have to wear a slip," Judith said.

"It's too warm."

"You have to. People can see every piece of you."

"A piece of this, a piece of that. *A-tisket a-tasket. A green and yellow basket.* Susan twirled in her bare feet. *I dropped it, I dropped it.*" There was a smell of charred lamb's fat.

"You will take a bath. I drew it for you. I scrubbed the tub. Your father wants you to take a bath," Judith said.

"My father? My father talked to you about my bath?" Susan laughed, her mouth wide open.

"You think you can do anything you want," Judith said.

"It's a free country."

"First you will take a bath. Then you will get dressed."

"First I will put on my socks and then I will leave. I want my white socks."

"I have them. I washed them." Judith walked into the bathroom. "Here they are. Here I am."

Susan followed her.

Judith knelt at the tub; her hand in the water, the tub half full, she stirred, making ripples, breaking up the surfaces that reflected the pink of the tiled walls.

"Just give me the socks," Susan said.

"You have to take a bath before you put on that clean dress. You are dirty. You have to wash yourself. Then you will put on clean underwear and socks. You will put on a slip so everyone won't see through your dress. The bath will cool you off," Judith said.

"I don't want to." Susan spaced out her words, spat the *t*'s. "You should take a bath. *You* are sweating," she said.

"You will do what I say," Judith said.

"You are not my mother."

Judith held the oval cake of new soap, its sugary smell filling the small room. She slammed down the soap on the edge of the tub. The soap slid, sank into the pink water. "You'll do what I say."

"No."

"I'll kill you," Judith screamed.

"You're crazy," Susan laughed.

"Don't you say that to me."

"You are. You're crazy. Crazy," Susan said.

Judith lurched to her feet and swung. She knocked Susan backward.

Susan banged into the half-opened door; the knob caught her in the back. Still on her knees, Judith lunged. "I'll take a piece out of you. You and your filthy father." She grabbed hold of Susan's white dress. She reached higher and hooked her fingers inside the collar and pulled.

Susan tried to pry off Judith's hand. "Don't, don't," she cried.

Judith pulled again and Susan's head jerked forward, slammed against Judith's hard shoulder. The thin cotton tore down to the waist, exposing Susan's chest, her small breasts. "You'll take this bath," Judith screamed, "if it's the last thing you do." With her left hand knotted in Susan's hair, she lifted her and plunged her into the tepid water. "Yes, you will," she screamed. "You'll wash under your arms and down there."

Susan tried to lift herself. She was on her back. Now with all her fury, Judith bore down on her, her hand against Susan's throat as she pushed her under. "You will, you will, you will," she said.

Susan could not hear her. Her head under water, she saw Judith's wild face above her, the bared teeth. Susan bent her legs to push herself up against the side of the tub and managed to grab Judith's hair. She tried to pull. To pull herself up. She kept slipping. She felt Judith's hand now on her stomach as Judith in her frenzy pushed the child up and down like a plunger.

Susan gasped, sucked, fought for air.

Judith tried to bang Susan's head against the bottom of the tub. The water impeded her. She couldn't push Susan down far enough. "I'll kill you," she gasped.

Susan's head broke the surface. She breathed in once before Judith drove her under. Bubbles of air broke from Susan's mouth.

Judith held her under. She felt Susan's body go limp. She did not release her. Susan floated, unconscious, her hair spread around her head, her eyes open. Her hair moved with the water, a violet bruise under her right eye.

Judith turned Susan over to cover her, folded her into the water, face down, one hand on her back, the other under her stomach, like a swimming instructor. She moved her hands to the back of Susan's neck, under the floating hair. As she leaned against the tub, her wild breathing slowed. With one hand she pushed back her own wet hair. Judith sat like this beside the dead child until she felt the water grow cold against her hand.

She staggered as she rose and looked down at Susan. She'll catch cold, she thought. She began to moan. She lifted her hands. "Oh, no," she called out. "Oh, no. No," as if she could turn things back. She ran from the bathroom and then from room to room. "God in heaven, help me," she moaned, as she slowed down, now swaying, swaying as she walked.

Wrapping her arms around her chest, she flung her head from side to side. Wave after wave of nausea rose from her stomach. Dizzy, Judith gripped the chairs, which slid away from her.

She was not alone for long. A neighbor, Ceil Roses, came from next door, rang the bell, an egg in one hand, a replacement for the one she had borrowed the morning before.

Judith pulled open the door and grabbed her neighbor's arm while Ceil struggled to hold on to the egg that lay in her hand. The pattern of violets printed on Ceil's housedress broke up, twitched, jumped in Judith's eyes.

"Don't come in." Judith pitched forward, her hands on her neighbor's shoulders. "We'll go to your house. We'll go there."

While Judith raved, Ceil called Doktor.

David Doktor swung his black-leather-shod feet onto the curb. His heavy black bag, which he had hoisted from the passenger seat with one hand, threatened to unbalance him.

Judith ran toward him, down the front walk of Ceil's house.

"What is it?" he said.

"I did a terrible thing. Oh God, I did a terrible thing. I did it," Judith said.

"What? What?" Doktor asked.

"Run!" she screamed.

Doktor lifted Susan from the cold water. The water dripped off her onto the floor, onto his shoes, as he lay her, face down, on the bath mat and knelt on the wet floor. The water wet his knees. For an hour Doktor pressed down on Susan's bare cold back, lifted her bent arms, pressed down on her bare back, lifted her arms, back and forth. He cupped Susan's head in his small hand. "Enough," he finally said to himself. "You'll hurt her." This last statement made no sense. Susan Shein was dead.

ON THE MORNING OF SUSAN'S FUNERAL, BRONA PLEADED WITH BEN, "At least drink something. Say something. You don't say anything."

"I said enough. I talked too much." He held up both hands and pushed against the air, pushed her away.

Ben spread out his dark gray suit jacket on the bed of his boyhood room on Manor Street. Grasping the jacket at the right angles made by the bottom hem and the front facings, he flung open the jacket so it made a triangle revealing the silky lining.

His feet were bare, and he wore only his boxer shorts, which now hung loosely around his waist. He hadn't eaten. His throat was dry.

I'm the one who should die, he thought. I picked a wife for myself, I found the right one to pick on. In his right hand he held a one-sided razor blade. This time he would not leave it to the rabbi. Pressing his left hand down on the lining just under the inside breast pocket, he slashed a rent the length of the span between his index finger and thumb. Using his hand like a ruler, he slashed again. He repeated the motions on the button side. The silky fabric yielded under Ben's expert fingers. There was no sound of tearing. Now he turned the jacket right side out and slashed again, this time a straight cut across the right lapel.

He turned his hands up and saw the blue veins bunched at the wrists. Angling the blade, he scraped it against his skin, over the veins, but he could not cut himself.

Ben's face loosened. The cheek muscles sagged. His ears throbbed as if he had been slapped hard across the face. "Why did I ever start with her?" he cried. He put his shaking hands to his face and sobbed like a child.

THE MOURNERS WHO CARRIED UMBRELLAS TO PASSAIC JUNCTION Cemetery didn't need them. The long, soaking rain that had fallen all night had stopped. By three o'clock the tombstones that surrounded Susan's grave had dried. But the narrow, rutted drive was still wet, and deep puddles reflected blue in the sunken road. The approaching cars moved so slowly there was no splash, only a sucking sound from the tires rolling through muddy puddles.

No graveside decorum constrained the mourners. They broke from their cars, leaving the doors open. Joan Englander ran, pulling her mother by the hand. The mourners rushed and halted.

A few people walked slowly—among them, Sophie Winik. She had rooted around in the back of her closet and found an old black toque that had belonged to her mother. The hat sat squarely on Sophie's large head, her thick white hair hanging down straight like a medieval knight's. She had an angry expression on her broad face, as if she had lost a battle. She gripped a furled black umbrella.

A rushing moan came from the mourners and rose to a fierce wail. "No," they called out at the sight of the bare wooden box that held Susan's body. The crude pine coffin hung at the lip of the raw grave, directly in front of her mother's tombstone, high and white in the June sun: *Tess Shein, Beloved.*

Ben threw himself on the mound of damp earth next to the hole in the ground. He pressed his face into the dirt while Nat crouched over him as if he were shielding him from bullets. When he lifted Ben to his knees, Ben's mouth was ringed with dirt.

He stood at the edge of Susan's grave, covered his eyes with his arm, and rocked forward. Nat caught him, held him until Ben sank against his brother and his head rolled into the hollow between Nat's neck and his shoulder. Ben sobbed. "No," he moaned.

A broken chorus of no's rose from the crowd.

Brona, her black veil lifted, her white face bare of makeup, saw and heard. There were her sons, but she couldn't take them in. They seemed like dark shapes ripped from a distant fabric and flung to beat and whip on the small patch of ground that heaved under her feet. She let go and swayed, her motion nearly imperceptible. She closed her eyes, and, wordless, she heard amidst the rushing moan, her own difficult breathing. Her heart swelled, and she thought she would never recover. She felt something pressing painfully against the ball of her foot and wiggled her toes, shifting the stone that dug into her foot. Standing on one leg, she reached down, took off her shoe, and shook out the stone. She lost her balance and was saved from toppling over by Renee Goldring's quick action. Grabbing Brona by the arm, Renee pulled her against her. Brona gave in and rocked against her daughter-in-law. Jeannette stood on her other side. Now Brona cried out and went to her, to her open arms.

That night Jeannette said to her husband, "They say coloreds carry on. My God, you should have seen them. Pitiful Sheins."

If Rabbi Monte Gelfand had raised his left hand and swung it a hand's breadth to his left, he would have touched Tess's gravestone. Between his straight, slim, dark-clad body and the white stone that marked Tess's grave, there was a strip of white light—as if the corner of a box had come apart to let light in. He waited. He wanted to reach out, to lean, but he kept his trembling hands at his sides. An hour before, at the new funeral home in Paterson, he had stood in the pulpit, looking down at Susan's coffin. Susan of Blessed Memory. His words had sounded hollow and wooden in his ears. Now he felt relieved to exhort the mourners. He urged them on to the Kaddish; he soothed as he recited, offering hope: "May the memory of the righteous be a blessing. May the memory of Susan Shein be a blessing."

Then he joined his voice with all the others.

Yis'gadal v'yis kadash sh'me raba. Amen.
B'alma di v'ra chir'ute.

"What are they saying?" Joan Englander asked her mother.

"They are praising God. They are blessing Him."

Joan listened to the rapid, low chanting. She heard the sob and spit.

They were cursing God. They were moaning out their sorrow. In praise. In despair. In anger. In praise. In greatness. In dirt. In the small grave.

The coffin dropped, tilted on the coarse ropes.

Joan saw the angle of the coffin slanting earthward, pointing to the hole in the ground where Susan would lie. Joan too would die; so would they all.

The sun was hot. It beat down on the mourners and on the tombstones.

"Gottenyu!" an old woman called out. Her old black dress had turned a reddish-brown. Her white hair had come undone and stuck out around her face. She lifted her arms and pressed her hands together, palms touching; the large umbrella hooked around her wrist threatened to drag down her arm.

Joan sobbed. She let go of her mother's hand and rubbed her eyes with her fists. Her back was wet with sweat. She reached up, sliding her hand between her shoulder blades and pulled her dress and slip away from her hot skin. Through an opening in the crowd she saw the stone wall that bordered the west side of the cemetery. A white and butterscotch cat stretched in the narrow strip of shade at the base of the west wall. The cat lay on its side, so that Joan could see the curve of its belly. The cat stretched out its paws as if it had found something to push its soft-padded paws against.

Yis'barach v'yish' tabah v'yis pa'ar
Y'yis'roman v'yis nase v'yis'hadar
V'yis'ale v'yis'halla?
Sh'me d'kud'sha, b'rich Hu . . .

Blessed and praised and glorified,
And exalted and extolled and honored,
And magnified and lauded
Be the name of the Holy One, blessed be He . . .

In the shade of the cemetery wall, the cat curled on its side and slept.

IT WAS THE NIGHT OF THE THIRD DAY OF MOURNING AT THE HOUSE ON Manor Street, where the Sheins would sit shivah for the seven prescribed days. Shaggy, unshaven, unbarbered, Ben Shein and his brother sat on the hard, low wooden boxes, which Jeannette the housekeeper had brought home from the grocer's to serve as mourners' benches. Trained by the orthodox family she had once worked for, Jeannette had also boiled eggs for the funeral meal and shrouded every mirror in the house with white sheets. She had even exceeded orthodox practice. If the Bible said Abraham had covered himself with sackcloth, so would the Sheins. Down south, where she had been born and where her grandmother still lived, Jeannette would have found sackcloth—sugar sacks, flour sacks. Clothes for the poorest of the poor stitched out of sackcloth, mourning cloth. That fit, yes it did. Dirt poor, sackcloth poor. Poor Sheins. Grieving poor. Sackcloth scratched the skin, made you remember how sorry and poor you were. In Paterson she had to settle for unbleached muslin. Brona, too weary to protest, had taken the cloth and put it away, but Nat wore it instead of a talis, the traditional prayer shawl. The plain cloth covered his head, his pajamas, the stiff folds falling over his shoulders, just reaching his knees.

Ben still wore his funeral jacket, the slashed lapel drooping forward, the slashed lining hanging like a fringe. A sour, stale smell came off him. Although the rules of mourning allowed the minimum ablutions necessary for hygiene, Ben had not washed himself at all since his return from the funeral, when, before entering the house, he had poured the ritual water over his hands from the pitcher Jeannette had left near the back door. The cool water had trickled down the steps and across the walk. He had shaken the water from his hands, refusing the towel Brona had held out for him.

One by one, the Sheins had washed their hands. "As if this is going to help," Rose Goldring had muttered to her daughter Renee. "You should be home. You're a pregnant woman." Renee had answered, "I'm staying with my husband." Rose Goldring had put her convictions aside and bent, the last in line to wash her hands.

On this night, Nat had heard Ben get up from the bed they were sharing in Ben's old room and had followed him downstairs, where Nat took some food from the refrigerator. The brothers sat in the living room; Nat with a meager plate of food in his lap, leftovers from the meatless meal that had been spread out on the dining room table after Susan Shein had been put into the ground. The bagel, because of its position at the bottom of the pile, had escaped the fine sprinkling of ashes Jeannette had dropped onto the platter in yet another mourning ritual. She had dug the ashes out of the wood fire she had kindled in the backyard pit her husband had cut out of the matted turf. Though she had raked the fire toward the center, the flames had scorched the new grass at the edges. "This is crazy," her husband had said to her. "More work for you. Why you do it? More work for *me*?" She had answered, "Somebody got to. Murder in this house. They acting like dead people theyselves." Nat ate a few spoonfuls of lentils and regarded the hard-boiled egg—white, shiny, bare. He split the egg, breaking the pale yellow yolk in two.

The egg was dry in Nat's mouth. "Let's have a drink," he said to his brother.

Ben did not move.

"You'll have something."

Ben shook his head.

"You'll come with me into the kitchen."

Ben closed his eyes. He seemed hardly to breathe.

Taking him under the arm, Nat guided him to his feet. The cloth fell from Nat's head, slipped from his shoulder, and he pulled it up, so that it partially obscured his face.

"Why are you wearing that rag?" Ben asked.

Nat shrugged, his broad shoulders falling, rolling forward.

"You're religious?"

"What do I know about religion?" Nat answered.

Outside on Manor Street the crows sent their wild cries into the darkness that would soon retreat.

The brothers stood facing each other. "If I could take my heart out of my body and cut it into pieces until it stopped beating, I would," Ben said.

"No. A man has to live."

"I'm a dead man."

"Come," Nat said. Taking Ben by the hand, he led him to the kitchen. The large seven-day candle burned white in its holder on top of a tin pie plate. "Jeannette's the good Jew, not me. She got it. Ma lit it. Me? I don't know what to do," Nat said and reached for the bottle of rye in the pantry. "I don't know what to do," he repeated, drawing his hand back.

At the sound of his brother's voice, Ben began to cry, choked back his tears. Nothing could be worse than this horror. How could such things happen? He wasn't even a big shot. He was Ben Shein. "I'll kill her. I'll take a gun and I'll kill her. You'll get me a gun. You know where to get it," Ben said.

Nat opened his arms.

"She should lie in the ground like—" Ben stopped: he couldn't say his daughter's name.

Their grandfather Jacob would have known what to say: 'Susan of blessed memory.' Never once had Jacob mentioned the dead without pronouncing the words, whether he believed them or not. The dead were dead, Ben thought. Never to breathe again. They had gone down to the pit from which no one had ever come back, not the Messiah, not one fly, not one little cat, not one baby, not one mother or father, not even the holy ones. The goyim were still waiting for Jesus—that's what Jeannette said—but they really weren't waiting: they were remembering, like good Jews. Jesus of blessed memory. And He hadn't sent them a word from the pit. But the living could speak. The words had been made for the living.

"Come on," Nat cried, his arms sagging.

"Let me kill her, let me," Ben begged, as if his brother could grant him his desire. "I'll do it."

"It's over," Nat said.

"Over? It'll never be over."

"Susan's dead." Nat had meant to comfort.

"Don't you say that," Ben screamed. He ripped the muslin from Nat's shoulders and tore at it. The tight selvage stopped him, and he fumbled for the cut edge.

"Give it to me," Nat said.

Ben held on to the cloth.

Nat gripped Ben's wrist and pried the material out of his hand. Facing his brother, he drew the material over his own head, covering the side of his face, as if he were a mirror that needed to be shrouded.

"What are you?" Ben asked.

"I'm your brother."

"Brother?" Ben shouted, beating his fists against his own head.

The long-necked bottle of rye stood on counter, amber and gold as honey. Leave it, Nat thought. Leave it.

Ben lurched toward the window. The sun had risen. He struck himself again, above the eye. His heart banged in his chest, jumped, danced. His heart would burst, and he would be finished. He would fall on his knees, his eyes would close, and he would go down to the pit.

"Ben," Nat whispered as he took his brother by the shoulders and turned him. "What are you doing?"

"I'm standing."

Nat pressed two fingers above Ben's eye, pressed hard against the skin, against the bone, to keep the swelling down.

His fingers can't go through, Ben thought, the proof of the hardness of his skull under his brother's hand.

Holding his brother by the arm, Nat opened the back door, letting in the warm morning air, warmer than inside.

The wind rose, stirring the air, raising with it the smell of ashes and must. There was nothing to say.

Ben let himself be led outside. A board had come loose at one end of the bottom step, pulling a rusty nail out of its hole.

Under the maple tree, winged ants swarmed over the deep, damp leaf mold—pale wing over pale wing; long, narrow body over long, narrow body, dark as soil. They had appeared without a sound. Ben went down the steps ahead of his brother. The ants spread out, the dirty lace of their wings, their stiff trains seeming to grow as Ben watched them.

"Bugs," Nat said. "Come inside."

"Where else can I go?"

Sophie Winik and her son, Theo, were among the visitors who came to the Shein house the week after the funeral. They arrived on the sixth day and followed Jeannette directly to the kitchen, where they put down their offerings: fresh black bread and a bottle of colorless eau-de-vie, distilled from purple plums.

"I'll put this away," Jeannette said as she took the bottle from Theo.

"Put it out, people might want. It's better than morphine from the doctor," Sophie said.

"No liquor," Jeannette said.

"Since when are the Sheins religious? Open the bottle. It wouldn't hurt nobody," Sophie said.

"You want liquor, you open it," Jeannette told her.

Sophie took the bottle. "We're not the family," she said. Scraping back the tight, binding seal, she pulled out the cork and poured a little of the colorless liquid into three wide-bottomed tumblers—so little that the plum liquor barely covered the bottom. "*Une larme*, a tear," Sophie said, holding out a glass for Jeannette.

"No, not for me. You go ahead," Jeannette said.

Sophie and Theo swallowed quickly, exhaled together, closed their mouths over their heated tongues.

In that brief moment the cork had swelled, and Theo had to push hard to get it back into the bottle.

"You'll see them," Jeannette said. "You'll see them all." Leading the Winiks, she went first from the kitchen into the dining room, past the shrouded mirror over the buffet, into the living room. How thin the sons looked, their hair growing over their ears, their beards thick, high on their white cheekbones. Ben rocked back and forth, his eyes closed. "Who is here?" Nat asked his mother as he adjusted the muslin rag over his head. Brona, her cheek red, still creased from the imprint of her pillow, motioned toward Sophie and Theo, who had just come through the door with Jeannette. As was customary, neither Winik spoke. They would take a drink in the house of the dead, but never would they speak first to a mourner. Besides, what could you say, "I'm sorry"? How sorry could they be compared to the father and the grandmother and the uncle, who had to sit there on the small stage their living room had become, the dead child in the box in the ground, while the visitors to the house on Manor Street watched the Sheins' faces and waited for them to speak first?

Though none of the Sheins were tall, their knees stuck up waist high, so low were the boxes. The wood was hard against their sitting bones. All of them wore the cracked, battered felt slippers Jeannette had brought down from the attic.

"Winik," Nat said.

"You remember," Sophie answered, but said no more.

People began arriving. First Yetta Mavet, her face still fleshy and full, wearing the second-hand suit Brona had given her; Marley Russoff's mother (but not Marley, who had not been allowed to attend the funeral); Jeannette's husband, with his hat on and a resigned expression; a few customers from the store; and finally Mary Elizabeth Moore, the art teacher. Their seats formed a little theater from which they watched the mourners. "I'm so sorry," Mary Elizabeth Moore said, rising from her seat between Sophie and Yetta Mavet, her hand extended.

Ben Shein opened his eyes and put his hands behind his back.

"You don't touch them," Sophie whispered, taking the teacher's arm and guiding her back to her chair, while the visitors regarded them. Sophie put her finger to her lips and turned her head back and forth, right to left and back again.

"Her teacher," Nat said.

"Art," Ben added.

"An art teacher." Yetta linked the two words.

Brona scanned the faces and found her lines, written long before she was born. "A sheyne meydel," she said.

Yetta whispered into Mary Elizabeth Moore's ear, "A beautiful girl, a maid."

Mary Elizabeth trembled.

"And she was good," Brona said.

"And you know what good is," Yetta said.

Brona's head tilted forward and back. "So good was she."

"A sweet, good girl," Yetta said.

Brona broke the form, "A sweet, wild girl."

Ben covered his eyes.

The visitors began whispering among themselves:

"It's cold for May."

"But not so cold."

"How is your brother?"

"My legs pain me."

Ben Shein rose from his seat, opened his eyes, spread his arms, and turned around step by step—as if a tailor knelt at his feet and pinned up the hem of his trousers.

"This is what a person comes to," Sophie Winik whispered to the art teacher, her voice so low Mary Elizabeth Moore could not make out the words.

"PICTURES," BEN SAID JUST TWO MONTHS AFTER THE FUNERAL, AS HE opened the envelope from Theo Winik, which Brona had handed to him.

Her face was powdered and rouged, her lips painted, her hair newly cut in the old bob, but she wore no jewelry. Bare of stones, her earlobes were shockingly naked. "What kind of pictures?" she asked.

"Of me."

"How do pictures come from him?"

"He took me. Before," Ben said and contemplated time locked into *before* and *after*. Between those seeming absolutes there was nothing.

"You're coming in to the shop?" Brona asked.

"You'll see me," he said. He hadn't been able to return to work.

"Better you should," she said.

"Better?"

When she left him, Ben slipped the pictures out of the envelope, staring at the top photograph, which at first he could not recognize. At last he made out the interior of the Winiks' store, taken from an angle he had never seen. Theo had shot from the back room through a series of doors, so that the store itself had become small, lit at one end by the window.

The light of that lost day was gone, never mind what the picture told him. He thought of the thin, reedy voices that had come out of the Victrola his grandfather had played. Back then, the singers had still been alive, but recorded they sounded like ghosts. There was no afterlife, so men made one. If Susan came back, she would sound like the voices on those records. Ben slid his hand over the glossy black and whites and saw his face, clean-shaven yet shadowed, a fleeting smile, a hidden shyness. He could not go back and change the day. And if he could, what would he change? All his crowded days spread out behind him—and Tess's days, her life and her death. "I didn't do it," he said to himself. He hadn't killed Tess. If only she hadn't died. Instead of her, better it was that an animal died under the knife, its throat cut. What was he saying? All those slaughtered creatures could not buy back Tess's life or Susan's.

Long before dawn he woke in his mother's quiet house. The August heat had gotten into the room, but although Ben was sweating, he did not throw the blanket off. Moisture covered his skin, coating him like sweat on a rock. He lay in the dark, empty for an instant, until he remembered.

"I have no strength, but I have to go," he said to himself as he sat up and swung his legs to the floor. The room was dark, not even the first weak light outlining the shades. Now he was on his feet, but weightless, insubstantial. He took a step and did not fall. Another step. Maybe he could get to work. He moved in the dark, feeling for the doorknob; he was wide of the mark. "Where is it?" he asked himself and finally found the knob. The walls of the upstairs hall were invisible in the darkness. He could have been on a catwalk. He found the bathroom, his hands on the sink, his feet on the hard tile. Feet, hands—nothing in between except the urge to pish. That he could do, feeling his way, sitting on the seat like a woman.

Ben opened his closet where his suits were lined up, the shoulders pointing at him. He picked one without thinking, but it was the right one, a lightweight gray, the finest worsted, almost as light as cotton. Worsted—it could keep a line better than cotton. I should put it on, he thought, but I'm so slow. What goes first? He tried to remember. Socks. He drew them on—black. His feet secured, he could find his underwear. He couldn't stand naked. He had to uncover a part of his body and then cover it—pajama top off, undershirt on; pajama bottom off, boxer shorts on. They hung on his thin hips. There wasn't enough air in the room. Ben put his hand across his throat and drew in a long breath. He cracked the paper that banded his shirt and unfolded the garment from the cardboard. The cotton was stiff from the laundry. Brona now sent his shirts out to save Jeannette work. The starched collar cut into his throat. Leaving his collar open, he rolled up his tie and placed it in his pocket. Though he cinched his belt at the tightest hole, his pants still hung on him. He'd put the tie on in the shop. No one would see him: it was too early.

Ben stepped from the August heat that had collected in the house into the cooler air of the street. He went down Broadway, past Tenth Avenue, the Kargers' street. How could the street still be there? How could a Karger be there? But they *were*—Estelle and the daughter, with a nurse to help take care of Judith. She had been bailed out to the custody of her mother until the trial. The charge of first-degree murder had been reduced, the doctors claiming Judith was insane. Ben wanted her dead. Let them kill her. Hang her. Did they hang now? No, they electrocuted. The thought of the electric current shooting through Judith's body sent charges into his legs, shooting up into his bowels, where they stung, cracked, and made him sick. But Judith would not be killed. She would go on living—like him.

"At least I can walk," he said to himself. The current was in him like a fever. He went past Summer Street, past Auburn—still dark—and took a shortcut on Church. "I'll go in to work," he said to himself as he came to Ellison, but he did not cross the street to his shop. What was he going to do there? There was nothing to do. He walked past the Shein salon, kept on, down the old way south toward McBride Avenue. Ahead of him, light came through the low cloud cover swollen across the sky, the clouds stretched and bowed. He couldn't tell whether the clouds were coming or going. Had it rained or was it going to rain?

Ben crossed Mill Street, where the old mills had been cut up into family shops, cockroach shops, greenhorns on the looms, dyers dipping the silk: you could have it. At least the fur was quiet—once Ben got it. The looms banged. Soon it would start—the whack. Banging with the silk. But the silk was shot. More business for dyers than weavers.

His feet found their way, the old way up toward the Falls, into the roar. It *had* rained. So what? Ben thought. Every time it rains it roars. McBride rose—Ben's breath coming hard now. Panting, he stopped on the ascending curve of the street to catch his breath. Ben could see the Falls. His heart slowed and he could go on.

He found the path, the footbridge—from the distance like a piece of lace—locked in its cage, closed to the public. Who walked there? The luggers from the electric plant. The path branched, and Ben took it, climbing from the electric plant to a rust-red ledge, where he crouched on soft stone above the Falls. The roar filled his head. Ben opened his mouth, and the pressure in his head eased. He got on his knees and sat down. Weeds grew in the cracks, choked and living. A bird dropped from an invisible shelf, diving into the spray. Ben didn't want to see the bottom: he crawled backward, his hands on the red shale, back, back, until he reached a scoured-out depression in the ledge where soil had collected and weeds crowded in. The light was brighter now inside the bowed clouds. There was heat. But not too much. Ben lay down in the weeds on his back in the depression, loosened his belt, and closed his eyes. No one could see him. The roar was in him, his scalp tightening around the noise in his head.

All day he lay as the clouds dissolved into fog. Moisture coated his hands and face, furred on his worsted. He sat up in the gray light and rocked forward on to his hands and knees. Cold metal pressed into his palms—coins that must have slid from his pockets—money for a paper, maybe a shoeshine, not for him, not today. But he picked up a few of the coins and went back to McBride, the roar of the Falls diminishing as he walked back toward home. But he did not go home. He wandered the city until he was sure Brona would be in her room when he came home. She didn't fool him. He knew what was behind her closed door: clothes for the baby—Nat's son, Joel. "Don't bring him here," Ben had said.

JOEL OPENED HIS MOUTH. HERE IT COMES, THOUGHT NAT. THE BABY mewed. The scream was on the way. Nat picked him up: there was no scream. Nat held Joel tucked against his side like a football, the baby's head in Nat's hand. There wasn't much to him—a crapper with tiny hands. But what a pair of lungs: the kid could scream. Joel whimpered, and Nat brought him to his chest, the baby's hot head under Nat's chin, the little puff of breath, the smell of milk. Taking care not to wake Renee, Nat walked with a light step, stretching the time between feedings, giving his wife a few more minutes. Her skin—pale gold when she was rested—was sallow: she was tired. Joel's body tightened as he tried to lift his head away from his father. Nat spread his fingers across his son's back and moved his hand in a circular movement with only as much force as it took to shift the surface—just barely. The infant's skin moved under Nat's hand, and Joel was quiet for a moment. Nat ran his index finger across the back of his son's neck, in the soft crease, but again the baby tried to lift his head. This time he got his face away from his father's neck and let out a cry. "All right, all right," Nat said.

Renee groaned as she opened her eyes, her hair snarled against the pillow. "What time is it?"

"Early," he said.

"Too bad you don't have milk in *your* breasts. Give him to me," Renee said. She cupped her breast, guiding the baby to her hard nipple held between her index and middle finger. Settled against her, the baby sucked, while Renee reached for her book with her free hand.

Nat turned on the bedside lamp. "I have something for you."

"I'm busy."

He went to his side of the bed and pulled out a bottle and opener from the middle drawer of the chest at his bedside. "Stout. The real stuff, from Ireland."

"I haven't eaten breakfast yet."

"Suck on this," Nat said and opened the bottle.

"Stout, the mother's friend," Renee said. She put down her book and took a swig from the bottle.

"How is it?" Nat asked.

"I like it," she answered.

"You'll come back when you're done with him," Nat said. He threw his chin toward the baby.

"Done?" She gave him that look: her sour and sweet eyes bit. "We'll never be done, not any of us." She picked up her book.

A long white envelope lay on the floor near the door. Nat gripped the knob, pulling so hard he could feel the disturbed air hit his face. There was no one in the hall. With the door open, his back to his wife, Nat bent down and picked up the mail. The white envelope lay on his palm—no return address, the postmark Paterson. "Must be from my brother," Nat said as he closed the door.

Renee turned her book onto its face, Joel quiet against her.

"My brother—I can't help him."

"Whatever you do," Renee said.

"I get it wrong," Nat answered. At the window, he held the envelope up to the light, turning it this way and that. "I never get mail." His name seemed strange in the black print: *Nathan Shein.*

Using Renee's nail file, he neatly sawed open the envelope and unfolded the stiff paper: "Dear Mr. Shein," the letter began. "My daughter has asked me to contact you. Though I cannot agree with her desire to see you, I have, because of her fragile condition, agreed to write to you. Judith wishes you to know she has certain things that belonged to your niece and which she would like to give you." Under the typed message, Estelle Karger had written her name in ink.

"It's from the mother," Nat said.

"The mother?"

"A mother of a killer can write a letter." What was it like over there, the two of them on Tenth Avenue? "Do you want to see it?" he asked Renee.

"Not now." She drew the blanket away and lifted the baby, rubbing his back. "He's wet. Everything. The 'waterproof' pants leak. I should have changed him before I fed him."

"Why make him wait more?" Nat bent down to the bottom shelves of the bassinet and picked out a clean diaper, undershirt, and blanket. Joel lay naked across Renee's lap, her hand spread across his chest and stomach, her wrist over the little prick, his eyes half open—thin strips of light between thick lashes, his hair scruffy dark gold. "Give me," Nat said. Renee handed Nat the small wet clothes, and Nat placed the dry changes next to her.

Joel turned his head toward the light coming through the window, his violet eyes open. The color wasn't set yet. "That violet, all babies have it; they all turn toward the light," Brona had told Nat. She was right. But did they see? Brona had said no.

Renee pulled out the open diaper pin she had stuck into the pillow.

"Don't hurt him," Nat said, before he could stop himself.

Nat called Lillian Tondow for advice. "Don't go," she said. "It could make her look good."

"Look good?"

"A Shein brother, the uncle, goes to see her; then she can't be all bad," Lillian said.

"No one's going to take my word for anything. I'm the bad guy, the bootlegger."

"You're a married man with a child, and you have no record," she said.

"What could she have?"

"It's always a surprise. If you want to go, get a lawyer."

"You know the law."

"Yes, and I told you."

"I want to see," Nat said.

"If that is really what you want, let me go with you. If they don't accept it, don't go. And don't write anything. Call them."

"I took these from her," Judith said to Nat, as Lillian Tondow watched her, the brim of Lillian's hat too narrow to hide her wide face. Judith held her hands over the collection of objects arranged on the tea table in front of her. Her mother at her side, Judith stared at her own long-fingered hands, unmarked, young, the veins hidden deep under the flesh, the closely cut nails childish and blunt. "I stole," Judith said.

"Judith, please," her mother said. "Mr. Shein, I never saw these things."

"Let her," Nat said. "No one can see us."

"I can see," Judith said as she scrutinized Nat Shein's face. Now that he had lost weight, he looked more like his brother, his face impassive, the scar high up close to his hairline like a tiny, closed eye, shrunken, hard. "Look, I'll show you," Judith said. She tried to keep her hands from shaking, but they fluttered over the pitiful things she had taken from her step-daughter—a single penny encrusted with green oxide, the stub of a pencil, a tiny safety pin, a bit of broken green glass, an empty wooden spool, a needle threaded with red cotton, the halves of a black button, a tiny piece of paper stuck with lint. Judith picked up the paper: "I stole it from her pocket." She plucked at the paper, unfolded it, crumpled it again.

"You took these from no one," Nat answered.

"I did. I know how to tell the truth. You can give them to your brother. I know how much he loved her. I took the hair from her head." Judith pulled at her own hair.

"Don't do that," her mother said and drew Judith's hand away.

"Everyone knows. You are smarter than your brother," Judith said.

Nat pushed away the compliment.

"I took money from her pocket, the tongue from her mouth. Listen, please, I stole," Judith said.

"You killed her," Nat said.

"I'm not a mother. I don't know how to take care of anyone," she answered.

"Be quiet," Nat said.

"I can't." The shock of her spinning mind exceeded the horror of the murder. Her thoughts leapt into words—one birth after another, the way dreams spawned. The words came—facile, no break between idea and language, no break between feeling and expression. Judith could stop eating, stop washing, stop moving. She knew she could stop herself from ever killing again. But she could not stop her mind from casting off words. "I took the blood from her womb," she said.

"She's not right," Estelle Karger cried.

"Terrible," Nat said.

"You don't know. You have no right to say what I am. I told you: you can give these to your brother." Judith's hands hovered over the scraps. "His daughter once touched them. She breathed on them," she said.

"I don't want anything from you," Nat said.

"It's not me. I swear to you. I took these things. I'm going to be punished. I'm pleading with you," she said and met Nat Shein's eyes. She needed to be rid of Susan's things.

"No," he said. "I can't do that."

She pulled at her tarnished, matted hair.

"Miss Tondow knows what to do," Nat said.

Lillian opened the white canvas bag she had brought with her: "If you can help us, Miss Karger." She held the open bag at the table edge.

No one wanted to touch the pitiful things. At last Estelle swept the tattered hoard into the bag.

"You didn't want him to marry me, did you?" Judith asked.

"No," Nat said.

"You told him, but he didn't listen. He never listened to me. I knew things he never knew. I should have killed him, not the child. I wanted to kill him," Judith said.

"I believe you," Nat said.

"You know what it's like to want to kill someone?" Judith asked.

She's wrong about me, Nat thought. I'm no killer. I know who I am, but do I? If I were crazy enough, who knows what I would do?

"Did you ever hear anything like that?" he said to Lillian as he stood with her outside the Kargers' apartment house on Tenth Avenue. Nat held the canvas bag, the material so thick and stiff he could not feel the tiny things inside.

"Burn it," Lillian said. "If she keeps talking like that, they won't put her in prison, at least not for very long."

Early the next morning, Nat went out to his car, took the bag from the trunk, and put it into the passenger seat. The Goldring fields stretched out on either side of the road, the corn cut, the dirt open: there had been no hard frost yet. He drove until he crossed the boundaries of the farm, intending to dump the bag into the deep clog of leaves that rotted at the footing of a stone bridge and that no one touched from year to year as more fell and were falling now, the last from the oak trees that held on to them for so long. He slowed down, changing his mind. He didn't want these things so close to the farm. The bag had now become a secret to be kept from Renee, from his brother, from everyone except Lillian and the Kargers. He did not want to share a secret with Judith and her mother. "I'm getting soft," he said to himself, "soft as a sneaker full of shit. This is not a body. Dreck, that's what she's got in there. Nothing but dreck."

The road widened where land had been cleared around what had once been a garage. Nat turned off and drove around to the back over the fragments of stucco that had fallen from the walls, revealing the bare metal grid. "I never liked stucco," Nat said to himself as he got out of the car, holding the bag by its drawn pull cords. There's nothing in here that can hurt anyone, he thought as he pulled open the bag. He grasped the bottom, turned the bag upside down and shook it. The little things fell out onto the broken pavement. Nat crouched down, sitting on his heels the way he had when he was a boy. A memory came back to him, of picking up little things from the gutter, from the sidewalk, years ago, when he had played hooky from school and roamed the streets, when he had had nothing. Maybe these things had belonged to Susan. Never, he thought: why would she save such junk? She had had beautiful new things, and so would his son, Joel.

Nat gathered the tiny hoard into one hand and made his way down the dry steep slope, raising his legs high as he stepped over the tangled blackberry canes arching red, hooked with reddish blue thorns. At the bottom, the ground was wet, and when he lifted his feet, moisture welled up in the footprint. Ahead of him to the right was high ground tufted with grass. Nat crouched again and lifted a rock from its tight bed. Brown ants scurried on the flattened earth strung with fine roots. With his pocketknife, Nat cut a neat rectangular hole in the ground. One by one he put the little things in it—green penny, green glass, broken halves of black button, empty spool—all except the needle, whose eye he could see was rimmed with gold metal. He pulled the red thread out of the eye, and the gesture gave him pleasure, as if he were going back in time. "It will disappear," he said as he placed the needle in the little hole. The thread he blew away, watching it drift to the tip of a grassy stalk.

IT HAD BEEN NEARLY A YEAR SINCE HIS DAUGHTER'S DEATH WHEN BEN came up the driveway of the house on Manor Street. He had walked the streets of Paterson, stopping to eat at the Robertson Cafeteria, where he spent part of every day, before he finally came home, tired. He wanted to sleep, but if he closed his eyes now, he would be up all night. The warm air was full of the scent of the lilacs Brona and Jeannette had planted. Jeannette had already cut branches to take to her cemetery. Where did colored people bury their dead? Ben didn't know.

The dining room windows were open, carrying the voices of the women, who would sometimes sew together at the table. As Ben walked past the window, he heard a stranger's voice and went back, stopping to listen, his head under the stone sill.

"Rock of Ages, granite from Vermont. You've made a good choice."

"It's time," Brona said.

A salesman: that's who they were talking to, a seller of gravestones.

Ben crept into the house, into the kitchen, and down the hall, stopping near the dining room door.

"A deposit now," the salesman said.

"What kind of deposit?" Ben asked as he walked into the room.

"Mr. Shein, how do you do. I'm here to help. Harris Lamell," the salesman said. He tilted his head to the side, the olive skin of his face supple over a thin pad of fat. "I was just telling Mrs. Shein." The salesman stood up, but he knew enough not to stick out his hand: he hadn't closed the sale. "Eighty percent now, twenty percent before the stone is set," he said. Lamell's samples were spread on the dining room table. "Your mother picked a good granite." He opened a loose-leaf notebook and propped it against his chest as he turned pages, showing Ben seven styles, not too many: Harris Lamell knew the art of selling. But he wasn't going to sell Ben Shein.

"I want something else," Ben said.

"What else?" Brona said. "There is no time."

"Susan dead almost a year," Jeannette said. "The stone *before* a year pass."

"What difference does it make? What month, what year, what day, what hour? Who is counting?" Ben asked. Susan was in the ground, and now they wanted to put a stone on top of her.

The salesman closed his book. "Mr. Shein, you don't need me now. If you do, we can talk." Lamell packed his samples and notebook. "You will call me if you need me. I know the way to the door." The salesman tilted his head as he backed out of the room.

Brona folded her hands on the table, her face hard, like Nat's. "You told me you would do it. What are you waiting for?"

"There's plenty of time. I want something special. I told you: I'll do it," Ben said.

"Let us do it, and it will be done. We cannot leave a bare grave," Brona said, opening her hands—the crooked thumbnail from the old wound, the joint below the nail bent.

"No more. I'll do it," Ben told his mother.

Ben would go to the maker. He knew where the stonecutters were—all Italians—one after another close by in Paterson on Totowa Avenue at the edge of Westside Park. Late one afternoon, after Brona had come home from the salon, he drove out to pick a stone. Ben reached Della Porta and went on to Contegiacomo, and Agnello. On the next block was M. Lucca and Sons, where Ben turned in and followed the curving drive to the gray stucco building trimmed in green wood.

Leaving the car unlocked, the window down, he walked on the fine-gravel path leading him to carved white lambs, crosses in dark granite, hearts dripping gray blood, angels smiling with closed mouths, heads between spread wings—each line of the feathers cut in a clear line. There were ropes of flowers, anchors, a stone in the shape of an airplane—fancy work, quality.

A man came out the side door, a handkerchief with knotted corners fitted over his head. He was built like Nat, broad in the shoulders, a little short in the leg—not the boss. "I want a stone," Ben said.

The man opened the door, and Ben followed him into a dimly lit room. When his eyes had adjusted to the murky light, Ben could see a small spare man seated at a table at the far corner. "Mister?" Ben said.

"I'm Lucca," the stonecutter said. He swiveled in his chair, reached for the switch, and turned on the lights.

"I come direct: Ben Shein."

The furrier glanced up. Above Lucca's desk, framed by a small curtain bunched into a tiny hook was a photograph: Sacco in front of a brick wall—a prison. So sharp and clear: had the photographer lit him, or was Sacco in the same light that shone on everything? "You knew him?" Ben asked, pointing to the picture.

"The man was a worker, Mr. Shein, like me."

"I remember when . . . ," Ben began.

"You want a stone?" Lucca asked, cutting him off. He motioned Ben to a chair near the table, and both men sat facing each other, nothing between them.

"Maybe you could help me," Ben said.

"Tell me what you want." Lucca's unblinking eyes met Ben's, his compact head motionless. "I can make you what you want."

"A good stone."

"My stone doesn't crack," Lucca said.

"I saw."

"Tell me—who is it for?"

Ben put his hand over his throat. "My daughter."

"No granite," Lucca said. "A white stone." He leaned forward, his hands on his knees. "Carrara marble; veins so pale you won't see them. You can give me a small deposit. If you don't like my work, don't pay me."

The man must know how to cut. "No pictures, no star, no fancy flowers." Ben drew a piece of paper from his pocket. "Just her name and these words."

At the unveiling when the white gauze would be drawn away from the stone, the mourners would see the words cut by Lucca in capitals:

AN INNOCENT CHILD

IS HERE AT REST

WHO DID NOT SEE

THE WORLD AT BEST

BRUTALLY CUT OFF

BY A VENGEFUL HAND

HAS JOINED HER MOTHER

IN THAT PROMISED LAND.

ON THE DAY OF JUDITH'S TRIAL, SHE WALKED BETWEEN TWO LAWYERS as she entered the courthouse. She wore a neat, close-fitting gray suit with a white collar. Not wanting to call attention to her hands, her lawyers had advised her not to wear gloves, and she had listened to them. She did not raise her hands to shield her face from the photographers who surrounded her. Instead she turned her face to the side as she lifted her right shoulder. She tried to hide her face against her own body, but she did not succeed. A photographer caught her in profile, her suffering face lit up with shame and knowledge, her hair restored to its placid coil.

In the courtroom Judith was silent. Her lawyers spoke for her, entering a guilty plea to the charge of second-degree murder. The judge, agreeing with the psychiatrists that Judith had been a victim of tempo-

rary madness, was inclined to impose a light sentence, but public opin-
ion was against Judith—"a monster," people called her. They wanted her
locked away for life, but he sentenced her to an indeterminate term in
the Women's Reformatory in Clinton, New Jersey.

IN THREE YEARS JUDITH WAS QUIETLY RELEASED TO THE CUSTODY OF
Estelle Karger. There was no mention of her release in the Jersey papers,
and the Sheins were not informed. In February, two months after Judith
went to live with her mother in the small apartment Estelle had rented
in Rutherford near the train station, there was a week of unrelenting
cold, finally broken by a sudden, tender thaw that carried the promise
of spring.

Judith had not slept for days. She was so tired, her body heavy, her
head aching. The heat had not gone on, and the air in her room was
damp. Judith got out of bed, careful not to wake her mother, who slept
in the adjoining twin bed. She put her hand against the glass pane where
the early morning sun came in. She wanted only to sleep.

Judith took the pillows from her bed and, pulling the blanket behind
her, went into the kitchen, where she dropped the bedding to the floor.

Still wearing the long pink nightgown her mother had bought her,
her feet bare, Judith left the apartment and stood for a moment on the
chilly landing before going downstairs to the front hall, where she stood
near the brass mailboxes set into the marble-faced wall. Mrs. Smith, the
landlady, had polished them the day before, and they gleamed. Judith
stared through the glass door that led to the street, as if she were waiting for the mailman. Her long hair, which now bore a gray streak near
the right temple, hung down her back, tangled and knotted. Her
streaked hair gave off a sharp feral smell. Judith hadn't washed for weeks.

As she stood there, twisting her nightgown with clenched fists, Eddy

Schneider, one of the few people in the building who knew the Kargers, came down on his way to work. He was a presser in a shop a few
blocks from the apartment. His sight was poor, and he pressed almost
entirely by feel, his heat-reddened, speckled hand smoothing, turning
the stiff shirts.

"What are you doing here so early?" Eddy asked. "The mailman
won't come for hours. You'll catch cold."

"It doesn't matter. I'm all right," Judith said.

"Every little thing matters." Eddy came closer. Smelling the rank
odor Judith gave off, he drew back and peered at her through his thick
glasses. "Go up. Your mother will make for you a nice breakfast. You'll
feel better. Later the mailman will come. You'll go out. Take a nice walk
in the sunshine."

"My mother is not awake, but I will go up," Judith said, twisting a
lock of hair around her finger. Her nightgown clinging to her thin legs,
she went up the stairs.

Estelle was still sleeping in the room they shared, her blue-veined
fingers curled around the frozen wave of sheet and blanket edge, the
knuckles swollen with arthritis. A little sunlight came in through the
open window, rinsing Estelle's hair with yellow. Her black eyebrows
seemed painted on, and Judith felt an impulse to stroke them with her
index finger, the way a child would explore a doll. Between Estelle's
eyebrows was a small, deep, perpendicular crease that gave her face a
perpetual frown, even in sleep. Looking down at her mother, Judith felt
an utter desolation. "What will happen to her without me?" she asked
herself. She felt an inexplicable pity for her mother.

Judith went to Estelle's dressing table and took her ivory-backed
brush. Closing the door behind her, she crossed the dark hall and
stepped into the bathroom. Standing before the mirror, she brushed her
hair, stroke after stroke. She ran the brush over her palm, then her fingers
over the brush, combing out the hair stuck in the bristles, her hair
mixing with her mother's hair.

She stopped to listen: no sound came from the bedroom. In the bathroom she found two bath towels, which she rolled into tight cylinders and pushed against the gap at the bottom of the bedroom door. When she was sure she had blocked the small space, Judith went to the kitchen, opened the oven, and slid out the metal racks. Leaning them against a chair, she faced the drawn window shade, the round crocheted pull hanging over the sill. Grasping the shade's hard edge, she pulled, keeping a firm grip to keep the shade from snapping, rolling it up all the way so the room filled with light.

Hurrying, Judith picked up the two pillows she had taken from her bed and stuffed one into the oven. She placed the other pillow on the open oven door. As she dragged the mat from in front of the kitchen sink to the stove, she heard a sound—a drip of water from the faucet. "I'll turn it off," she said to herself, but the faucet would not budge. My mother will take care of it, she thought as she turned on the oven gas jet.

Drawing the blanket around her shoulders, Judith knelt down and put her head on the pillow that lay on the open oven door, her face near the escaping gas, her mouth half open. Her left hand rested close to her face, her right arm extended as if she were reaching for something at the back of the oven. At last she could sleep.

Wakened by the smell of gas, Estelle Karger ran from her bed and pulled Judith away from the stove. She struggled to turn off the gas jet. Her hands stiff and her body slow, she opened the window as far as it would go.

Hooking her hands under Judith's limp arms, Estelle managed to drag her to the window and haul her up so that her head rested on the windowsill. Estelle held her there. Her daughter's arm hung out the window; saliva trickled from her open mouth.

She knelt next to Judith, oblivious to the hard floor under her swollen knees. "Get up, get up," she kept saying as she awkwardly stroked Judith's hand.

Judith opened her eyes. "No," she said when she realized she was alive.

That night, as they lay in the dark, in their twin beds, Estelle spoke her last command to Judith: "Don't do that again." The dark gave authority to her voice.

In a week, Estelle, who had never worked outside her home, found a job in a stationery store. "We need the money," she told Judith. She received a ten percent discount on anything she bought, but she bought very little, having no one to treat except Judith. On her daughter's birthday, she would dutifully buy a card, from mother to daughter, invariably decorated with flowers. Above the rhyming verses Estelle would write "Judith dear," and below, "With love from your mother." Once she wrote, "I will never forget you." Judith kept every card.

While her mother worked, Judith took care of the house, shopped, and cooked their simple meals: canned soup, a chop and a baked potato, tuna salad. Every morning after she had washed and dressed herself, she would make a detailed list, which she would carry with her, checking off items one by one as she completed her tasks. She made her rounds—library, post office, bank, grocery store. She would exchange a few words with clerks and shopkeepers, quickly moving on, careful to say little. She told no one her name and at the library used her mother's card. She would eat her lunch alone, standing by the window watching the sky as she chewed on her sandwich, a single slice of American cheese between two pieces of packaged bread.

BEN SHEIN HAD TAKEN TO WEARING A HAT. HE HAD BOUGHT IT AT Mendy's on a hot day when he had been roaming the streets, not wanting to go home. The black straw narrow-rimmed hat shielded the top of his head from the sun, and he got into the habit of wearing it everywhere, even in the house on Manor Street. Early in the morning and late in the evening, Ben would sit in the living room with his hat on, as if waiting for a guest. His mother would find him there, and at first she would tell him to take off the hat, but after hearing his habitual reply, "What for?" she had stopped mentioning the hat. It had become a sign of Ben, the absent Ben. "Oh he's *here*. But . . . ," Brona would say to Nat and Renee when they came to visit. Her son was as present as his hat: a fact, a thing that did not seem to eat or sleep. He wouldn't come to work. "What do you need me for?" he would say. "You're selling ready-made, and Moe's keeping up the fur repair. And the storage business."

Mundane things would drive Ben into a frenzy, even something as trifling as having to salt an egg. He renounced everything. He did eat, though not at home. With his hat on—in fall, a gray felt fedora trimmed with black grosgrain ribbon—he became a habitué of the Robertson Cafeteria, joining the old men who took their main meal of the day at noon. He would fill himself, eating blindly, never stopping, even to lift the salt shaker, always sitting at a tangent to any group, which he would acknowledge with a shrug, as if to say, "Look at me, look at what I've become." He would pick up the cast-off newspapers and in this way follow the news of the war.

"What do you think, Mr. Shein?" Hy Katcher asked him one day.

"I'm not a *mister*," Ben said and ran his fingers along the brim of his hat.

About the war?

"I'm too old to go," Ben said.

"What about the Jews?" Hy Katcher lowered his voice.

"They should all kill themselves. We should have done it long ago."

"What are you talking about?"

"You asked me, I'm telling you, Mr. Katcher." What was so good here on earth that anyone should live? If we were all gone, thought Ben, there would be no more trouble. Did a lion worry about killing, about anything? What did the animals need us for? To tell them, 'What a beautiful coat you have'? Let them keep their fur. Without us, the trees would flourish, the ants would multiply, the roads would crack, the dams would collapse, the rivers would flood, the grass would cover everything. The grass had shot up and covered Susan's grave.

Ben would sit all evening in the cafeteria, always ordering the same thing, a dairy dish, since he had eaten heavily at noon: a baked potato and sour cream or a cup of soup. Late one night, as he methodically ate his potato, he looked up to see a man staring at him. It was Theo Winik, thin as a pole, a camera slung over his shoulder, a cup of coffee on his tray. As he walked to Ben's table, the coffee sloshed into the saucer.

"Have something with it," Ben said.

"I'm not hungry."

"You wouldn't eat their lousy Danish. It's dreck. You're a baker: you should know. But a person can get used to anything. Some people don't know what good is. How is your mother?" Ben asked.

"She gets along. The old man is gone."

"Even Sophie Winik couldn't keep him alive," Ben said.

"My father stood up from his chair, the first time in years. He said a few words. He said he had to go. She thought he meant to the toilet."

"That was it?"

"No, my father smiled. His face moved. For years he hadn't smiled. Then he smiled once, and his heart stopped. All those years she took care of him, and she didn't know whether he felt anything. Better he hadn't felt anything, better he had dreams, nice dreams," Theo said.

"Maybe he did." Ben picked up Theo's camera, which the baker had put on the table. "You still have time for this? Maybe you could show me."

"You're a *furrier.*"

"No more. I'll pay you for the lessons," Ben said.

"I don't need the money."

"You'll take it. You'll give it to your mother. She's a good woman."

"My mother does what she has to, day after day, the way the sun comes up. I don't know how she does it, but she finds the sugar to bake," Theo said.

Once a week, through the winter, Ben Shein took lessons from Theo Winik. He soon learned the basic operations of the camera and corrected his beginner's errors—finger over the lens, underexposure, overexposure—so that by spring he was able to get a tolerable picture.

With his camera Ben Shein emptied the world of people. After he had drunk a glass of water at the kitchen sink, he would leave the house early in the morning, his narrow-rimmed black hat firmly on his head, his camera over his shoulder. He shot the empty streets, doorways, trash-cans, fire hydrants, lampposts, smoke stacks. Corners interested him—the way the brick of an apartment house met the concrete sidewalk. He searched for lines, chance patterns. He grew to like trees, a bare shapely branch against the wide expanse of a factory wall. He began to shoot trash, a piece of paper blowing down the street, a discarded apple core. He tried for weeks to catch the mist rising from the Paterson Falls. The picture blurred. Down on his hands and knees in the dirt, he shot anthills, which in close-ups looked like mountains. He shot down alleys. It was a point of honor for him never to arrange a shot, never to move an object. Not once did he take a picture of a human being, not even a shadow of a person, not the smoke curling up from a cigarette, not the cloud of human breath on a cold day. Sometimes he would talk to himself, as children talk to themselves while they play. He was not always aware of what he was saying or to whom the words were addressed. Though he avoided thinking of Susan and could not imagine an after-life, he made his pictures as if he could send them to her with a message: *This* is what it's like here—beautiful, serene. In his pictures he had erased people. They were the source of evil, he believed.

His days became a series of scenes. When he had finished with his camera for the day, he would sit in the Robertson Cafeteria, a cup of coffee in front of him, his black hat on his head. Always he wore a dark suit and a tie. He would stare at the curve of the thick white cup, the fine brown scratches on the saucer.

When the war ended and the pictures of the concentration camps were published in *Life*, Ben felt justified in never having taken a picture of a human being. "They all should have killed themselves," he repeated when the subject came up at the Robertson, "before the Germans could touch them." Yet people wanted to live no matter what. Look at Ben Shein. Every morning he got up, drank a glass of water, put on his hat, said good bye to his mother, went out into the street, did no good for anyone. No, that wasn't true. He had given money to Yetta Mavet, who would come into the Robertson.

Yetta sat down, her scarf slipping forward over her full, flushed face, her shoulders rounded under the heavy winter coat buttoned tightly around her neck.

"Let me treat you," Ben said. "Be a lady."

"I don't know what I want," she said.

"So you'll decide."

Soon Yetta Mavet had a bowl of mushroom and barley soup in front of her.

"Your Tess took care of me," she said.

Ben didn't answer.

"May she rest in peace," Yetta said.

Ben laughed in one rapid exhalation.

"And the little one of blessed memory," Yetta said.

"No more," Ben Shein raised his hand.

"Who knows why things happen?" she said.

Ben Shein didn't know.

"Why should I, Yetta Mavet, have a brother who doesn't know who I am? And when he *does* recognize me, he tells me I'm going to die. My parents—it's a good thing they never lived to see such a thing. He'll never get out from there. I saw him. I took the bus. He had on one shoe, and he danced, waving his arms, like he could fly. Everything he knows. That's what he says. He knew about the Germans, about Hitler. Hitler: may his memory be erased."

Ben Shein had not heard these words since he was a child and his grandfather Jacob had pronounced them after the death of a man who had cheated him in business.

Now on those terrible days when Ben thought of Judith, he would pronounce the words, *May her memory be erased*, though he didn't know whether she was dead or alive.

EPILOGUE

*J*udith would sometimes wake from nightmares—her hands around a child's throat. She would sit up in bed, gasping, sweat pouring off her. "Are you all right?" her mother would call out, and Judith would answer, "Yes."

After a few years they moved to Florida, where they rented a small apartment in Miami, away from the beach. The terrible dreams became less frequent. In the winter months, Judith went out almost every day in the mild air. In summer, she liked the heat that stunned her. She continued to shop and clean for her mother, who found work in another stationery store.

The neighborhood changed. Cubans moved in, and a *botánica* opened across the street from the Kargers. Its owner, Felicia More, a tiny, big-headed woman, whom her friends called *Muñeca*, doll, treated patients in the small back room and dispensed herbal remedies. Judith shopped often in the *botánica*. She bought soap; she bought perfume. Sometimes she bought nothing.

"You're very pretty—still," Felicia More said to her. "But you're a sleepwalker. You should wake up."

"I'm too old," Judith answered.

"In your thirties! Look at me." She put her face, fine up and down lines cutting through her lips, close to Judith's. "I'm older than you. You should live your life."

Ultimately Felicia offered Judith a job. For a few hours each afternoon, while Felicia More ate lunch and took her siesta, Judith would sweep the store and straighten stock. She would move her straw broom over the bare wooden floor. On the shelves were bottles of Florida Water cologne; in the corner near the back door, a jar of dried plants half submerged in dark green liquid. Felicia treated her patients with the infusion. The orange cat would rub against Judith's legs. The parrot in its cage near the window would squawk, "*Oye, cabrón.*"

When Felicia brought children to the back room to treat them, Judith would run away.

"What's the matter with you?" Felicia once asked her.

And Judith told her. Just like that. How she had drowned her stepdaughter.

"*Madre de Dios.*" Then Felicia was struck silent. Finally she said, "A person only does that once. But I take you seriously."

She began to treat Judith. And Judith, without believing, lay down under Felicia More's hands. Felicia did not expect to cure her, only to give her some relief. She kneaded her stomach. She gave her tea of *yerba mora*. She treated her for fever, though Judith had no actual fever. She gave her the Rose of Jericho. She brewed a decoction of herbs and river ferns for Judith to pour into her bath.

"I don't believe in this," Judith would say.

"I don't either," said Felicia More. She did not know why these things helped. But she was sure her patients liked her attentions. She was assiduous. People trusted her. Men would reveal their weaknesses. "I'm out of business," they would say to her. "My bird is dead. Don't tell anyone. My wife thinks I'm tired." Felicia promised not to tell. "I'm quiet as the tomb," she would say. In the narrow closet in the back room was a dismantled skeleton that had belonged to her pharmacist great-grandfather. Brown bones jammed the shelves.

Their third winter in Miami, Estelle began to suffer from blinding headaches. Judith would give her Felicia's linden flower tea and chamomile infusions flavored with anise. For a few months the herbal mixtures soothed, until one night, waking in agony, Estelle staggered to the bathroom and fell. An artery had burst in her brain. "Mother?" Judith whispered as she got down on her knees and crept toward Estelle's body. Estelle lay near the sink. Her eyes were open; above her tongue a glint of gold, her bare arm caught behind her waist, forcing up her ribs. Judith sat back on her heels, away from her mother's twisted body. The cry of the fish peddler rose from the alley, *Pescao bueno con ojo que te mira.*

Less than a year after Estelle's death, Felicia's grown son, Rufino, arrived from Cuba. With his limp, his right leg withered from childhood polio. With his raised comb of black hair. He had his mother's large head and small body, her sensitive hands. Even before his illness, Felicia had not warmed to him. She had given him to her mother to look after. Now the husband she had left behind in Cuba sent their son.

To torment me, Felicia thought. She had no patience with Rufino, but Judith did. She spoke to him in her newly acquired Spanish with a firm authority she had never commanded in English. He was terrified of making mistakes and would constantly ask her questions.

Judith became Felicia's partner and more and more took over management of the *botánica*, freeing Felicia for her patients.

"They are eating me alive," Felicia would say. "I'm no saint. I need to rest."

Felicia decided Judith and Rufino would marry. She spoke to Judith first. For the first time in memory, Judith laughed out loud. "You're crazy," she said, in her emphatic Spanish.

After the civil wedding, Judith slept in her old apartment on week-days. "You can be a *chica* and a wife," Felicia told her. On Friday nights, Judith would cross the street to her mother-in-law's house to spend the weekends with her husband. She grew to like the foreign formality of her visits. In the tiny pink parlor, seated side by side on the sofa, she and

Rufino would first exchange polite greetings and then each drink one glass of the red wine Felicia had left for them before she had gone down to the store.

In their bedroom, red votive candles burned on the blue dresser, white candles on the night tables. A crucifix, tiny drops of painted-on blood dripping from the wounded Christ, hung above the bed, where Judith would sit on the edge of the mattress, and Rufino would kneel, his head in her lap. He behaved as Felicia said he would, like a child. Judith stroked his hair. She spoke to him in Spanish and told him what she wanted. When she was angry with him, she told him. *Bruja*, he sometimes called her. Witch.

Downstairs, Felicia would wait on customers. At ten o'clock she would close the shop and go to the back room to sleep. She lay down on the narrow bed and drew up the light blanket. Sometimes she would think of Judith and Rufino upstairs in the same bed—the murderer and the cripple. The rare times when Judith woke sobbing, Rufino would wake his mother, and she would make a calming tea to help her daughter-in-law sleep.

ON AN AUGUST NIGHT, MANY YEARS AFTER SUSAN SHEIN'S DEATH, BEN left the small cabin where he stayed occasionally when he was a guest at the Goldring Farm Camp. The white gravel path through the mowed field where the Goldrings had once grown corn was bright and clear, but Ben felt his way, pulling himself forward with a silver-topped walking stick. Cataracts clouded his eyes. Years ago the doctor had pronounced them ripe for surgery, but Ben had refused. At my age, he thought, I don't need an operation. He saw clearly only in bright light. And now it was dusk.

He wore a black gabardine topcoat that came to his ankles, long as the coat crazy Joe Mavet used to wear. His black hat, fresh from the hatbox—round dome, upturned brim—accentuated the pallor of his face and hid his white hair, his mouth framed by deep lines.

Ahead of him yellow light streamed from the open doors of the barn, now the theater of the Goldring Farm Camp for the Arts. It had become a Goldring tradition to welcome parents with wine and sweets before the season-end student performance. Tables were laid out just inside the door, and visitors were already helping themselves to food and drink.

The farm had metamorphosed into a camp after the war. It had been Renee's younger brother and sister, the twins, who had come up with the idea. Some friends of the Goldrings argued against it. Art, they said, was regressive. The twins, the Julliard graduates, persisted. They argued with their grandparents and their mother. Art, they had learned, took work. There would be junior campers. Why not let them regress? What was childhood but regression? Were they supposed to come out of the womb with shovels and pails in their little hands, ready for work?

The twins went to Nat for help. He backed them completely. Their vision became his. He outdid them. He had to fight Rose Goldring, Renee's mother. He had been fighting her for years. It was Nat who raised the money, from Ben, from Lillian Tondow. He put on a suit and went to see her. "You've done well, Lil," he said. "I've never asked you for anything." Lillian gave him the money. "Without interest," she said. She had not expected to be paid back. But Nat had repaid the debt—handsomely, with interest.

Renee did what she did best: she managed the finances and kept the books. Nat built. But they crossed the lines of their talents. Nat learned finance. He helped with the books. Renee had ideas—build the studios in the sheds, call the largest one the Shed, leave the wood bare. Bunkhouses rose on the foundations of the chicken coops. Renee picked up a paintbrush and helped Nat paint the barn.

He could sell. The parents liked him. Nat Shein, in middle age, exuded quality. He delivered. He made sure the food was good.

He wanted an athletic program. He fought for a swimming pool. "We'll dig it out of the cornfields," he said. "What do you need it for?" Rose Goldring had shouted at him. "These kids don't swim. They're musicians. A pool. That's for people like you. People who go to Florida. You'll ruin us."

"What do you mean?" he had said. "Look what you would have done to your daughter. Married her to an accountant. Both of them with the books. She was hunched over when I met her. Don't tell me what people need." Nat won. He hired an athletic director. "No competition, no teams," he told him. "Just get them moving. Teach them to swim."

The young, brainy, romantic campers, the artists, saw the older generation as incarnations of their heroes. Never mind that Nat Shein had only painted walls, he—the artists said—looked like a taller version of Picasso, Picasso in a bathing suit, barrel-chested in old age. Renee Goldring Shein—they announced—was a woman out of Kokoschka, the ugly beauty, the bulbous nose and the sardonic eyes.

A young artist at the camp had painted Nat stripped to the waist, bare feet, chino pants. The boy had caught something. He had found Nat's thought—an intimation, a sweet scowl, a yearning. In the painting, which hangs in the Museum of Modern Art in New York, the angular planes of Nat Shein's face are tense with meaning.

Ben gave money to the Goldring Farm Camp. He had endowed the theater but refused to have his name inscribed on a plaque. Once a year, at season end, when he visited the camp, he appeared like a statue taken out on a saint's day.

The younger Goldrings and Sheins moved out through the big doors to greet him. Joel, Nat's son, took Ben lightly by the arm and guided him to a chair in a quiet corner away from the tables. Ben didn't speak, not when Nat came up to him, not when Renee bent to kiss him, not when the twins pressed his hands, not when the nieces and nephews called out their greetings. His silence was immense. Since his return from Israel, where he had gone the year Brona had died, he had said little. The doctors thought he might have had a stroke, but they found no organic evidence. Ben Shein had—for the most part—stopped speaking. For years he had been moving toward silence, and in Israel what had been a growing habit became an act of will. He had stood at the Wailing Wall, awkward, angry in the stifling heat; he had waited in the line of men swaying toward the wall. Now they were rocking back and forth in that old bowing, davening motion as they recited the daily prayers in front of the massive stone blocks.

At one point an old man standing next to Ben stopped praying and with a shaking hand raised the corner of his own prayer shawl, so Ben could see his face. " 'Pity will take away sorrow,' it says that here, we're saying it. But you know? Maybe it's true and maybe it's not, but I pray anyway," he said to Ben. The man's eyes glittered and seemed to shrink behind his thick glasses; adjusting his prayer shawl so the embroidered edge threw a shadow over the side of his face, he turned to the wall, lifted his book and opened his mouth about to speak the first word of his prayer.

Ben pressed toward him. "Who asked you?" Ben said. Face to face with the old man, he crowded him against the stone blocks, his hands clenched at his sides. The old man cried out and two young men, throwing down their prayer books, pulled Ben away.

"What kind of thing is that for a human being to do?" The old man was shaking. "He's not right in his mind. Let him go," he said.

They held on to Ben. Two pairs of hands on him, around his wrists, his arms bent to his sides.

Ben didn't move. "I'm guilty," he said.

"Nothing happened," the old man said to his rescuers. "I'm all right." They let Ben go.

What's the use of talking? Ben had asked himself. The malignancy of his words had frightened him—again.

His silence had another use. With silence he guarded his unrelenting irony. If he had spoken, he would have said as year by year he watched the smiling parents at Goldring Farm Camp, 'What do you know?' He regarded himself as the holder of truth: life wasn't what you thought it was. 'So what are you smiling about?'

He gave his money to the camp and kept quiet. He grew protective of his secret, believing it belonged only to him. The strangers he met— they would never hear his story.

He had chosen not to talk, and then he could not talk.

In the Goldring camp hall, Nat came toward him. His hair was completely white, shocking above the black eyes. He led a young couple. The woman was long-waisted, long-armed, long-necked, her thick, straight brown hair parted in the middle and drawn back into a short brush at the back of her neck; the man, dark, large, with the mass of a football player but not the muscle. They were lawyers. "I want you to meet someone," Nat said as he drew Cynthia Richardson and Orlando Salinas close to his brother. "They bought a house. In Paterson."

The couple bent low, but even so Ben had to look up. He had nothing to say.

Cynthia bent closer, taking his hand.

He felt the dry heat of her skin, the steady heat of her firm fingers. She did not release him.

"In Paterson?" Ben repeated in disbelief, his first spoken words in years.

"On Jerome Avenue, the east side, near the park," Cynthia said. "It took workers a year to scrape away paint and dirt. They saved the garlands of carved flowers. We flashed the roof with copper."

Rose House, Cynthia and Orlando called it.

In the entry hall were paintings of their first homes, their root homes: hers in Ohio, white shingled, a little bridge, a stable where she had kept her horse; his, a violet-painted shack on stilts in the Dominican Republic.

They were the new pioneers—in Jersey.

"I love the blankness, the lack of society," Cynthia loved to tell people, as if it were the nineteenth century and she were surveying the wild open plains of Nebraska, where—she seemed to believe—no one had ever lived and nothing had ever happened. Cynthia knew better, of course. But the people and events that had come before her had to be unreal, so she and Orlando could have their adventure, their new beginning.

She knelt down next to Ben's chair. He could not make out the color of her eyes. He could not see the flash in the yellow, but he heard her belief and it disarmed him.

Flanked by the pioneers, Ben went in before the crowd, into the empty theater. The bare wood walls were dry and worn to silver; the grain showed. The seats were covered in red plush. Ben took his seat in the small curtained box Nat had built for him close to the stage. Cynthia drew back the curtain, and they waited without speaking for the guests to assemble. They came up the aisle, some of them carrying glasses of wine, some of them with bunches of flowers—zinnias and sunflowers cut from the Goldring fields—yellow, pink, and red. Ben felt tired, tired already. He closed his eyes and leaned his head back against his chair. His head fell to the side as he dozed.

The high cool notes of the piano rose in the small hall—like a shiver. Distinct. A sad, delicious silence between the notes. Ben woke.

"It's Pippin," Cynthia whispered, her lips close to Ben's ear.

"I don't know it," Ben said.

"Listen." She put her hand on Ben's arm, just above the wrist. She kept her hand on him.

Ben took the pressure of her touch. His hand fell open. He waited. A boy, no more than thirteen, was alone on the bare brightly lit stage. He wore a short brown tunic held close to his thin sides by a wide belt. His dark blond hair hung straight to his ears. He rested his hand on the hilt of the sword hanging from his belt. In the stage light his face was pink and gold; the gold seemed to swim in flecks—like pollen. His lips were painted red. He took a few light steps; the long muscles of his legs—in smooth tights—seemed older than his voice. When he sang the first notes, his voice, a pure tenor, wavered then held as he found his way, but even as he held the notes, Ben heard, deep under, a raw, trembling, unfinished sweetness.

David Lane

Born in Paterson, New Jersey, MIRIAM LEVINE is the author of *Devotion: A Memoir*, three poetry collections, and *A Guide to Writers' Homes in New England*. A recipient of a National Endowment for the Arts fellowship and grants from the Massachusetts Artists Foundation, she was a fellow at Yaddo and Hawthornden Castle. Her work has been published in such venues as the *Paris Review, Kenyon Review*, and *Harvard Review*. Levine chairs the English Department at Framingham State College near Boston and divides her time between Massachusetts and Miami Beach, Florida. Currently she's at work on a new novel and a poetry collection.